DEAD OF WINTER

DEAD OF WINTER

DON D'AMMASSA

FIVE STAR

An imprint of Thomson Gale, a part of The Thomson Corporation

THOMSON

™

GALE

Detroit • New York • San Francisco • New Haven, Conn. • Waterville, Maine • London

THOMSON

GALE

LIBRARY OF CONGRESS CATALOGING-IN-PUBLICATION DATA

D'Ammassa, Don, 1946–
    Dead of winter / Don D'Ammassa. — 1st ed.
      p. cm.
    ISBN-13: 978-1-59414-495-0
    ISBN-10: 1-59414-495-8 (hardcover : alk. paper)
    1. Widows—Fiction. 2. Country life—Fiction. I. Title.
PS3604.A46D43 2007
813'.6—dc22   2006027878

First Edition. First Printing: January 2007.

Published in 2007 in conjunction with Tekno Books and Ed Gorman.

Printed in the United States of America on permanent paper
10 9 8 7 6 5 4 3 2 1

CHAPTER ONE

Laura felt an odd sense of timelessness as she returned to her hometown for the first time since she'd run off to be married. They said you could never go home again, that even a year away from a place left enough time for it to change in subtle if not dramatic ways, subtle but still significant enough to make it differ from the place you remembered. As she slowly drove down Main Street, her eyes flicking back and forth to survey the storefronts, she realized that some of that change was subjective. Everything seemed smaller and dingier than she remembered, as though some of the depth of the very colors had been leached away while she was gone. The displays in the windows were different, but only in detail, and the names on the signs were all the same. She even thought some of the faces she passed were familiar, although she couldn't point to any specific individual and say: There! I know that person.

It was comforting to know she was back where she was known and where she knew what was happening around her, although not as comforting as she had hoped. She was looking forward to re-creating her life, in a context where the person sitting next to her didn't change personalities almost from one day to the next. The way Sean had changed. She shook her head, willing herself to forget about Sean, at least for the moment. He was gone forever, and the sooner she accepted that and moved on, the better. Maybe here, back in Dorrance, she could find the peace that had eluded her in the days since his death. Her mother would be pleased to know she was back, and would effortlessly renew her campaign to manage her daughter's life just as she had before, probably vowing this time to be more successful at protecting inexperienced and naïve Laura from her own ignorance and impulsiveness.

Anticipation of the coming struggle drained some of the pleasure out of the moment, but it also caused her to recollect herself. She'd made certain silent promises before turning toward the town she'd once called home, promises she meant to keep. Dorrance was probably no safer a refuge from the terrors she carried around inside herself than any other place she might have chosen; its advantage was that she was already familiar with the outside distractions, the town's virtues and its flaws, its habitual staid conformity and its occasional quirk, and she understood her place in the scheme of things, even if that place wasn't always a comfortable one.

Winter had come early this year; the trees were dark skeletons standing in formation down the median strip and scattered through the neighborhoods that huddled against the back of the small commercial district. The heater in her car had been working fitfully for the past two hours and she was chilly as well as hungry. She had thought about stopping to eat an hour earlier, but her mother would insist upon feeding her and would be insulted if she picked at her food. This was going to be difficult enough without providing an extra excuse for conflict.

Once past the diminutive downtown, she turned right at McAlester and started up the gently curved incline toward Taggart Hill. With the foliage gone, she caught brief glimpses of the house sitting astride the distant crest. Like the town, it appeared unchanged—a sprawling farmhouse that dominated the town physically just as Laura's grandfather, Leonard Rustin, had dominated it financially, politically, and through force of will. Old Leonard had died while Laura was still a child, but she could remember him vividly, partly because his portraits were displayed in almost every room of the house where she'd grown up, partly because he'd made such a powerful impression on his young granddaughter that she felt his presence even when he wasn't there.

The road became steeper as it neared the driveway. When John Dill had been appointed town manager, he'd objected to the expense of plowing McAlester Road. "The Colliers are the only ones who have property along the road, so it's almost a private drive. It takes almost as long to clear it as far as the crest of Taggart Hill as it does the whole rest of the town combined."

Mary Collier, Laura's mother, had calmly pointed out that she also paid almost as much in property taxes as the rest of the town combined, and when Dill had still balked, had calmly referred him to her attorney. At the next snowfall, McAlester Road had been promptly cleared. They had crossed swords a few other times as well, but Dill generally emerged from these encounters beaten if not bloodied, and although she'd won all the major battles, Laura's mother made no secret of her animosity towards the town manager. Mary Collier had inherited Leonard Rustin's will to win along with his physical estate and a remarkable similarity in physical appearance; Laura had never known her to lose a battle over anything that really mattered to her, unless it was the conflict with her husband that had driven him to leave. When Laura's father had abandoned them, he'd done so secretively and quickly, leaving behind no hint of where he had gone or what he was doing.

Whatever she might have thought privately, Mary kept up a brave face in public and her criticisms of Ben Collier were always at least loosely veiled. "Your father was a good man in his time, Laura, but he became weak as he grew older. It was tragic to watch that decline and I suppose it's a small mercy we were spared what must have followed. No, I don't miss him, although I occasionally miss the man he once was." Having characterized the desertion as a minor blessing, she had deprived her many critics of a major weapon, and had if anything enhanced her position of influence within the community. No one had ever resisted her for long, not even Laura.

Except once, she told herself. She didn't want me to marry Sean. The one time I stood up to her and won, and it turns out she was right about him all along. Not in the way she had believed, of course, but ultimately it had come to the same thing. So now Laura was coming home, and even though she had given no warning of her decision, she knew her mother would accept her arrival without ruffling a feather. She had wanted her daughter back, and now she was home. What was there to be surprised about, after all? The universe itself was no match for the will of Mary Rustin Collier.

But her return was conditional, and her mother would not like the conditions. She'd accept them initially, though, convinced that she could wear down her daughter's resistance, erode her self-confidence, and ultimately get what she wanted. Laura knew her tricks, had learned most of them the hard way, and she had steeled herself for this. Despite a tremulous feeling in her gut, she was convinced that she could stand up to her mother this time; she'd been tested in an even hotter fire, bending but not breaking. And if she discovered that the battle was going badly, she could pack up the few belongings that mattered to her and move on. It wasn't the most glorious way to win, but in this case, a successful retreat would in itself constitute a sort of victory.

The large wooden gate was open, which surprised her. It was almost as if her mother knew that she'd be coming home today. Or perhaps it was left open routinely now. No one would dare to call upon Mary Collier without an appointment or invitation, so closing the gate was superfluous. Laura took her foot off the gas as she approached, feeling a momentary reluctance to commit herself, but it was too late now. If her mother was home, she'd almost certainly have seen that a car was making its way up McAlester. She'd have fetched her binoculars and had probably already catalogued every dent and scratch on Laura's aging Chevy Nova. The Vermont license plates would be a dead giveaway.

She stepped on the gas and turned into the private driveway. "Yes, Mother, I'm home," she said aloud. "Please don't tell me you knew I'd be back, at least not until I've been here for a while."

The fields looked well maintained and Laura wondered, not for the first time, why her mother bothered. The income on her investments subsidized the farm, which was a marginal operation at best, and even in the face of the current stock market rockiness, she felt certain her mother had weathered things well and had managed to safeguard her portfolio. It had been years since the farm had been profitable to operate, barely covering expenses most years, expenses which included the full-time manager and temporary help during planting and harvesting.

"It's our legacy, entrusted to us for safekeeping," she had responded the one time Laura had broached the subject. "My family built this farm and to a large extent built the town of Dorrance as well. It wouldn't be very loyal of me to abandon it just because times have changed. You'll understand that as you grow older and recognize your own responsibilities."

Laura had abandoned that argument, as she had so many, without pointing out that her mother had provided a somewhat edited version of history. The farm had been profitable for several generations, unquestionably the most productive land in the area. But Leonard Rustin had been more than a simple farmer, and it had been his avocation rather than the farm that had made him such a wealthy and powerful man in the community. Not even Laura knew the specifics of the matter, but her grandfather had been feared rather than respected by the people of Dorrance, a fear that had spread down to his children and their children so even his granddaughter Laura enjoyed, if that was the word, respect for her power if not for her person. She'd heard rumors as a child, of course. Other kids in school had called her grandfather a smuggler, a gangster, even a killer. But the charges had all been nebulous and it was, in any case, past history now, a history that held no interest for her.

There was no obvious sign of life from the house, but Laura knew that someone was home. There was a brand-new Jeep parked at the side, the curtains were open, and a thin plume of gray smoke wavered above the kitchen vent in addition to the thicker, darker one from the main chimney. Laura felt her foot easing up unnecessarily on the gas pedal and realized she was trying to delay the moment of confrontation as much as possible. Impatient with herself, she pressed down more firmly and had to struggle to take the sharp final corner without swaying too far to one side.

She parked and turned off the ignition, and the sudden silence seemed louder than the engine noise. Her failing muffler would have announced her arrival even if her mother hadn't been watching, but no one came to the door. Typical, she thought. Won't budge an inch. I have to be the one to go to her. She leaned forward and pressed her forehead against the top arc of the steering wheel, her fists clenched tightly at her sides. I can get through this, she told herself. I'm a big girl now and I know all of her tricks and games.

She opened the car door and stepped outside.

It was cold, of course, but it felt good somehow. Maybe it was the smell of the air here, or the aromas drifting from the sprawling house ahead of her, but despite her conviction that this was going to be less than a joyous reunion, it felt good to be here, good to be back home. There were a lot of pleasant memories connected to this house, even memories of her mother from the times when the two of them shared a less adversarial relationship. They had never been as close as, retrospectively, she might have wished, but they had rarely been distant until the last few years, following the mysterious abandonment by her father, her short and controversial courtship with Sean, the decision to move out of Dorrance. But all of that is past now, she told herself. Mother and I will have to find new things to argue about.

She knew it wouldn't take long.

Suddenly impatient with herself, Laura walked toward the house quickly, noticing that the porch had been freshly painted and that all of her mother's plants had been taken to the greenhouse to await spring. The curtains in the windows were just as she remembered them and the wicker furniture scattered across the porch remained unchanged. She skipped up the three steps and reached for the doorknob, then hesitated. After all, she didn't really live here anymore, did she?

She pressed the doorbell and waited.

It took a few seconds longer than she expected and Laura wondered if the delay was deliberate, but then the inner door swung back and Laura herself opened the storm door and there was her mother, looking as though she hadn't aged a day in the two years that had passed since they had last seen each other. Her mother had come out to Vermont once, just after Sean's death, but Laura had refused to see her, had become hysterical when pressed.

"Good morning, Mother. I'm back."

Mary Collier's face radiated satisfaction. "I know, dear. I saw you coming up the hill. I would've met you but I thought I'd put the kettle on first, and it never occurred to me that you wouldn't just walk right in. This is your home, you know. You don't have to ask for permission." To illustrate her point, Mary stepped aside and as she did so, Laura felt herself falling back through time.

Not literally, of course, but it was as though she'd shed a few years the moment she stepped across the threshold. The living room opened off the vestibule to her left, the small utility room that served as the farm office was to the right, and a staircase to the second floor stretched straight ahead of her. She followed her mother into the living room, feeling just slightly distanced from reality. The room was exactly as it had been the last time she'd been here, the thick drapes partly drawn so that the interior always seemed just slightly too dark, even on a very bright day, which this wasn't. The overstuffed furniture was arranged as it had been since she was a toddler; Mary Collier wasn't one of those people who constantly fiddled with her environment. "Once I've found what I want, I keep it. I don't object to change, but I draw the line at change for its own sake." The only thing new was the local newspaper, neatly folded in its place on the table under an ornate antique lamp with a hand-painted, rose-tinted shade.

"Sit down, Laura. You must be exhausted. The tea should be ready by now. I won't be a minute."

Laura didn't want tea, had never cared for tea and wanted coffee, as bitter as possible, but she knew better than to try to persuade her mother otherwise. Tea was required in this situation and tea would be served, consumed, and appreciated. It didn't matter if she liked it. The Colliers, like the Rustins before them, were acutely aware of their duty, and it was her duty to submit to her mother's errant hospitality just as it was Mary Collier's duty to see that each element of the homecoming ceremony was properly observed.

She settled into a chair, her usual chair in fact, and smiled slightly at the familiar little squeak as her weight placed a strain on one of the joints. Despite all of her anxieties about this moment, and all of her ongoing concerns about dealing with her mother, she had to admit that it felt good right at this moment to be back in familiar territory, with someone else worrying about propriety and appearances. She started to open her purse to find a cigarette, then remembered that she had quit, and wondered once again why she had done so. Was it her last gift to Sean, who had never liked it that she smoked? He didn't deserve a gift, did he? Not after what he'd become. But that hadn't been his fault. The doctors insisted that it was a physical problem, a malignancy in the brain that had remained dormant, only to awaken swiftly and terribly and to change the man she had loved into a monster she had loathed, and feared.

She shook her head suddenly, as though trying to physically expel the memories of those last months from her mind. But they hung on stubbornly until she was distracted by the return of her mother, bearing a silver tray and a tea set with two delicate china cups.

"I'll just put this here." She set the tray down on the coffee table and glanced sideways at her daughter. "Still one sugar and light on the cream?"

Laura nodded, not trusting herself to speak. She suddenly felt oddly light-headed, as though this was a dream rather than an actual encounter. Her mother prepared both cups before handing one to Laura and settling herself at the near end of the settee. "Everyone will be happy to have you back, Laura. Mason Cortway was asking about you just this past week. Ashley Sothern's home, too. The job in Buffalo didn't work out any better than the last one."

Laura nodded again, then realized that wouldn't be adequate. "I'd like to see Ashley again. We lost track of each other after . . ." She let her voice trail off. After the wedding, of course; Ashley was supposed to have been maid of honor. Laura would have asked Kathy Peebles, her best friend all through high school, but Kathy had left town right after graduation and never responded to her letter.

"She hasn't been looking after herself very well, I'm afraid. She's put on some weight again. It's a real shame. She has such a pretty face, but she's always had trouble with her figure, on top of everything else."

Laura sidestepped the issue of Ashley's personal appearance and her life choices, the latter of which had been the focus of more than one argument between mother and daughter in the past. "I apologize for showing up without warning, but when I left Vermont, I didn't have any real plans. I just needed to get away from there and think by myself for a while. So I drove around a little bit, pretty aimlessly, stayed in a few places for a while, and then one day I realized I was on my way back to Dorrance."

"No need to apologize. This is your home, Laura. You're always welcome here. Your old room is just the way you left it, in fact, and Alice has been keeping it nice and clean for you." Alice, the maid, wouldn't dare do otherwise.

"Thank you. I'm sorry for putting you out this way."

"Nonsense. I've been expecting you. After everything that's happened, I was sure you'd want to get back to something safe and familiar."

Laura almost disagreed on principle, then realized that her mother was exactly right. "I'm over the worst of it, really. I don't even have nightmares anymore." Well, not very often, at least. "I just want to put that all behind me now and get on with my life." She laughed nervously. "That sounds pretty trite, doesn't it?"

Her mother shook her head. "Not at all. You've been through a lot, more than I can imagine, I'm sure. If you weren't so strong, if you didn't have those Rustin genes, I don't know what would have happened to you."

Laura set aside her teacup, only half empty, and started to get up. "I have to bring in my bags before I collapse. I drove straight through last night."

Mary Collier was up before her, urging her back down. "Don't worry about it. Del will be back in an hour or two and I'll have him unload the car. It sounds to me like you need your bed more than you need your bags."

Laura opened her mouth, prepared to protest further, but she knew it was a lost cause, that it was such a minor battle that it wasn't worth fighting, and most of all she knew her mother was right. She was exhausted. Her hands were shaking and her thoughts were muddled and the tea tasted like rainwater in her mouth, thin and tasteless. She needed to sleep and recover her wits, because if she was going to survive in the face of her mother's indomitable urge to manage everyone and everything, she'd have to do it with a clear head.

"Thanks. You're right. I'll talk to you later."

Her feet seemed to find the right room without guidance from her brain, and she collapsed across the familiar bedspread on the familiar bed without a glance through the adjacent window at the familiar countryside.

It was dusk when she opened her eyes again, disoriented and still disturbed by vaguely unpleasant dreams. She was startled to discover that she'd slept through most of the day, although darkness came so early now that it wasn't quite as extraordinary as she first thought. Habit was strong; she reached for the bedside lamp without even glancing in that direction and a soft glow spread through the room, chasing shadows into corners. Laura sat up and slowly let her eyes roam through her surroundings.

It was exactly as she had left it slightly more than two years earlier. The stuffed animals were arranged in the right order, the items on her dresser—those she hadn't taken the night she'd stormed out of the house—were in their proper places. She had no doubt that if she opened the closet door or pulled open a drawer in the dresser, she'd find all of the clothing that she had left behind. Probably freshly laundered.

She slid her feet off the side of the bed and stood up a bit unsteadily, then walked over to the mirror and appraised the young woman who stared back at her. Two years older, Laura, she told herself, but you've aged a lot more than that. Some of it shows—there are new lines in your face and something different about the eyes—but most of it doesn't. And the parts that didn't show were far more significant. There were scars inside that would heal with time, and there were other scars that she would have to live with forever.

Her luggage was in the hall just outside the door, all of it. Laura frowned. She had only wanted her overnight bag and the smaller suitcase, but she hadn't specified. Her mother obviously assumed that she was back to stay, but Laura had made a promise to herself when she first realized what her destination was. She was back in Dorrance and maybe that was going to be permanent, but she would not be staying at her mother's house, not for the long term. This was a visit, nothing more, a temporary refuge while she decided what to do next. It was going to be a tough battle. Her mother would employ every weapon in her arsenal to keep her daughter close now that she was back—guilt, sympathy, logic, duty—each chosen at the appropriate time and wielded with consummate skill.

Laura had beaten her once, two years ago, beaten her by retreating into what was supposed to have been a new life with Sean Brennan. Well, it had been a new life, all right, and then some. But she had changed a lot in those two years, changes her mother couldn't possibly know about, and she felt better prepared for what was to come than she ever had before.

Not that confidence assured victory, of course. Her mother was relentless. What she didn't overcome with a frontal assault had always succumbed eventually to attrition. Laura knew that tactic as well, and told herself that she had to be on her guard at all times, even now before the battle was at hand. Mary Collier was certainly plotting her strategies, planning for every contingency.

Laura moved all of the luggage into the bedroom, but most of it she just piled in a corner. It would eventually have to be taken back down to the Chevy, but now wasn't the time for that. Now was the time, however, for a shower and a change of clothes, and then she'd deal with her stomach, which was enthusiastically complaining about the long gap between meals.

A short while later, scrubbed, wearing jeans and a bulky pullover, Laura ventured downstairs. It was very quiet and the grandfather clock in the front hall clicked away contentedly, cutting the day into tiny segments. Laura moved from room to room, feeling the presence of her mother even when she was absent. The house seemed empty and a glance out the side window confirmed it. The Jeep was gone.

Laura returned to the kitchen in search of a snack, and this time she spotted the note on the kitchen table, handwritten in her mother's meticulously clear cursive. "Went for groceries. There's salad and cold meat in the fridge. I don't have any beer but I'll pick some up on my way back. Love, Mother."

The salad was freshly made. Laura cut up a few thin strips of ham and laid them across the top, suddenly ravenous, and was only mildly disappointed when the only salad dressing she could find was diet French. She had eaten almost the entire bowl full before it occurred to her that she probably should have taken only a portion, but it was too late for that now, and she finished what remained with only a mild twinge of guilt.

Her hunger dealt with, Laura made a more leisurely tour of the house and confirmed what she already suspected. The only changes in two years had been superficial ones. The familiarity was comforting and helped drive away the feeling of disorientation and unreality that had troubled her ever since the problems with Sean had begun to grow serious. She felt a slight loosening of her constant guard against anything unsettling or unexpected, but she knew better than to relax completely. Her mother had the instincts of a predator. If she detected weakness in her daughter, she'd exploit it ruthlessly. It would be for Laura's own good, of course, but it would still be a suffocating application of force.

The house was uncomfortably warm. Her mother always kept the thermostat up high, and Laura was more used to the inefficient heating of her car, or the grudging warmth of cheap motels or rooming houses. Her sinuses felt dry and she grabbed her coat and then set out to walk around the property.

The ground was already partially frozen and there would be no more farming until the thaw. Del Huggins would be in maintenance mode now, tuning up the tractors, checking the barn and silo for pests or deterioration, preparing the crop rotation schedule for her mother's approval, after the inevitable changes she would make just to ensure that Del knew who was the boss. Laura wondered how and why he had put up with her for so many years. She treated him like a flunky and made no secret of the fact that she didn't trust his judgment. It was hard to feel sympathy for him, though. Del was a taciturn, irritable, and irritating man who had never made any attempt to disguise his disapproval of Laura, perhaps because of her perpetual battles with her mother, perhaps just because she was young and, to his way of thinking, privileged. Del lived alone in a tiny house out beyond Sharp's Curve, never entertained visitors, was rarely seen in town. He never ate in local restaurants or drank in local bars. As a child, Laura had always thought of him in much the same way that she thought of her mother's small herd of milk cows.

The flower beds, though presently colorless, were as well maintained as ever, and the vegetable garden in the side yard had been plowed under in anticipation of the spring. Mary insisted upon maintaining this small farm within a farm by herself, and never let Del or the hired hands or even Laura help with the work here. Even at fifty years of age, Mary Collier was a strong and active woman. She worked with shovel, hoe, and rake, planted the seeds by hand, weeded and pruned and eventually harvested beans, peas, corn, radishes, turnips, lettuce, carrots, celery, and a variety of herbs and garnishes.

"Our family is connected to the soil here, Laura. I keep up the garden so that I don't lose that connection. You don't appreciate what you have unless you really work for it. You'll learn that one of these days." Laura had been offered a plot of ground for a garden of her own, but she had less than graciously declined. Her mother hadn't insisted, which was fortunate, because Laura was quite sure she'd have been bullied until she too spent a little time each day tending crops that could much more easily have been extracted from the farm's commercial output.

The toolshed was closed and locked and the ground hard and bare, but Laura was quite certain it would be torn and tilled at spring thaw. Shaking her head, she went back into the house and began rehearsing her arguments for the inevitable confrontation. Her mother wasn't going to like her plans, not even a little bit.

CHAPTER TWO

It was slightly after six when her mother returned, the Jeep's headlights visible through the denuded trees. Laura had grown increasingly restless and nervous, anticipating the argument that would inevitably follow when she made her plans known. There was nothing in the house to distract her. Her mother's television only picked up two channels and those just barely, and she didn't own a VCR. The only reading matter in the house consisted of farm journals and a collection of books dealing with crop rotation, fertilization, and other agrarian issues. Laura had suggested using a computer to manage much of the farm's business, but her mother wouldn't have one in the house, and always referred to them as "those damn black boxes." She insisted on keeping the ledger and all other records manually, occasionally using a typewriter but most often inscribing the figures by hand. Fortunately, her handwriting was neat and legible, a talent she had managed to pass down to her daughter.

The new Jeep was the only change Laura had noticed. Mary had traded in her vehicles every three years with relentless regularity, so even this one bit of novelty was paradoxically familiar. Laura opened the door as her mother stepped up onto the porch, carrying a small bundle clutched against her chest. A sharp, cold wind had sprung up during the past hour, and Laura closed the door quickly.

"I was beginning to worry." She followed her mother through the living room to the dining room, where the older woman placed her package down on the oversized mahogany dining table.

"Don't be silly, dear. You haven't known where I was or what I was doing for more than a year, so why worry about a few hours?" It might have been meant as a jab, but her mother was smiling broadly as she slipped out of her coat, and Laura decided to accept it in good spirit.

"You're right, Mother. Can I make you some tea? You must be cold."

"No, thank you. The Jeep stays quite warm. And I have something else for us to drink." She dropped her coat over a chair and walked to the antique hutch in the corner, where she carefully selected two crystal wineglasses. "There's a bottle opener in the drawer, dear, if you don't mind."

Laura automatically did as she was told, retrieving the bottle opener and turning just as her mother removed a bottle of champagne from the bag. "I thought we'd celebrate your homecoming. I remember you always liked champagne."

This was definitely a change, and Laura hesitated warily. Her mother had never really approved of alcohol, only allowed it in the house when they were entertaining, and almost never took any herself.

"Open it, will you? I've never been very good with that thing."

Laura blinked and licked her lips, then crossed to the table and accepted the bottle. Actually, she didn't care for champagne, although she enjoyed wine. A snide inner voice was shouting that Mary was well aware of that fact, but the rest of her believed that it was a sincere, if slightly misguided, attempt to patch up old quarrels. Even the hint of possible compromise was welcome.

It was actually a very good champagne. They sat in the living room and Mary waited until Laura had poured them both a second glass before the inevitable shift to the business at hand.

Laura was mentally reviewing the various opening gambits she'd rehearsed in anticipation of this moment, trying to decide which would be the most effective, but just as she was about to say something her mother effectively preempted the issue.

"It will be so nice having you back at home. The house is really too big for one person. I feel lost in it sometimes."

Laura doubted her mother would feel lost if she were alone in Buckingham Palace, but she let it pass. "This is only temporary, Mother. I'm not moving back in."

Mary blinked but there was no other visible reaction. "But this is your home."

"I know that and I am going to stay in Dorrance, at least for the time being. But not here. I need to be alone for a while longer. After everything that's happened, I realize that I don't know myself as well as I thought."

"No one will bother you here. It's a big house and you know I'd respect your privacy."

Laura struggled to keep her expression neutral. Mary Collier could no more resist the temptation to insert herself into her daughter's private affairs than she could commit suicide by holding her breath. It was temperamentally if not physically impossible. Oh, her intentions would be good. She would blithely walk uninvited into Laura's bedroom without knocking, or read her private correspondence, and listen in on a telephone conversation without feeling any guilt. "I was just concerned about you" or "I just noticed it lying there and picked it up without thinking" or some similar excuse. She would honestly believe it, too. It would never occur to her that the standards she applied to others differed from those she tolerated when applied to her own privacy.

"It wouldn't be the same. I'd feel like a kid again and it's time for me to starting feeling like an adult. And acting like one."

"Don't I treat you like an adult?"

Laura considered that, and answered it honestly. "Most of the time, yes, you do. I'm sorry. I don't mean to sound ungrateful or unfriendly. I'm really not. But I've been through a lot lately and there's some kinds of healing that you just can't do with other people around." She leaned forward and touched the back of her mother's hand. "I'll get a job in town somewhere, look up some of the old gang. I just need to ease back into things slowly." Not that she'd ever had much of a "gang." Laura's memories of her childhood were predominantly ones in which she was alone. She'd had only two close friends in high school, and even they'd grown apart.

"But where will you stay? I don't think there's anything for sale or rent in the area and Jo Kaplan closed down her boarding house last year when her arthritis got so bad."

"I was thinking about opening up the cabin." More than thinking about it. It had been her plan almost from the outset. Her memories of the sturdy cabin up at Moon Pond were almost exclusively pleasant ones. She and her father had spent many a happy weekend there, fishing, hiking, shooting cans off logs, or even just working on the cabin. Her mother had come occasionally as well, but had never been willing to spend the night. The only heat came from a woodstove and a small electric space heater and there hadn't been running water or a flush toilet until the year before her father left.

"The cabin? The place must be filthy. No one's been in it since before," she hesitated, "since before you left. Del drives by once a month or so to make sure no one has broken in or burned it down, but there's no phone and no electricity." She seemed more puzzled than disappointed.

"I can have the electricity turned on and a telephone installed. And if it's filthy, well, maybe that's what I need, a project to fill the time and give me a feeling that I'm accomplishing something. And if it doesn't work out, I can always move back." This last was an attempt at mollification, and it appeared to have worked because her mother visibly relaxed.

"Well, that's certainly a possibility. They did finally finish Moon Pond Road, you know. It connects to the feeder road for the highway now."

Laura's eyebrows went up and she pretended enthusiasm, although she was actually disappointed. Part of the charm of the cabin was its isolation. She had inherited it from her father's sister, Aunt Olivia, along with a small trust that paid for the annual taxes and insurance with a little left over for maintenance. "Or if I decide not to stay, maybe I could sell the property and buy something closer to town."

"Oh, I doubt that. The land on this side of Moon Pond is almost worthless. There's no reason for anyone to invest in Dorrance, I'm afraid. When the interstate bypassed us, the property values here all dropped like stones. I'm afraid you'll be stuck with that white elephant forever."

"At least I won't have to worry about paying rent." Mary's subdued opposition had caught her off guard because she'd expected a major brawl. Could it possibly be that her mother might actually be trying to see her point of view for a change? Laura remained skeptical, but she decided to offer a small concession. "I promise I'll come by regularly. I'll even be pleasant to Mason, if he's speaking to me again."

Mason Cortway was a year older than Laura, and had declared himself in love with her while she was still a high school sophomore. She'd dated him briefly, very briefly, and turned down three marriage proposals over the course of three years. He had been furious when her engagement to Sean Brennan became common knowledge, refused to come to the wedding, said some unpleasant and untrue things about Laura and Sean behind their backs. Not as unpleasant as the eventual truth, though, she admitted to herself. Mary had liked him, or pretended to, anyway. Mason came from a "good" family, was heir apparent to the second largest farm in Dorrance as well as his father's store, and was not by nature a strong-willed person. In Mary's distorted scale of values, he was a near-perfect catch.

"I'm sure he's forgiven everything by now. I know he can be very annoying sometimes, but his intentions are good. He's like your father in some ways; neither of them ever really grew up." Laura suppressed a flash of annoyance, because she knew there was some truth to that. Her father had always seemed more at ease with younger people than with his own generation. "Mason thinks he's in love with you and he can be very thoughtful when it occurs to him."

"And when he thinks it's to his advantage. Did you say Ashley was back?"

A flicker of a frown passed briefly across the older woman's face. "Yes, indeed. She lost another job in Buffalo, fired again. Told a customer off or something like that. That girl always did have a temper."

Laura laughed. "You can say that again. How many fights did we have when we were kids?"

"I couldn't possibly have counted them all. You had more black eyes than most of the boys in town."

"I gave back as good as I got."

Mary smiled, remembering. "I always thought you were a bit of a tomboy, but you couldn't hold a candle to Ashley Sothern. She was a pretty child, though, could have caught herself a good husband if she'd kept her looks. It's too late now, I suppose."

"Mother, she's only twenty-three, same as me."

Mary nodded. "I realize that. But you have Rustin blood in you. When you're knocked down, you eventually spring back. I think Ashley has already given up the fight. You'll see what I mean when you talk to her. I won't say anything else right now; I don't want to prejudice you."

They spent the evening talking casually while Mary made supper. She could afford a cook as well as having Alice in three times weekly to clean, but Mary always insisted on preparing meals herself, sometimes grudgingly allowing Laura to help in small, insignificant ways. Tonight Laura made no effort to volunteer her services, correctly interpreting her mother's mood, but sat at the table drinking coffee throughout the process. Within the past hour she had heard a summary of two years' worth of gossip and nodded dutifully through a short flurry of complaints about the way small farmers were being treated by the State Board of Agriculture. Over supper she acquired a working knowledge of town manager John Dill's latest shortcomings, some of which were probably valid. Dill was a charmer who, according to her mother, kept his job solely because of his personal popularity and not because of his performance. She characterized him as an indifferent administrator, timid, unimaginative, inflexible, and lazy. Laura thought her mother was exaggerating, but it was probably true that his periodic sparring with Mary Collier was part of an effort to build support among the large faction in town who had resented the Rustin line for generations and considered the present matriarch aloof and overbearing.

"He did try to patch things up last year, but I know how his mind works. He just wanted to play both sides of the fence. I let him think I'd forgiven, if not forgotten, that the past is past, but I have a long memory. Sooner or later, Mr. Dill will make a fatal mistake. Did you know he tried to take part of the farm away last year? Wanted to put a new section of road across the southwest corner. Said it was because the curve was dangerous. Even got Chief Clay to support him after the Langston boy crashed his car and killed his girlfriend."

"Oh, just forget him, Mother. He's a little man in a big body and he probably hates his life here. Does he still talk about moving back to Buffalo?"

"Probably. I don't take much notice of what he says anymore. His wife left him, you know."

"Yes, so you said. They always seemed so close."

"Appearances can be deceptive."

They finished the champagne with supper. Laura felt exhausted and excused herself early. She considered unpacking her suitcase into her old dresser, but decided against it. Her mother would be watching for just such a seemingly innocuous sign of weakness and she didn't want to offer even minimal encouragement for a prolonged campaign to keep her at the farm.

Laura had to admit that she felt more at peace than she had in a long time. She made a slow circuit of the room, lightly touching the ghosts of her childhood, the dolls, stuffed animals, and the row of Nancy Drew mysteries she'd devoured during a single summer. The ridiculously ornate mirror still stood above her oversized dresser, and the wicker chair under the window looked as comfortable as it had when she'd curled up on its fat cushion to stare outside and wish to be older so that she could run away and have adventures.

Well, I had my adventures, she told herself, and they're not nearly as much fun as I thought they'd be. No fun at all, as a matter of fact. She put one hand on the back of the chair and then impulsively sat down, pulling her legs up under her and wrapping her arms around her shoulders tightly. It was dark outside, the night held at bay only by a security light on the toolshed and some spillover from the back of the kitchen. The sky was cloudy, the moon and stars invisible.

Laura was just turning her head away when a slight shifting of the shadows caught her attention. She turned back, convinced that something had moved just outside the pool of light beside the shed. Leaning forward, nose pressed against the cold window pane, she tried to focus and for a second she thought she saw someone standing there, but she blinked and when she refocused there was no sign of anything out of place. Del Huggins maybe, making a last check of the property before going home? It seemed unlikely. Maybe her mother had gone outside for a second. Or most likely, her eyes and her imagination were playing tricks on her. She'd spent a long time jumping at shadows while the business with Sean was resolving itself, and even longer afterward. His death should have ended all that, but she had trouble believing that he was gone even now, that she no longer had anything to fear from him and his crazed obsessions.

She slept better that night than she had in a while, and if she tossed and turned at times, disturbed by old memories and old fears, they were not strong enough to remain long in her mind, and she woke the following morning more refreshed than she had felt in almost a year. It was almost enough to make her reconsider her mother's suggestion that she remain at the farm permanently. Almost, but not quite.

Her mother had already left the house when Laura came downstairs that morning. Alice was cleaning the kitchen and greeted Laura as though she hadn't been gone for more than two years. They had a cup of coffee together and Alice told her that she was about to become a grandmother. Alice had, to a limited extent, been Laura's co-conspirator during her childhood, occasionally helping her thwart one rule or another. She seemed smaller and frailer now than when Laura had last seen her, but she supposed the change was in her eyes and nowhere else.

The temperature had dropped since the previous day, so

Laura put on her heaviest sweater under her coat before venturing outside. The Chevy miraculously started up on the second try and minutes later she was at the foot of Taggart Hill, headed toward downtown Dorrance. She gassed up at Ed's Service but the attendant was a stranger to her. He gave her the once over, not being too obvious about it, but bundled up as she was she figured it was habit rather than actual interest. With a full tank and a thinning wallet, she followed Main Street back in to town.

Dorrance had always been a bit of an anomaly. It had been strategically located a century earlier, but the interstate had shifted traffic away and the Indian reservation to the north restricted its growth in that direction. To the south the soil was poor and, with the exception of Moon Pond, unattractive for development. Most of the local farms were so small that they were at a disadvantage dealing with wholesalers; even Rustin Farm was only marginally profitable.

Laura parked in the small municipal lot next to Davenport's Hardware Goods. The wind had died down considerably, but dead leaves and occasional pieces of debris were still airborne and she leaned forward to shelter her face as much as possible. The next door down was Slade's Café. She wasn't hungry, but Slade's was always the best place to find out what was happening. Of course it worked both ways. Everyone in town would know she was back once she put in an appearance.

Only two of the booths were occupied when she pushed through the door, shutting it quickly behind her to hold out the chill. There was a trucker sitting in one and he glanced up at her disinterestedly before returning to his ham and eggs. The Jensons were two booths further on. Mrs. Jenson looked older than ever, but she smiled and nodded her head and said something to her husband, who slowly turned to glance in Laura's direction.

Not that he would remember me, she thought. He was barely

able to remember his own name when I left. Mrs. Jenson insisted he was just "forgetful" and no one used the word "Alzheimer's" in her presence.

Kevin Slade emerged from the kitchen, carrying two plates. He stumbled slightly when he saw Laura stripping off her coat, then delivered the food to the Jensons.

"Hi, Kevin. Remember me?"

" 'Course I do, Miss Laura."

She took a stool at the counter and he walked around and down the other side, snagging a pot of coffee and an empty cup as he came.

"How are your parents?"

Kevin kept his eyes on the coffee so that it didn't overflow. "They're good. Mom's back in the kitchen. She'll want to come out and say hello. Dad's at the house. He doesn't come in until later. You still take it black, just sugar?"

She nodded. "Looks like business is slow this morning."

"It'll pick up after a bit. You moving back here like your Mom said?"

Laura sighed, but she had expected no less. She wondered how many people Mary Collier had spoken to during the last twenty-four hours. "I'm thinking about it. I don't suppose there's anybody looking for paid help this time of year."

"Nothing nearby except maybe the Dairy Stop down the end of town. Bud Wiegand caught one of the kids stealing the other night and fired him." Kevin scratched a shoulder absentmindedly, as if it helped him to think. "Tom Bailey retired this year, but his nephew got the job. Sorry, but that's all I can think of."

"I didn't expect much." She suddenly realized that she was, after all, hungry. "Do you suppose your mother would make me one of her special omelets?"

Edna Slade brought it out herself, turning sideways to edge her bulk through the narrow doorway. She'd supposedly been on a diet when Laura left town, but if anything, she looked even larger now. The omelet was presented as though it were an award, rather than being worthy of one.

"How are you doing, child?" Edna was smiling but not with her eyes. Like everyone else in town, she must have known at least approximately what had happened between her and Sean. "I'm doing okay, Mrs. Slade." Edna Slade had been a surrogate mother to Laura at times, particularly after her father was gone. Sometimes she'd been allowed to sit in the kitchen while Edna worked, simultaneously listening to Laura's list of grievances against her mother, the kids at school, the world in general.

"You're not really planning to move in with your mom, are you?"

Laura shook her head. "She thinks so, even though I've told her otherwise. I'm looking around for a job right now. I'd like to stay in Dorrance if I can, at least for a while. I'm thinking about opening up the cabin on Moon Pond."

Edna nodded. "I could send Kevin up with a half cord of wood for you. You wouldn't have to pay us until you were settled."

"I'll let you know. I haven't even looked at the place yet. It might be falling down or infested with rats or something. And last time I was there, there was enough laid away to last me through the winter. It'd sure be well seasoned by now."

"You just stop by if you need anything. Bill and I were real pleased to hear you were back."

The omelet was every bit as good as she remembered and she left her plate almost clean enough to reuse without washing. Two more parties entered the diner before she left, a pair of complete strangers and a farmhand who'd worked for her mother a couple of times. He glanced at her with a puzzled expression, as though he almost, but only almost, recognized her.

It didn't feel as raw when she went outside again, but she was still glad that the police station was only two blocks. The desk sergeant glanced up as she entered. "Good morning, Mrs. Brennan. What can we do for you today?"

That name sounded strange but she supposed that was still who she was, Laura Brennan, although she'd already started thinking of herself as Collier again. She'd have to ask Ted Catterall about the legalities of changing it back when she went to see him.

"Nothing special. Just wanted to let you know I was back in town, in case my mother actually missed someone."

He chuckled. "She stopped by and told the chief yesterday afternoon. Looked pretty pleased with herself."

"My mother is always pleased with herself, Sergeant Anders. Oh, and I'm thinking about opening up the cabin on Moon Pond again, so any activity you see up there in the next few weeks is likely to be me. Assuming it hasn't burnt to the ground by now."

"Oh, it's fine. Your mother asked us to keep an eye on it, make sure no one was camping out there or anything, and you know how persuasive she can be."

"Yes, she does make a habit of getting her way. I hope it wasn't too much trouble."

"Well, since they finally finished that last stretch of road, we actually run a regular patrol back and forth along there at least twice a day, so it's really no trouble at all." His smile faded slightly. "We heard about your trouble, Mrs. Brennan, and your loss. If there's anything we can do, I'm sure the chief would be happy to oblige, even if your mother wasn't, well, your mother."

Laura forced herself to smile. "Thank you, but I'm pretty much all right now. Just have to get off to a fresh start."

"That's usually best." He glanced over his shoulder at the closed door to the rear. "Would you like to see Chief Clay?"

"I don't want to disturb him and I'm sure I'll run into him soon. I've got to run."

"You take care now."

She returned to the Chevy, which stubbornly refused to start this time until she was on the verge of tears, then kicked over just as she was about to give it up as a wasted effort. Whispering thanks to whatever god watches over automobile ignitions, she pulled out of the lot and turned left, then took a sharp right and threaded her way through a residential neighborhood. She almost missed the dirt road because it was heavily overgrown, but at the last minute she recognized a particular gnarled tree and slowed, then turned off the pavement. The dirt track ran about a tenth of a mile and provided a shortcut to Moon Pond Road, where she turned right this time.

The first thing she noticed was that the roadbed was better maintained than it had been in the past. The second thing was the scattering of trash along both sides. Two years ago, there had been little reason for anyone to come this way. Teenagers would drive up to the pond to skinny dip sometimes, but they usually left their trash on the shore. Charlie Mason had occasionally used his cabin, not too far from hers, but he had died a few weeks before the wedding. The connection to the interstate feeder road not only provided a quicker route from Dorrance, but also shaved several miles off the trip from at least two other nearby towns, Nickleby and Shawcut. The increased traffic through Dorrance might marginally help a few of the businesses in Dorrance, Ed's Garage, the McDonald's, and Plato's Pizza, but was otherwise probably more trouble than it was worth. Her mother had already expressed her resentment that the town had been forced to add two full-time officers to the payroll.

"And they still won't be around when you need them. I don't know what Chief Clay is thinking of. If the state people want to build their roads, then they should provide the policing for them, but no, they'd rather put the burden on the public. Next thing you know John Dill will be raising the taxes again to pay for the new help and threatening to cut town services if he doesn't get his way."

Laura drove more slowly than necessary. It was still windy but the road was clear and dry. She was savoring the anticipation. Although she would never be so cruel as to tell her mother, it was the image of this cabin that had drawn her back to Dorrance, not Mary Collier's arms. Laura supposed she loved her mother, although she'd never been quite sure. Mary seemed so disdainful of emotional attachments that Laura often wondered how she and her father had ever decided to get married. There had been little obvious love or even affection between them for as long as Laura could remember, but they had never argued in front of her, and perhaps not in private, either. Their relationship had just come to an end as far as she could tell, and then her father had disappeared one day, taking only a suitcase full of clothing plus the cash that he'd drawn from their joint account that same morning. No one had heard from him since, and her mother had refused to make any serious effort to locate him.

"If he wanted to go so badly that he couldn't even say goodbye to us, then he certainly wouldn't thank us for tracking him down. If he decides to come back someday, we can ask him then what was so terrible about our life together that he had to run out the way he did. But until then, I'd rather just not think about him at all."

It was the only time Laura had seen Mary Collier on the verge of tears.

The road swerved gently back and forth at first, then turned sharply to the left, inclining slightly upward. Just over the crest, Laura spotted a jagged rock on her left and slowed even further. It was her unofficial signpost. There were a few fallen branches on the unpaved driveway, and she avoided them as best she could until the Chevy was well off the road. She stopped short of the cabin, locked the car, and picked her way carefully across the ground because puddles of water had accumulated and frozen and the footing was slick and treacherous. It had rained briefly during the night; she had wakened long enough to identify the sound.

Laura walked slowly up to the cabin, examining it critically as she did so. The windows were all covered with shutters and looked to be intact. There were a few shingles missing from the roof, but it seemed to be sound otherwise. The tiny outbuilding that housed the emergency electrical generator appeared to be undisturbed; it would probably need an overhaul but she'd deal with that later. A call to the electrical company should get the main power restored, and then she could find out if the pump that drew water from the well was still functioning.

The front door was closed, padlocked as well as more conventionally secured. Laura had both keys on her keychain, but before going inside she wanted to check out the exterior. There was a porch in back, positioned strategically so that someone could sit there and stare down across the small, mostly open meadow that led to Moon Pond, just visible in the distance. The sun rose in that direction in the morning, which provided a quite spectacular dawn whenever the sky was clear.

There were more fallen branches on this side of the cabin and she had to pick her way more carefully, watching where she placed her feet. That's why she didn't notice the cat until she reached the bottom step and stared up directly into its face.

It was hanging from the same hook she'd used for her wind

chimes as a child. Someone had sliced its belly open from throat to tail.

CHAPTER THREE

For the first few seconds, she thought her heart had stopped beating. It hurt to draw breath, and not just because the air was so cold. She had unconsciously reached out to grasp one of the guardrails on the stairs, and now clutched it so tightly that her fingers were starting to cramp. Look away from it, she told herself, but it was hard to turn her head, because she was afraid to see what might be lurking to either side, hidden in the shadows, waiting to spring out at her. The way Sean had sprung out at her a year before.

It's day, not night. There are no shadows. And most importantly, Sean isn't there anymore. He can't hurt me. He's dead and buried and I'm safe now. She ran through the arguments in her head, knew they were true, but felt only slightly better. Slowly her fingers uncurled, and briefly they ached even worse as the circulation returned.

Laura glanced up, hoping it had just been a flashback. She'd experienced them periodically in the months following Sean's death, although she hadn't had one now for several weeks. But the cat was still there, swinging back and forth as the wind buffeted it. The blood was dried and the small body stiffened by cold and rigor mortis. "Kids," she said aloud. "Drunken teenagers playing a cruel prank." But against whom? The cabin had been empty for at least two years and the cat was recently dead.

She backed away from the porch, her eyes remaining locked on the tiny corpse until she had retreated around the corner of the building. Then she sank against the rough wood, closed her eyes, and waited until her heartbeat and respiration returned to normal.

Although she was tempted to return to her car and leave, Laura stood huddled up against the cabin wall until she felt she was in control of herself, then fished the keychain out of the pocket of her jeans with fingers that were numb with more than just cold. The padlock was stiff and turned reluctantly, but she managed to open it; the regular lock worked normally. Laura pushed open the door and stepped into her cabin, her place, the only real property she owned now.

It didn't look very inviting.

For one thing, it was dark. Laura took a flashlight from her jacket pocket and flicked it on, playing it around the room. Everything was as she remembered it, except smaller somehow. There was a lantern on a shelf beside the fireplace with a working mantle and at least some fuel left. Her hands were trembling so much that it took three matches before she could get it lit, but when she succeeded, it drove off most of the shadows, although they lurked in the corners, waiting for their chance to return.

Laura slowly turned and looked around and her first impression was that everything was filthy. There was dust everywhere, and a few leaves had managed to get in somehow, which was puzzling because the cabin was well caulked and close to airtight. Her mother must have sent Del Huggins over with the spare key to check the place at some point and he'd tracked them in.

Otherwise, she was happy to note, things seemed to be in good shape. There were linens in the cupboard at the foot of the presently bare bunk beds in their corner room, although she'd have to wash them before she could use them. The kitchen, adjacent but separated from the main room by only a half wall, was fully stocked with pans, plates, and utensils, although there was no food left that she'd risk eating. There were spare mantles for the lantern but no more fuel for either that or the propane stove, some work clothes and a pair of heavy boots in good condition, a small tool chest, a very dusty but usable first aid kit, and a collection of mops, brushes, and other cleaning supplies in a metal cabinet next to the sink. The tiny bathroom had neither towels nor toilet paper, but since the water wasn't running, that wasn't an issue yet. She found lots of spiderwebs and other evidence of insect life, but the squirrels hadn't gotten in and, as far as she could see, neither had the mice.

She returned to the main room thoughtfully, then rummaged in the tool drawer until she found what she was looking for—a hatchet. After taking several deep breaths to calm herself, she unbolted the second door, a narrow one that led out onto the porch. Just concentrate on the rope, she told herself, letting her eyes trail across the underside of the porch roof. There it was, tied to the metal ring her father had installed when she was ten years old. It was heavy twine, not rope. She stepped onto one of the weatherbeaten wooden chairs, still not allowing herself to look down, reached up with her free hand to force the twine against the wood, and swung the hatchet.

It took three tries because the angle was awkward, but then the twine was severed and she heard the dull thump of something falling to the porch floor. She stepped down and returned to the cabin, dropped the hatchet on the table to her right, and retrieved several moldy newspapers from the stack by the fireplace. A few minutes later she left a loosely rolled package in the brush a few dozen steps from the cabin so that nature could take its course.

The dead cat had spoiled her mood but not her determination. If anything, the surprisingly sound condition of the cabin had only encouraged her to act more quickly. She made a quick mental list of things she'd need, most of which she'd try to borrow from her mother, although Mary would undoubtedly refuse payment, then locked both doors again and returned to her car. It was almost calm now, the cold crisp but not biting, and she glanced around a final time, then got inside and drove back to Dorrance.

Some things went well, and some things not, but on balance, the rest of her morning was a success. Ted Catterall, the attorney who administered the trust fund, was able to see her almost immediately. He was a disturbingly thin man with a pinched face and a perpetual expression of pain, but it was wrapped around a genuinely pleasant personality. After the obligatory reminiscences about old times, he told her that the trust had actually outstripped its expenditures during the past two years.

"I don't see any problem about using those funds for improvements, and a telephone and electricity certainly fall into that category."

"I'd like to have the pump and the generator looked at, too."

He nodded. "You might want to try Ed down at the garage. He'll give a fair price and he stands by his work. Bud Davenport can bring in a contractor if Ed's too busy, but you never know what you're going to get."

"How about Bill Forrester? He's the one who installed the pump in the first place."

"Moved to Schenectady to be closer to his daughter."

"Is there anything else I need to do?"

Catterall drummed his fingers on the desk while his face grew even more pinched in thought. "You didn't mention the post office."

"Oh, right." Not that she expected to get much mail. Her life outside Dorrance was ended, at least for the time being, and Dorrance was small enough that people rarely wrote to one another. But there'd be bills. "I'll take care of that. Have to buy a mailbox."

She decided the post office could wait, but stopped at Ed's garage on the way back. Edwin Burgess was Catterall's opposite, pudgy and soft looking, with a face that looked like a Santa Claus, and a raspy voice. As a child, Laura had thought of him as a gigantic troll. His gruff exterior was misleading and he had a good reputation; even Laura's mother had nothing bad to say about him. When Laura described the work she wanted done, he quoted a price that was much lower than she had expected, and let her use his phone to call the electric company.

"No point in going up there till the juice is on. Tell them it's an emergency or they won't be out for a week."

They promised to have it done within two days. The telephone company, on the other hand, was less than cooperative. "There are no lines along Moon Pond Road, Miss. The work is scheduled for this coming spring. May I suggest a cell phone until then?"

She stopped at the post office and notified them that she'd be opening up the cabin. "Better make it a week from today. I'll be staying at Rustin Farm until then." The clerk was a stranger to her, a dour-faced woman whose lips were so thin they occasionally disappeared entirely.

"All right, Miss Collier."

She had given her name as Laura Collier, but had explained that it was possible that some mail might come addressed to Laura Brennan. "I'm recently widowed," she'd explained.

"Sorry for your loss, Mrs. Brennan." The clerk didn't sound sorry at all, and Laura left feeling vaguely offended.

Her adventures were not over for the day. She just had time before lunch to run out to the Dairy Stop and check the place out. It looked even dingier than she remembered, but she pulled into a poorly marked parking space and sat there for a while. There wasn't much violent crime in Dorrance, but during her senior year the convenience store had been robbed late one evening and the clerk assaulted. New lights had been installed at the time, and assuming they were still working, it looked as though the surroundings were pretty well lit up after dark. There was a Laundromat to its left, which hadn't changed at all, but an antique shop had replaced the thrift store on the opposite side. The sign on the Laundromat door warned that it closed at eight; the antique shop seemed to have gone out of business.

Laura went inside and glanced around at the usual selection of packaged foods and incidentals. The far wall was completely concealed by a cooler stocked with milk, juices, and soft drinks. The teenaged boy behind the counter was sitting down when she came in and he didn't rise, hardly even glanced in her direction. The magazine in his lap was clearly of more immediate interest. His sweater was covered with flaming guitars and she could hear heavy metal playing, though not loudly, from under the counter.

It was chilly inside, but that suited her fine. She hated going back and forth from bitter cold to oppressive dry heat, which was another reason for not moving back in with her mother. A quick walk up and down the aisles provided no surprises and suggested no problems, so she grabbed a bag of chips she really didn't want and brought them to the counter.

"Hi. Not very busy this morning." She nodded to indicate the empty store behind her.

The teenager's face reflected a brief struggle before he decided to be sociable. "We were mobbed earlier." He picked up the chips and glanced at the price before turning to the register.

"I see there's a Help Wanted sign in the window."

He nodded. "Yeah. Know anyone who wants to work nights?"

"Actually, I was looking for something myself. Do you have an application or something I can fill out?"

The kid snickered. "No application, lady. Here." He tore off a piece of the register tape and wrote a phone number on it. "Just call old man Wiegand and tell him you want the job. He'll probably hire you over the phone."

"How much does it pay?"

"Minimum." He stared at her intently for a moment, as though trying to decide whether or not she could be trusted. "Wiegand's a bastard. The shift's supposed to be six hours and that's what he pays for, but you'll have to clean up the backroom and cash out your register on your own time. No discount for anything you eat or drink and, trust me, he'll know if you're taking anything on the sly."

She laughed, trying to sound like a co-conspirator. "No health plan, I take it?"

This time his laugh was a snort and he looked away self-consciously. "No vacation, no sick days, and the only holiday he pays for is Christmas, and you won't get that because you have to be here a full year first." He laughed again, more restrained this time. "As far as I know, no one's ever made it a full year, so I guess he doesn't pay for that one, either."

"Sounds like the job of my dreams." She put the slip of paper in her pocket. "Thanks for the help. Maybe I'll be seeing you."

Laura had intended to return to the farm for lunch, but she stopped at the drugstore across the street from the Dairy Stop to pick up a local paper, the weekly *Dorrance Courier*. She had already opened it to the single page of classified ads when she reached the counter, and set it down without looking up. She was fumbling in her wallet for change when a familiar voice startled her.

"Are you shoplifting again or are you paying this time?"

She looked up, startled, and saw Ashley Sothern staring at her. "Ashley! Mother told me you were back. What are you doing here?"

Ashley pointed at the name badge pinned to her shirt. "Working. What does it look like? Which is more than I can say for you, I imagine."

"Well, I'm trying to do something about that." Laura turned the paper so that the classifieds were showing. "Looks like you grabbed the only good job in town."

Her friend huffed. "If this is a good job, there's no hope for any of us. It was the only thing available except for the Dairy Stop, and I wouldn't work there on a bet." Laura's face fell slightly, and Ashley picked up on it immediately. "Oh no, you're not going to do that, are you? Bud Wiegand is the boss from hell."

Laura shrugged her shoulders. "Beggars can't be choosers. It's the only thing available."

"Your mother will be pissed. She hates his guts. Or is that just another reason for doing it?"

"No. Mother and I are actually getting along pretty well. Of course, I've only been home for one day. How long have you been home?"

"I came back during the fall. You can take the girl out of the small town, but you can't take the small town out of the girl, or something sappy like that. I hated Buffalo even worse than I hated Dorrance, and the ratty little apartment I had wasn't any better than living at home. The landlady watched me closer than my mom does. No visitors in the room after eight, no loud music, no loud noise at all, in fact. No pets, muddy boots to be left in the back hall, thermostat locked so I couldn't adjust it. And the job wasn't much better. So I chucked it and here I am, just like you, living with my mom and wondering if I'm going to end up stuck here for the rest of my life."

"I'm not living with my mother, or at least not for long. I'm going to open up the cabin on Moon Pond."

Ashley frowned. "Isn't that kind of primitive? Camping out is fun in the summer but it gets real cold out here, in case you've forgotten."

Another customer made an impatient sound so Laura stepped out of the way. No sooner had the woman departed than another appeared. Ashley gave her a martyred look. "Hey, I'm off for lunch in twenty minutes. Why don't we grab a sandwich at Slade's?"

Laura was acutely aware of the thinness of her wallet. "It's really kind of early for me yet, Ash."

But her friend correctly diagnosed the problem and brushed it aside. "Hey, I'm sure you can force something down. My treat, to celebrate having you back." Laura must have still looked doubtful, so Ashley sweetened the pie. "There's nobody here in town I can talk to, Laura. C'mon, give me a chance to get some of the last two years off my chest."

"Okay, you're on. But when I get my first paycheck, it'll be my turn."

On a warm day, they might have walked the eight blocks, but today they rode in Laura's car. She apologized for its condition, but Ashley just laughed. "At least you've got a car. My dad drops me off and picks me up most days. The rest of the time I have to walk to work."

Slade's was much busier now, and they managed to snag the last open booth. Bill Slade, Kevin's father, was working the counter while Kevin and a young girl waited tables. He gave Laura a brief wave when she came in, but was obviously too busy to talk.

It was inevitable that the subject of Sean Brennan would arise. They had just placed their orders when Ashley's face turned serious. "I know you probably don't want to do this right now, but we have to talk about Sean."

Laura sighed. "What's to say? I'm sure you read the newspaper stories like everyone else. They got things mostly right." They had gotten the facts right, with one notable exception. Facts didn't tell the whole story, though; there was no way that the printed stories could possibly have conveyed what she had experienced during those last few months, and particularly the final two weeks.

"I don't mean that. I'm talking about the way I acted, you know, before that. I was out of line and I guess I knew it even back then. But you know how hard it is for me to admit it when I'm wrong. I'm so sorry, Laura."

It had been Ashley who had introduced her to Sean, Ashley who had been dating the handsome young farmhand and who had been hoping for a proposal. The proposal had eventually gone to her best friend. Laura had wanted her to be maid of honor, but Ashley had packed up and moved to Buffalo without a word of explanation. Probably just as well, since Mary Collier's opposition had forced Laura and Sean to elope and get married by a justice of the peace.

"It was perfectly reasonable for you to be angry, Ash. You don't need to apologize for the way you felt."

"Yes, I do. We were friends, are friends, best friends, and I should have been happy for you. If I'd been honest with myself, Sean and I never had a chance together. He was always so conventional and well mannered and I was always acting crazy." Her eyes went suddenly wide with horror and she reached across the table with both hands to hold Laura's wrists. "Oh my God, I can't believe I said that! I'm making this worse instead of better."

Laura took a deep breath and forced herself to remain calm. "No, you're not. You don't need to watch every word you say around me. It was a bad time when Sean got sick, worse than you can possibly imagine, but he's gone now, it's over, and I need to have people treat me normally so that I can feel normal again myself."

Ashley slowly relaxed her grip and pulled her arms back, looking relieved but still wary. "Do you want to talk about it? Sean, I mean."

"Not right now, no. But eventually, yes, I do. I'm just not sure how to say what I need to say yet."

"Well, whenever you're ready, I'll be around if you need someone."

They spent the rest of the meal talking trivialities, local gossip, the comparative disadvantages of life in Buffalo, New York, and Burlington, Vermont. Laura noticed that her mother was right, Ashley had indeed gained some weight again. It was a battle she'd fought constantly during high school, slowly and painfully shedding twenty pounds over the course of months, then gaining it back in a matter of weeks because she ate compulsively when she was depressed, and she'd been depressed a great deal during those four years. She had a pretty face and a sharp mind, but her tongue was even sharper and she was rarely troubled by inhibitions. She had been suspended twice for talking back to teachers, sported a black eye from one of her boyfriends when she humiliated him publicly, and spent several hours sitting in the police station once when she got stopped for running a red light and gave Officer Spellman a hard time about it.

Ashley had a salad for lunch and declined dessert, but joined Laura in a cup of coffee. It was getting close to the time to take her back to the drugstore when a silver-haired man came through the door, crossed immediately to the cash register, and began paying for a takeout order.

"Isn't that John Dill?" Laura moved her head, trying to get a less obstructed view.

Ashley leaned back for a better look, then turned back to her coffee. "That's him, all right. Still has a poker up his ass, too."

"He looks awful. Has he been sick?"

Ashley shook her head. "No, but he took the business about his wife pretty badly." Her eyes suddenly widened. "You do know about Mrs. Dill, don't you?"

"Mother said she walked out on him."

"Well, she's gone anyway, but no one's quite sure she walked. Left him a note typed on his computer screen and drove off to her mother's in Oklahoma. Except she never got there. She gassed up out near the highway and that was the last anyone ever saw of her or the car."

"Kidnapped?"

"Not likely. Dill spends all of their money living up to the community's expectations. He can't even collect on her insurance until they find a body or declare her legally dead in, what, six or seven years? My mom thinks he killed her and hid the body somewhere, and the state police did come down a few times and question him about it. But I don't think so. Say what you will about the bastard, he did love his wife, and for some reason she found something to love in him. They were inseparable. No one ever heard them fight about anything, and he was so broken up about it, I even felt a little sorry for him. No, I think she was carjacked and dumped in a ditch somewhere and they'll find her in the spring when they go out to patch the roads."

That image was a little too morbid for Laura, whose own brush with death had been similarly ugly. She set down her coffee cup and made a show of looking at her watch. "We have to get going if I'm going to get you back on time."

After dropping Ashley off, Laura realized that despite a few awkward moments, she had really enjoyed herself. She hadn't had time to develop new friends in Burlington before Sean's problems began to emerge, and she'd been too preoccupied after that to spend much effort on her own needs. His breakdown had manifested itself very quickly once it started. A few months after they'd moved, he began to experience brief periods of irritability that seemed to have no external cause.

Laura had interpreted this as a reaction to their new environment, a new job, the effort of sharing living quarters for the first time in his life. Sean had been an only child whose parents died within months of each other when he was seventeen, cancer for his mother, a stroke claiming his father.

He started to have wild and extreme mood swings, anger, happiness, sadness, any emotional response became disproportionately intense. She found it endearing the first time he cried during a movie, but was less pleased when he alienated their next-door neighbors in a silly squabble about an encroaching tree. Their lovemaking grew more energetic and prolonged, but sometimes she didn't think he was actually enjoying what was happening. On other occasions, a mildly funny remark would result in raucous, uncontrolled laughter. Worst of all, he grew sullen and uncommunicative whenever she tried, ever so delicately, to point any of this out to him.

As pleasant as the talk had been, Laura felt exhausted and drained. She wasn't used to dealing with so many people in such a short span of time. After Sean's death, once the police were satisfied, she had hidden in her home for weeks, refusing to go outside and risk encountering a reporter, leaving her phone off the hook so long that the telephone company sent someone out to check it, venturing out only when absolutely necessary or for a session with her therapist. Ultimately, she had realized that she couldn't stay in Vermont. She had no job, no husband, and thanks to his secretive and unexplained draining of their bank account, she had enough money to live on for perhaps a year, if she was careful. The therapy was only minimally helpful, perhaps because she was unwilling to tell even Dr. Scribner the entire truth about Sean's death. She'd notified the real estate agency that she was abandoning the lease, and they were so happy to have her go that they even returned her damage deposit.

She sold what she could for far less than it was worth, keeping only what would fit in her car. When she left Burlington that last time, she had no idea where she was going or what she would do when she got there. The last thing that would have occurred to her was that she'd return to Dorrance, but here she was. Life was full of surprises, pleasant and otherwise.

When she reached home at two o'clock, her mother's body language expressed her displeasure even before she spoke. "Where have you been, Laura? Alice said you left first thing this morning. That car of yours looks like it's ready to fall apart and I had visions of you lying in a ditch somewhere freezing to death."

The image of Colleen Dill lying dead in a ditch came so sharply to mind that Laura missed the next few words. "I'm sorry, Mother. What did you just say?"

"I said that we were expecting you for lunch. Have you eaten?"

She nodded her head. "I had a sandwich at Slade's. What do you mean 'we'?"

"Slade's!" Her mother made it sound like a curse. "Well, I suppose you could have done worse. Come in and have tea with us anyway."

Curious, Laura followed her mother to the kitchen. Supper was always served in the dining room, but lunches were more casual and could be consumed at the table in the kitchen, or even on the porch, weather permitting. But never in the living room. That was for entertaining or for tea and coffee and perhaps cookies, but nothing else. There were very strict rules in her mother's house, rules that had frequently seemed nonsensical to a young Laura Collier, although she'd learned very early to question them in silence and obey them without argument.

Alice always left at noon, so Laura was quite puzzled until she stepped through the door and saw Del Huggins sitting at the table, staring blankly at the far wall, his large, gnarled hands curled around a steaming cup of coffee, a sheaf of papers in front of him.

"Look who's here, Del."

His head, which had always seemed too large for his body, slowly turned in her direction and he nodded at her. "Welcome home, Miss Laura."

His voice was completely without warmth, which didn't surprise her at all. Del Huggins never seemed enthusiastic or excited or pleased about anything. His eyes blazed at her with an animosity so intense that it felt as though he'd physically attacked her. Sean's eyes had been like that, right at the end. It was something she would never mistake again.

CHAPTER FOUR

Laura kept her eyes averted as she sat and accepted the unavoidable cup of tea. Del hadn't looked at her since that first glance, but even though his eyes were directed elsewhere, she could feel his awareness of her as though it was a physical link. The intensity of it puzzled her and disturbed her. Relations between them had never been warm; he'd frequently complained about her youthful pranks and her reluctance to help out with farm chores, had shouted at her more than once when she was caught at something she wasn't supposed to be doing, but it was a neutral kind of animosity, the same he displayed toward everyone else.

Had something happened to change things while she was gone or had she just been oblivious to his hostility in the past? She doubted strongly that it was loyalty to her mother. Could it have something to do with Sean's death? Laura couldn't remember ever seeing the two of them together and they certainly hadn't been friends.

"Have to get out to the barn and finish up the thresher." Del backed away from the table and stood up. "You still want me to look at the Jeep?"

"Yes, Del, sometime tomorrow. I won't be needing it until evening."

He made an inarticulate grunt of acknowledgment and pushed out the back door without sparing Laura so much as a sidelong glance.

"What's put him in such a bad mood?"

Mary laughed. "When have you ever known Del to be anything other than miserable? So what did you do today?" It was a demand rather than a casual inquiry, but Laura chose to ignore the tone and provided a brief summary. "Oh, and I had lunch with Ashley. She's working the register at the drugstore."

"You're not really still thinking about opening up the cabin, are you? I assumed you were just too tired to think straight yesterday."

Laura told herself to remain calm and control her temper. "Yes, I am. I checked it over and it's in good condition. Once the electricity is on and the pump is working, I'll have heat, water, light, and a working shower. They won't install a phone that far out so I'll have to get a cell."

"But you'll be all by yourself out there. It's better than four miles to the next occupied house. If anything happened and your car wouldn't start, you'd be stranded. And there have been some bad rumors about that area."

"That's why I need to get a cell phone. It's not like I'll be on the moon or something." She squinted her eyes. "And what kind of rumors are you talking about?"

"Oh, you know. People going up to Moon Pond to use drugs or worship the devil, that sort of thing."

Laura answered with an exaggerated sigh. "Mother, you need to get out more. The kind of people who drive out to remote rustic spots to use drugs aren't going to bother anyone who doesn't bother them and Satanism went out of style a while ago. It's too cold for a black mass, anyway. Drunken skinny dippers are more likely to be my problem, and not until the spring."

"It just seems foolish to me, that's all. There's lots of room here and you won't have to pay for your utilities or food. At least stay long enough to find a job and accumulate some savings first."

"I'm fine for money," she answered shortly, which was a lie, "and I think I've already found a job." The latter was potentially true, but she didn't mention that it would be part-time and at minimum wage.

"A job? Where?"

Laura realized she shouldn't have said anything this soon. Her mother would disapprove of any job she took, of course, but clerking at the Dairy Stop would be right down there with call girls and disco dancers. "There's an opening at one of the stores in town. I'm going to call about it this afternoon."

"Which store? Leonard's? The IGA?"

Laura sighed. "No, it's the Dairy Stop."

Mary Collier's eyes widened and for a few seconds she seemed incapable of speech. "Are you out of your mind? Bud Wiegand can't even get teenagers to work there for more than a few weeks. He's a foulmouthed old lecher."

"I'll be working for him, not with him. The night shift. And I'm old enough to take care of myself. If he gets out of line, I can always sue him for sexual harassment and live on the settlement." She had meant the remark to be funny but all it did was make her mother's eyes narrow even further.

"Laura, maybe you should just take things more slowly. You don't want to rush into a decision and make another . . . make a mistake."

Laura felt a flash of anger and had to fight the impulse to clench her fists. Her voice trembled ever so slightly, but enough that her mother certainly detected the change. "I'm not rushing into anything. I've been thinking about the cabin for weeks. This isn't a snap judgment. I know the job isn't a shining opportunity, but it's just to tide me over until I find something better. I'll have more choices in the spring. I'm a hard worker and you know it and so do a lot of other people."

"But it's all so unnecessary."

"No, that's just the point. It *is* necessary. I need to do something other than sit around and mope and remember what's past. It's gone, it's over, and I can't do anything about it. I know I made bad decisions, but I don't think we'd agree about which ones they were. The most important thing is that they were my decisions, and I'm going to have to live with the consequences. And that's why I'll make the decisions about my future as well."

She tried to soften her voice and derail her mother's inevitable counterattack. "Look, I know you're just trying to help and I appreciate it, really. But I'm going to open up the cabin with or without your approval. I'm going to need all sorts of supplies and if you want to help out there, I'd be really happy. Just don't fight me about this, please."

There was a long pause and Laura thought, my God, it's working, and then her mother slowly nodded. "All right, I guess you've inherited your willfulness from the Rustin side of the family, so I can't really complain about it, can I? If you really want to stay at the cabin temporarily, then that's what you'll do."

Laura blinked at the modifier "temporarily" but decided that a qualified victory was the best she could hope for at the moment.

"Great. And now I guess I'd better call Bud Wiegand before some pimply faced teenager beats me to it."

Laura had rarely interacted with Bud Wiegand in the past, but remembered him as an overbearing, unattractive man with a raspy voice and a bad temper. He proved to be just as offensive and uncouth on the phone as he was in person.

"Who? I never heard of any Laura Brennan."

She had given her married name through force of habit. "I'm Mary Collier's daughter. I got married a couple of years ago."

"Oh yeah, heard about that. Killed himself, didn't he?"

"Something like that. Is the job still open, Mr. Wiegand?"

"Could be. I don't usually get someone like you applying." Which Laura assumed meant that no one who wasn't desperately in need of cash was willing to work for him, but that's exactly what she was at the moment—desperate.

"I'm looking for something part time," she lied. "I worked as a cashier in Vermont." She didn't add that it had lasted less than a month. When Sean lost his job, she'd hoped to make enough for them to get by without touching their savings, unaware of the fact that Sean had already drawn most of the money out.

"Well, I suppose I could let you try it. Suppose you come by the store around seven tonight. I'll meet you there and we'll see what we see."

"All right. I'll be there." She hung up the phone, wondering if she'd just made a mistake.

Laura thought about moving most of her luggage back to the car, but decided that would be provocative and let it remain in the house, untouched. Her mother was in and out of the house that afternoon, once running an errand in town, twice huddling with Del Huggins, who had apparently discovered more problems with the heavy equipment than expected. Laura tried reading a novel that she'd bought at a rest stop several days earlier, but the story of a happy family facing what by her standards were trivial problems differed so dramatically from her own experience that she couldn't identify with any of the characters. She finally lay down on the bed, fully clothed, and dozed for a while, until wakened by the sound of rapping on her door.

"Laura! Are you in there?"

She sat up blinking. "Yes, Mother. Is something wrong?"

"No, but you have a telephone call."

"Who is it?" Bud Wiegand? Ashley?

"I didn't recognize the voice. Do you want me to ask?"

"No. No, I'll be right down."

She had kicked off her shoes and the floor was cool, so she slipped her feet into them, rubbing her eyes. Her mother was nowhere in sight as she came downstairs. The telephone in the hall was off the hook and she picked it up. "Hello?"

The line was silent, not dead, but silent. No voices, no background sounds, no carrier hum.

"Is anyone there?" She waited a few seconds. "Hello!" There was still no answer, so she hung up just as her mother descended the stairs. "There was no one there." Laura shrugged her shoulders. "Was it a man or a woman? Did they say anything?"

Mary shook her head. "It was a man, sounded like he had a cold. He just asked to speak to Laura Brennan and I said I'd call you. Were you expecting anything important?"

"No. I guess whoever it was will call back. It might have been Ed Burgess, or someone from the electric company. I hope it wasn't Bud Wiegand calling to tell me he'd found someone else for the job."

Her mother laughed. "If he had, do you really think he'd have done you the courtesy of calling?"

Laura smiled. "No, I guess not. How are things going with Del?"

Mary half turned her head toward the barn complex. "Oh, he's a bit of an old woman at times. Just because a part shows some wear doesn't mean it has to be replaced right away. But he's good at what he does so I don't object if he complains a little."

Del didn't join them for supper, although he'd been invited, so Laura didn't see him again that day. She spent more time than was necessary trying to decide what to wear for her job "interview." Should she play it mildly sexy and take advantage of Wiegand's voyeurism, or sexless and professional to discourage him from being too forward? She decided on the latter. There was a suitable sweater and slack set ready at hand; it was probably best to set an impersonal tone with Bud right from the start.

Mary offered to let her use the Jeep but Laura declined. "The Chevy works just fine, Mother. I know it looks like it's ready to fall apart but I had it tuned up just before I left Vermont." It was already dark when she drove down McAlester, darker than usual, in fact, thanks to a bank of heavy clouds that had rolled up during the day. The forecast was for snow during the night, probably light, possibly heavy if the front stalled.

It only took ten minutes to reach the Dairy Stop. She parked next to a rusting Buick and walked to the entrance, feeling unusually nervous. This wasn't her first job interview and there was no real reason for her to be as edgy as she was, but her stomach was fluttering and her hands shook slightly as she pulled open the door and stepped inside.

There was an acne-scarred teenager behind the counter, not the one she'd met before, although she had to look twice to be sure of that. He also wore a heavy metal emblazoned sweater, but he was slightly taller and bulkier. His head never even bobbed when she entered, but he wasn't reading a magazine. Instead, he stared distractedly out through the window into the street.

Laura approached the register. "Excuse me. I'm supposed to be meeting Mr. Wiegand."

His head turned slowly, grudgingly. "Yeah. He's in the back. He'll be out in a minute." His eyes moved away and Laura felt mildly annoyed.

"Shouldn't you let him know that I'm here?"

The eyes didn't return. "Nope. Can't leave the register while there's a customer in the store. It's a rule."

Laura turned around. Except for herself, the store was empty. She was tempted to say something sarcastic, but was saved the effort when Bud Wiegand emerged from a doorway behind the counter.

He didn't look as bad as she remembered, but the last time she'd seen him had been during her teens. Wiegand was a large man, would have been quite powerful if he hadn't been so soft. He was unshaven rather than bearded, and his last haircut had left him with unmatched muttonchops. He was wearing a badly stained flak jacket over a heavy red flannel shirt and blue jeans.

"You the Brennan girl?" He edged around the end of the counter and came much closer than Laura would have preferred.

She stood her ground and met his eyes, was delighted when he looked away. "Yes, I'm Laura Brennan." She extended her hand and, after a brief hesitation, Wiegand shook it briefly. His grasp was hot and moist and she had to resist the temptation to wipe her palm against her slacks.

"Still want the job?" His eyes roamed around the store. "Gets pretty lonesome here at night. Wouldn't keep it open even except I have to in order to keep my franchise. That's why I can't pay more than minimum."

"I understand that. Minimum wage will be fine."

Wiegand snorted. "Surprised your mother lets you work at all. What happened? She cut off your allowance?"

Laura knew that her face was coloring but she couldn't let that pass. "My mother doesn't support me, Mr. Wiegand. I have my own place here in town and I'm planning to make my own way."

"Yeah, all right, don't get your dander up. I was just wondering is all. So let me show you what's involved, and you can stay with Scott over there for the rest of the shift to train."

It was about what she expected. The rear of the store was a mess. Old stock and new had been inextricably mixed together, and the chips on the shelves might be three days or three months old. There were spiderwebs in the corners, but the floor was dry and the walls were sound enough to keep the wind out, although the heat had been turned down to a point just high enough to keep the pipes from freezing. There was a small toilet and sink, partitioned off from the rest of the storeroom by two blankets hung from the ceiling, neither of which was particularly clean. The roll-up delivery door was locked from the inside and seemed secure.

"There's a slot under the desk where you drop any big bills you get," explained Wiegand. "Falls into a safe that I empty out in the morning. You never keep more than twenty dollars in the register, just enough to make change. Keep the shelves full, but don't leave the register if there's anyone in the store. Your shift, there should be plenty of time for that. Just toss the empty boxes over there." He pointed to an empty corner. "When your shift ends and your replacement arrives, you clock out. Before you leave, toss all the empties into the Dumpster out back. That's pretty much it. Any questions?"

She thought about pointing out that he was violating labor laws by requiring her to work after she'd clocked out, but she wanted the job first. Bud Wiegand could be dealt with later. "I don't see anything I can't handle. What will my shift be?"

"Have to start you on graveyard, midnight to six, Thursday through Saturday." He sounded regretful, almost apologetic. "Might be able to shift you to evenings in a few weeks."

"That's fine with me." Eighteen hours wasn't much, but it would pay for groceries and electricity and gas for the Chevy.

She operated the register to prove that she knew how. On at least two occasions, she caught Wiegand checking her out, as best he could through her bulky sweater. She kept her jacket on; the store proper was heated, but still chilly, and would be cooler if the doors opened and closed more frequently. Only one customer had stopped in while she was there, for a pack of cigarettes and a tank of gas. After Wiegand left, she sat next to Scott who responded to her occasional conversational overtures with noncommittal grunts, and who made no effort to tell her anything further about the job. When their shift ended and a gangly man with several missing teeth arrived to take over, she made a point of saying "Good night and thanks for all the help" very sweetly, but if he noticed her sarcasm, he didn't respond to it.

During the drive home, she kept telling herself that it could have been a lot worse.

Ed Burgess gave her the good news two days later. "The juice is on and all the outlets are working. You'll need some new bulbs, though. The pump needed cleaning and the filters were completely gone, but there's no rust that I can find, and after I pumped out the pipes for a few minutes, the water came through sweet and clean. I took a look at the roof while I was there. It should last you the winter, though I'd think about replacing some of the tiles come spring."

She thanked him and paid him from the funds Ted Catterall had advanced her, then drove out to the cabin to look things over and make up a shopping list. Her mother would insist on providing the bulk of what she needed, and Laura would accept whatever she offered along those lines, at least partly because it co-opted her mother into giving tacit approval for the move.

This time she checked the grounds more thoroughly, greatly relieved when she didn't find a dead animal hanging anywhere on the property. The underbrush had grown thicker and one of the pine trees had been struck by lightning and was split up the center. If it fell, it might just possibly reach the cabin and do some damage, so she'd have to think about taking it down in the spring. She found traces of campfires near the edge of Moon Pond, and there were beer cans and other debris scattered through the bushes there and probably lying under the water as well. It was about what she'd expected, and in fact she'd come up here with Ashley and some of her other friends for an illicit drinking party more than once during her high school years, so she supposed she shouldn't begrudge the same pleasures to the current generation of teenagers. There wasn't much of a beach here, but people went swimming anyway. There was a secluded cove nearby which she and Ashley and Kathy favored, mostly because it was so well hidden that they didn't always have to wear swimming suits.

Inside the cabin, she saw that Ed Burgess had done more than she'd paid for. Most of the dust and dirt had been cleared away, the sink was freshly washed, and the shower stall had been cleaned. The small electric heater provided warm, if not hot, water, all the faucets worked, and the toilet flushed, though perhaps a bit reluctantly. He'd also brought in an armful of wood for the stove and he'd left a box of long stemmed matches on the kitchen table. Laura's childhood image of Ed Burgess had been of a rather forbidding though not actively unpleasant man, and she was touched to discover that he was actually so thoughtful.

She spent the next hour making a list, light bulbs, toilet paper, batteries, towels, a can opener, and other durable supplies. There was enough kitchenware to get by, but she'd need to stock up on groceries. The last thing she did was a more thorough check for rodents; there had been mice in the cabin years earlier and it had taken forever to get rid of them. Laura went down on all fours, peering into nooks and crannies with her flashlight, emptying cupboards to examine rear walls, moving furniture, searching closets. All she gained for her trouble was the stub of a pencil, seventy-eight cents in change, and a small, flower-shaped pin that was actually pretty enough that she decided to keep it.

After making a last pass around to make sure she hadn't forgotten anything obvious, Laura gathered up her notepad and keys and stepped outside, locking the door behind her. She was halfway back to the Chevy when another car came up the dirt roadway and stopped just behind hers.

It was Mason Cortway.

It took her a second to recognize him. He'd grown a moustache and changed his hairstyle to a crewcut. Mason had always had a reputation for immaturity, well deserved, and she suspected this was his latest attempt to change his image. His quilted hunting jacket was new and sported a prestigious logo on one shoulder. Mason stepped out of the car, waved cheerily, and started toward her.

She and Mason had some history, not all of it bad. Her mother had always favored him as a potential son-in-law, perhaps because in addition to his family connections he was also obviously malleable. Mary Collier preferred men who deferred to her and even in high school Mason had deference down to a fine art. Laura had not been popular because her family had always kept a distance between itself and the rest of the community, but the male to female ratio in her age group had been so heavily slanted that she did get asked out, at least by boys who had never actually met her mother.

That, unfortunately, was Laura's handicap. Her mother insisted upon meeting everybody she went out with, and when she disapproved of a boy, she always made her feelings known to all concerned. Danny Hewitt had left the house practically in tears, and two other boys had avoided her assiduously and without explanation after their first date. There were two or three whom Mary tolerated, but only two she had actively liked,

Mason Cortway and Alan Ross. Alan dropped out of high school and joined the Army during his junior year, but Mason remained in town and was at the top of Mary's list of prospects for her daughter.

"He's a very nice boy. He comes from a good family, respects his elders, stays out of trouble, and works hard." Unfortunately, Mason had to struggle to get passing grades, lacked even an ounce of imagination, and hadn't been more than sixty miles from Dorrance in his entire life. His father owned a small farm that was no longer commercially viable, plus the only furniture and appliance store in Dorrance. He was a deacon at the Baptist Church and a member of the town council, one of the few willing to take Mary's side during her periodic campaigns against John Dill's policies.

They had dated a few times during high school, and Mason had gotten quite serious during their senior year, proposed in an indirect fashion shortly before graduation, and more seriously afterward. Laura had tried not to hurt his feelings, but not as hard as she probably could have, and there had been at least one very loud public scene when he'd found her having coffee with newcomer Sean Brennan at Slade's. Sean had just been an interesting new friend at that point, nothing more, but Mason had railed at her "betrayal" of him and had knocked over a bowl of soup before Bill Slade calmly but efficiently escorted him outside.

Their encounters after that had been cool but polite, even after it became obvious that she and Sean were more than just casual friends, even when she began telling people that they were going to get married. After that, when her mother finally realized that she was serious, things had become so strained and emotional that she might have walked right past Mason without recognizing him. She'd been very preoccupied in those last few weeks before the two of them just threw up their hands and sneaked off for a quickie wedding and the long drive to Vermont.

"Hi, Mason. What brings you out here?" She met him halfway, not wanting to have to invite him inside.

He was rubbing his gloved hands together briskly as he approached. "Just thought I'd stop by and say hello, find out how you were doing, if you needed anything."

Laura wondered if her mother had put him up to it, but then dismissed the thought as too cynical. "I'm fine. Just getting the cabin ready so I can move in. How've you been? Married yet?"

That brought the familiar giggling laugh that had driven her crazy in high school and she had to struggle to keep the pleasant expression on her face. "Me? Married? Not likely. I've been too busy for that sort of thing. Dad took me into the business as a partner, you know. His health's not so great, so I'll be taking over more and more in the next few years."

"I'm sorry to hear that, about your father, I mean. He was always very nice to me. How's your mom?"

"Still working on her causes." Helen Cortway spent most of her time writing letters of protest or traveling to nearby communities to participate in protests of one form or another. There were lots of things she objected to—abortion, property taxes, fantasy literature, violence on television, rock lyrics, the 21st century—and she'd probably added to the list since the last time Laura had met her. How she'd ended up married to Mason's father, who was tolerant and good-natured, was a mystery she'd never solve. "So. You planning to move in here?"

"That's the plan, Mason. It's not as primitive as it looks."

"Kind of lonely, though."

"Well, that's really what I'm looking for right now. I want some time to be by myself."

Mason suddenly looked uncomfortable and his eyes skittered off into the uncertain distance. "Yeah, I heard about what happened. With your husband, I mean."

Laura didn't want to talk about Sean, particularly not with Mason Cortway. "Look, it was nice seeing you again, but I've got some things I need to do in town."

But Mason ignored her, apparently hadn't been listening. "He wasn't right for you, Laura. I knew that right off. There was something strange about him even back then."

Laura felt a flare of anger, and didn't even attempt to keep the edge out of her voice. "That's enough, Mason. I don't want to talk about it, all right? Now if you'll just move your car, I need to be leaving."

He turned to face her and this time she saw something new in his eyes, something she'd never seen there before and couldn't quite identify. It was an intensity beyond anything Mason had ever displayed when they'd been together in the past, and it disoriented her, even frightened her slightly. She backed off a step.

"You're better off without him, that's all I wanted to say. You deserve better. You deserve someone who really appreciates you." His voice was thick with emotion.

"Please move your car, Mason. You're going to make me late." She had a sudden inspiration. "I'm meeting mother for lunch and you know how mad she gets when she has to wait for someone."

His eyes blinked and, that quickly, the intensity was gone. "Sure. Sorry. I'll back right out. Say hello to your mother for me."

"I'll do that, Mason."

Her hands didn't stop shaking until she was back in Dorrance.

CHAPTER FIVE

She wasn't actually meeting her mother, but she was meeting Ashley for lunch. Laura had decided she could afford one meal at Foster's, the closest thing to a fancy restaurant available. People in Dorrance generally cooked their meals; dining out was reserved for emergencies and special occasions.

"So how's the cabin coming?" They had been offered a table but Laura had asked for a booth.

"It's a little rough around the edges, but it's livable. I'm going to move in tomorrow."

"Have you told your mother yet?"

Laura sighed and her face fell slightly. "Yes. More than once, in fact, but I don't know if she actually heard me. She has this trick hearing system that filters out anything she doesn't want to know."

"So how's the new job?"

Laura made a face. "Wiegand's a dirty old man. He dropped in twice the first night, supposedly to see how I was getting on. I think he even scared off one of the customers." She paused while the waitress delivered their food. "Believe it or not, he actually turned the heat down. Said he was trying to reduce overhead. He probably still has the first dollar he ever made. Did Dill ever get him to paint his house?"

Ashley laughed. "Not last time I looked. He must have been heartbroken when his old Ford finally broke down and he had to buy the Buick. Did you know he tried to buy your cabin?"

"No! Really? When was this?"

"I'm not sure exactly. Dad told me he heard he made your mother an offer."

"Wouldn't do any good. It belongs to me. I wonder why he wanted it."

Ashley smirked. "Maybe his house is falling down and he thought he could get the cabin cheaper than fixing his place up."

"That must be it." She put the matter out of her mind, though not completely. "Guess who came out to visit me today."

"I haven't a clue."

"Mason Cortway."

"Mason? God, I haven't seen him since I came back and I admit it, I kind of forgot about him. He's still here, then, in Dorrance, I mean?"

"Well, of course he is. I don't think Mason believes the outside world really exists. Remember when we were kids and he thought the television programs all came from Shawcut because his father took him along once and he saw the big transmitter?"

"So what did he want? Tried to flirt with you, I'd guess."

"Sort of, but he's still the same social klutz. He started talking about Sean and I'm not ready to do that, and I'll probably never be able to talk about him with Mason."

"Well, I'm here when you are ready if it'll help, and I'm not going anywhere soon." She sighed theatrically. "Maybe never."

Laura reached across the table and touched her friend's forearm lightly. "I know, Ashley. Thanks. And you will get out of Dorrance. We both will, when the time comes."

Although Laura had wanted to get the confrontation over with, she waited until her mother had driven into town the following morning before lugging her bags downstairs and repacking the

Chevy. Her mother had told her to "take what you want" from the pantry, and she did so, collecting her selections in a large cardboard box. This went onto the front seat, passenger side. She was just closing the car door when her mother returned, the Jeep's wheels following precisely in the worn ruts of its previous journeys.

Her face was expressionless as her eyes took in the suitcases in the backseat, but she returned to the house without saying a word. Knowing it wouldn't be that easy, Laura told herself to be firm and followed.

"You didn't need to sneak out of the house."

"I'm not sneaking out, Mother. I told you I was moving either today or tomorrow. Things went faster than I expected and there's no reason to put it off. I'll be fine, and if it doesn't work out, I can always come back." If hell freezes over, she added silently.

"The toilet doesn't work right, you know. Your father insisted on putting that in himself and he never was very good with plumbing."

"Yes, Mother. I know. I think I can deal with a plugged drain." Laura was intimately aware of every error of judgment, thoughtless word, and hasty decision Ben Collier had made during the twenty-six years he'd been with her mother. Mary had them all thoroughly catalogued and cross-referenced, and could summon an appropriate example to suit any occasion.

"I just don't understand why you want to go off and live like that when there's plenty of room for you right here." Here was admittedly ample space. The house had been more than adequate for the three of them during Laura's childhood, physically at least. Emotionally it had apparently been too small for her father to endure. A few months before she met Sean Brennan for the first time, Ben Collier had withdrawn exactly one third of the funds from their joint bank account, told one or two people that he was leaving his wife, and then disappeared so completely and efficiently that he might have taken a starship to another world. He had never called or written or sent a message to either Laura or her mother, and that was a deep wound that Laura had never acknowledged, not even to Sean.

Mary Collier had never displayed any of the hurt or anger she must have felt, not even to her daughter, but she'd held herself even more aloof from the surrounding community, her dislikes hardening into fervent animosities, and the already considerable gap between her and Laura had widened appreciably, culminating in her vehement opposition to Sean Brennan and the subsequent elopement. Widowed in effect if not in fact, she had armored herself with the Rustin aura and refused to show weakness, but now that Laura was herself a widow, she felt that some common ground had begun to open up between them. She was endangering the tenuous peace by moving to the cabin, but in the long run it would be easier to stay on good terms with her mother from a distance, however short.

"Have I made you feel unwelcome here?"

"Of course not, Mother. It's just that you have your own life and I feel like I'm intruding."

"You're my only child, Laura. How could you feel that you'd ever be unwelcome? Have I been such a bad mother that you'd rather live in a shack than in your home?"

"It's not a shack; it's a cabin."

"It's dirty and squalid and I think there are rats living under the floor. In fact, I'm sure of it; I've heard them moving around down there and chewing. The whole thing is going to collapse someday, you mark my words." Mary had wanted to sell the property immediately after the will was read, and had waged an intermittent campaign to that effect, but as sole trustee, Ben Collier was the only one authorized to approve the sale, and he had stubbornly and uncharacteristically refused to budge.

"It's the girl's property," he'd say over and over again, keeping his voice low but not low enough that she hadn't overheard him more than once. "When she's old enough to make her own decisions, she can sell it or keep it or burn it down."

"Why are you in such a hurry? I thought we had agreed you were going to wait until after Christmas."

"No, Mother, you decided I was going to wait. I never said any such thing." Laura drew a deep breath, refusing to be drawn into an open argument. "Look, I really appreciate your offer, but if I stayed until Christmas, then we'd put it off until after New Year's, and by then it would make more sense to wait until spring, and by spring, who knows what else might have come up."

"It's just that I don't think you've considered the consequences."

She hadn't finished, but Laura raised her hand, surprised at her own temerity. Mary was not a person easily interrupted. "I've considered everything that I need to consider. If this is a mistake, then it's my mistake."

Mary seemed ready to respond angrily, but she must have seen something in her daughter's face, perhaps a reflection of her own stubbornness, that made her hesitate. Instead, she let her shoulders slump. "I'm only thinking of you, Laura. You've been through a lot, and you were away so long, I hoped we could get to know each other again."

Although she recognized this as just another tactic, Laura relented slightly. "We will, Mother, I promise. It's only a few minutes from here, you know."

"Well, then, I suppose you'll have to try it and see for yourself. Just remember, your room is always here if you need it."

"I'll remember." She stepped forward impulsively, kissed her mother's cheek, then turned and was out the door and in the

Chevy before any of the many doubts freshly tilled in her mind could break the surface and bloom.

It started snowing while she was carrying in the last of her mismatched luggage. It wasn't a very big place, but Laura had always felt a sense of open space because of the high, vaulted ceiling. It didn't take her long to unpack. Laura had fled rather than left Vermont, abandoning much of her clothing and other possessions to whoever bought the small house she'd called home for two years. If anyone ever did. People were funny about living any place where a violent death had occurred.

She hastily dropped that line of thought.

It was cold at first, but she started a fire in the woodstove and she had the electric space heater plugged into the outlet by her bed. The dry heat from the fire took away the dampness along with the chill. When she went outside to open the shutters, she discovered that almost an inch of snow already covered the ground, and the rate of fall had increased. She checked to make sure she'd locked the car, which was probably unnecessary this far from town, then went back inside, securing the door from habit rather than nervousness. It was still chilly enough that she wanted to stay active so she moved some of the furniture around a few times before deciding that it was best in its original position. All of the furnishings were solid and heavy and she was thankful that she'd inherited her mother's considerable physical strength if not perhaps her strength of character.

The snow seemed to be falling even faster outside as the red rim of the sun dropped far enough that she could no longer see it through the pine forest and a few minutes later full dark was gently lapping at the outside walls. Laura welcomed the snow. She felt as though it and the encircling trees and the cabin itself were wrapping themselves around her, shutting out the world and all of its hard edges. Shutting out the memories.

She went to bed early, setting the alarm for eleven. It was

Saturday; she was working, midnight till dawn and still hadn't completely adapted to her new sleep/wake cycle. The last two nights had been troubled by dreams which she was unable to remember when she awoke, although on both occasions she'd felt a sense of danger that had persisted well into the morning. This night's dream was more distinct, and the central image would remain sharp and clear long after she was up and had driven to the Dairy Stop. She'd dreamt of Sean; Sean standing in their living room, next to the Christmas tree, using the sharp edge of his hunting knife to sever the strings that attached each individual ornament to the branches. Those that hadn't shattered when they fell had been ground to powder under his boots. It wasn't an imaginative dream but rather a memory, faithful in every detail to what she had actually been through.

It was disorienting to waken in the dark, the alarm complaining shrilly. Laura threw off the covers and slowly climbed out of the lower bunk, blinking sleepily and shivering. Even with the area heater buzzing in the corner, it cooled down noticeably if she wasn't feeding fresh wood to the stove. She put on her heavy terrycloth robe and washed her face and hands before dressing. It was very quiet other than the noises she was making; the burning wood had stopped crackling, there was no wind, and she was far enough back from Moon Pond Road that she couldn't hear even its infrequent traffic.

She made herself a cup of coffee on the propane stove, hot water with instant stirred into it. There was a tiny refrigerator where she kept milk and a few small perishables but she'd need something better come spring. While waiting for the water to boil, she glanced out the rear window, noticed that the snow had stopped falling after leaving a blanket of perhaps five inches. She couldn't see enough of the sky to tell whether or not it was completely clear but the moon was out because a pale blue glow flooded the meadow leading down to the water.

There was movement to her left, right at the limit of her vision. Behind a screen of thick brush, an indistinct shape was moving, an animal of some sort, she thought, probably a deer. It was too big to be anything else; they hadn't seen moose in this area since her grandfather's time. It was a cautious animal, careful to stay out of the light, and she wondered if it was predator or prey. The wind gusted just then, and a few flakes of snow began to fall once more, the dying gasp of a storm that didn't know it was dead.

Laura pressed her nose to the cold glass and watched as snow sifted down through the evergreen trees that surrounded the cabin. In the moonlight, the snowflakes had an eerie, ethereal look and formed vague, phantom patterns that shifted and disappeared before she could bring them into focus. The first week of December had been unusually warm and dry, but the first substantial snowfall of the season promised an end to the respite.

The tip of her nose tingled when she turned away and she rubbed it with the back of one hand, encouraging the blood to circulate. Years earlier, Laura had suffered a mild case of frostbite, and her flesh had always afterward seemed peculiarly sensitive to the cold. A board creaked loudly underfoot and she hoped she wasn't going to have to think about repairing the floor any time soon.

The woodstove crackled at the far end of the room. Sparks threw themselves against the screen and died with tiny hissing screams of protest. Laura finished her coffee, drinking it down quickly, and then went out to clean off her car and go to work.

The snow came and went during the rest of the night, and so did the handful of customers, mostly truckers taking a shortcut back to the interstate. Despite Bud Wiegand's grousing, the store did pretty well even on her shift. She had brought a book along just in case but only managed to read a few pages. Wiegand didn't drop by this time, which made her feel more comfortable. He hadn't done anything obviously objectionable, but she felt his eyes on her even when he was looking in a different direction.

She drank three cups of coffee, paying for each even though Scott had told her not to bother. Eventually she would adjust to this unnatural sleep schedule, she supposed, but so far it had proven more of a strain than she had expected. The last two hours dragged by inexorably, and then Winifred, the overweight matron who had the morning shift, was twenty minutes late and so obviously belligerent that Laura wisely chose not to say anything. The snow had stopped completely, the sky was clear except for some thin clouds hovering at the horizon, and Dorrance was already wide awake. Even in the winter a farming community is a busy place.

But not Moon Pond Road. She didn't see another vehicle traveling in either direction after she took the turnoff, and felt so sleepy that she opened her window partway so that the chilly air would revive her. It worked well enough that when she finally reached the cabin, she no longer felt as though her first priority was to fall onto the bed and take a nap.

It was actually a very pretty view from her porch windows. Under its fresh covering of snow, the woods outside seemed a brand-new universe, ripe for exploration, reawakening some of the enthusiasm she'd felt coming here as a child. And this time she had sole control over the rules; it was up to her what chores got done and which were deferred. She could have spaghetti for breakfast or sleep in the nude or do whatever she wanted. Even with Sean, even before he'd begun to change, she'd never felt that freedom.

She made herself a hearty breakfast, no spaghetti. With scrambled eggs and coffee warming her stomach and the freshly lit woodstove warming the cabin, Laura bundled up in a pair of old jeans and a faded sweater, insulated boots and a thickly lined jacket, and went out to explore her new world.

The hatchet was old and chipped in a couple of places, but the leather cover had protected its head from years of neglect and the edge was sharp enough to suit her purposes. Laura suppressed a momentary queasiness as she tested it, a fragment of her dream stirring in memory. Closing the door behind her, she set off to find herself a Christmas tree.

Her mother would not have approved. For as long as Laura could remember, they'd had an artificial tree, one that wouldn't shed needles everywhere, that wasn't a fire hazard, that could be decorated symmetrically. She and her father had won a concession on wreaths, which they made by hand each year, but only so long as they were confined to the enclosed porch and the exterior of the house.

This year her mother had seemed oblivious to the holiday, hadn't put up any decorations, and had only mentioned the subject of presents in passing over breakfast one morning. Laura knew that it was a difficult subject for them both, since Sean had died on Christmas day a year before, but the way her mother carefully avoided talking about it only made it worse. On the other hand, she had never really enjoyed Christmas. Her mother had always characterized it as overly sentimental and "a tool to make people spend money on things they wouldn't otherwise buy," and even her father had admitted that it didn't feel the same as it had when he'd been a kid.

Their one conversation on the subject since Laura's return had been brief, and for Laura acutely painful. Her mother had glanced up from her coffee after a long silence. "Under the circumstances, I assume we'll forego exchanging gifts this year."

"Don't be silly, Mother. I've already picked something out for you." That was a lie. She hadn't been able to bring herself to think about Christmas, but she didn't want to admit weakness, any weakness, until she was ready.

"I just thought it might be too soon. You're still having those nightmares, I know. I've been listening for them."

"The doctor told me that they'd stop eventually, and that trying to pretend that nothing happened was the worst thing I could do. I won't spoil your Christmas over this, Mother. And I won't spoil mine, either."

They'd dropped the subject then, and Laura was pretty sure her mother had bought something the following day, because she looked mildly furtive after she'd been to town on a mysterious errand. But she also noticed that every time a Christmas card arrived, it was promptly thrown into the trash rather than displayed on the mantel as was their usual custom.

Laura found the perfect tree a hundred meters from the cabin. It only came up to her chin, but she wanted a small one because she had very few ornaments with which to decorate it, a small box of them that she'd found in the back of her bedroom closet at the farm. Some of them she'd made with her own hands, at school or at church. Memory of church reminded her that she should visit Reverend Gorse soon or he'd be offended, but she wasn't ready yet. One of the manifestations of Sean's breakdown had been prolonged bouts of furious, audible prayer, and at times he'd insisted that she participate. Laura considered herself a good if casual Christian, but she was disturbed by Sean's sudden devoutness, particularly when he was begging forgiveness for things she knew he hadn't done, and even more so when he tried to intercede for sins of which he believed her guilty.

The chopping down went quite well. The dragging back to the cabin was another matter entirely, a tedious, tiring struggle in snow which had inconveniently drifted to almost waist level across her path. But eventually it was done and she felt quite pleased with herself. It was too soon to bring the tree inside; the dry air would wither it quickly. Laura's arms and thighs hurt from the unaccustomed exertion, and she realized how badly out of shape she'd gotten recently, but she was determined to finish what she'd started. She rummaged through the toolshed until she found a rusted ripsaw, evened off the stump, then set the tree upright in a bucket of snow. It was already above freezing and water was dripping from the trees and spattering the ground. She propped up the tree in one corner of the small porch and slid a chair in place to support it in case the wind came back.

"That should hold you for the time being." She straightened up, stretched her back, stared up into the weak sunlight. The cold felt reassuringly clean and fresh. "You're going to come out of this okay, girl," she said aloud. "Just give it some time."

She was making up a shopping list when the lock on the front door clicked distinctly and turned.

"Hello, Mother. Come to see if I survived the night?"

Mary stepped inside, a bag of groceries clutched in one arm, and closed the door behind her. She didn't answer at first, just let her eyes trail around the room.

"It's been a while since I've been inside here. It's as bad as I remembered. Here, I thought you could use these."

"Why thank you." She knew what was expected of her, emptied the bag item by item, expressing amazement at her mother's ability to guess just what she needed. Even when she didn't. The olives were very welcome, for example, but why prunes? And there was a box of filters for a coffeemaker she didn't have.

"So how did it go?"

Laura blinked. "Oh. You mean my first night out in the wilderness? Fine, honestly. A band of marauding Indians woke me up once or twice but they couldn't force the door."

Mary ignored the levity. "It must be cold back where you're sleeping."

"I have two blankets and a down quilt, wore my wool pajamas, and I have a space heater right next to the bed. It was very cozy."

Mary was walking slowly around the large room, examining it critically. "Come spring, you'll have to have the exterminators in. Bugs. And I told you there are rats under the floor."

"Yes, I believe you did mention that once or twice. It's not much more than a crawl space, Mother. I have no reason to go in there so the rats and I will co-exist just fine. Can I make you some tea?"

"No, I can't stay. I just wanted to make sure you were all right. You are all right, I take it?"

"I'm fine. You worry too much."

She had a second visitor later that morning, and this one didn't have a key. In fact, he knocked.

When Laura opened the door, she experienced a moment of absolute terror. It was Sean, returned from the dead, standing on the doorstep leering at her, and his hand was coming up from his hip lifting that shining blade toward her throat.

Except that it wasn't Sean, although there were some strong similarities, and it was a handheld radio that he was lifting and a tentative, professional smile that shaped his lips. A police emblem was visible on one shoulder of his jacket and the name on the pocket read "Sievert."

"Morning, Ma'am. Hope I'm not disturbing you?"

Laura had to try twice to get her voice to work. "No. No, you're not. I mean, you just caught me by surprise." She remembered her manners. "Would you like to come inside, Officer?" The temperature had dropped into the single digits, and there was a nasty wet wind coming in from the direction of Moon Pond.

"Thank you, yes, I would if you could spare me a minute."

When she looked closely, the resemblance to Sean Brennan seemed quite superficial. "Is anything wrong, Officer?"

"No, not at all. It's just that this place has been empty for a long time and the chief asked me to stop by and introduce myself and find out if everything was okay."

"Did the chief ask you to keep an eye out for evidence of wild drinking parties? He used to come up here personally to collar us when we were kids. I imagine the current generation does the same thing."

He sketched a smile. "I think they've found themselves a new spot. Haven't seen anyone up here drinking since I've been in Dorrance. We have had some trouble with squatters, actually. A couple of summer places on the other side of Moon Pond have been broken into this fall."

"Well, I'm Laura Collier." She offered her hand and he shook it briefly and warmly. "I can show you some identification."

He laughed dutifully. "No, that won't be necessary. I've met your mother and you look a lot like her."

"Mother always makes a strong impression."

He smiled again, more genuinely this time. "That she does. Anyway, sorry to have bothered you."

Laura felt suddenly unwilling to have him leave. It wasn't because he attracted her; she wasn't ready to consider a replacement for Sean yet, might never be. But he was the first normal person she'd met in Dorrance who wasn't aware of her past, who didn't seem to be treading on eggshells around her, and she was reluctant to let him go so quickly.

"Would you like a cup of coffee? It's pretty raw out there and I was just about to make some for myself."

He hesitated and she hastily put the water on, hoping to tip the balance in her favor. After a brief moment when it appeared he'd refuse, Officer Sievert accepted first a chair and then some coffee, and if he drank it a little more quickly than usual, then she decided that was because he was cold and thirsty and not because he was in a hurry to get away.

Although he turned down a refill, and in fact asked to use the bathroom before leaving, he was calling her Laura by then and she was calling him Dan. For the first time it felt as though something had begun to heal inside her, and when he was gone and Laura laid down for a short nap, she slept peacefully and without any trace of a disturbing dream.

Chapter Six

Laura slept late on Sunday and woke refreshed and feeling more optimistic than she had in over a year. The prospect of four straight days without having to go to the Dairy Stop helped lift her spirits. She spent the morning in the cabin, moving things around experimentally, deciding once again that they looked best the way they had been, then fried a hamburger for her lunch. The air was calm outside, so she took a walk, kicking at the snow playfully, marveling at how dramatically it changed the appearance of the nearby woods. She also did a very slow, deliberate transit of the cabin, looking for potential maintenance problems that Ed Burgess might have overlooked, but found nothing amiss.

She drove into town, intending to find out how much it would cost to buy a cell phone, but she'd forgotten that few businesses in Dorrance operated on Sunday. Slade's was open, of course, but the hardware shop, drugstore, and virtually everything else were all closed. She would try again tomorrow, and made a mental note to open a local bank account as well. She still had a few travelers' checks and some cash, not enough to make her comfortable but too much to carry around, and she'd need to be able to cash her paychecks.

There were a few things she wanted to retrieve from the farm, and she decided to get it over with so that the drive wouldn't be a complete waste of time. She might even catch her mother in a mellow mood.

She was halfway up McAlester when a police car passed her going the other way. Chief Clay was driving and there was another officer she didn't recognize sitting beside him. Clay glanced in her direction as they passed, but his face remained expressionless.

Laura parked, knocked at the door, hesitated, and then walked inside. It felt strange waiting to be admitted to what had been her home for twenty-two years, and she knew Mary would be annoyed if she continued to act like an outsider. She heard voices from the living room and found Del Huggins and her mother standing very close together. Del looked angry, which wasn't unusual, but her mother's expression was strange, somehow more intense than usual.

"What's going on?"

"Your mother's seeing ghosts," Del replied gruffly, then brushed past her and out the door.

"Ghosts?"

Mary shook her head. "Not ghosts. Prowlers. One prowler to be exact. Last night something woke me up and I thought I heard someone walking around on the porch. I came down and looked but no one was there so I assumed I'd just been dreaming, or maybe a raccoon had wandered in to forage. Anyway, I went back to bed and nothing else happened, but this morning when I came down I looked again and the bolt on the back door was bent. Someone tried to force it open last night."

"So why does Del think you're seeing ghosts?"

"Because I was foolish enough to tell him that I'd been dreaming that someone I knew was trying to get into the house." She looked away, biting her lip. Mary Collier never liked to admit to anything even approaching human weakness. "And he and that fool Nathan Clay think the bolt was already distorted and that I'm imagining the whole thing."

"Who was it you dreamed about, Mother? Was it Dad?"

There was just enough hesitation that Laura knew that Mary Collier was about to lie. "Yes, it was your father. I guess I still wonder why he's never let us know where he is or how he's doing." She shook her head and shrugged. "Come on. I'll make us some tea. You must be half frozen."

For a change, her mother didn't try to monopolize the conversation. She seemed preoccupied and even a bit nervous. When the obligatory tea had been consumed and Laura indicated that she was going to move some more things from her room, hand towels, a spare pillow, a heavy comforter, and some old clothing, Mary just nodded. She was still sitting in the kitchen, staring out the window, when Laura was ready to leave.

"Maybe you should have Del put heavier locks on the doors, Mother. Just in case."

"Don't worry, dear. I'll be careful. And I still have your father's guns in the den and I know how to use them."

"All right. I'll be seeing you. Oh, can I use your phone?"

"Of course you can."

Ashley's mother answered on the third ring and they talked for a few minutes before she let her daughter take over. Laura had always gotten along well with Mrs. Sothern, sometimes better than with Ashley, who had always had a sharp tongue and a short temper. Kathy Peebles had been the perfect third member of their triumvirate. She ignored Ashley's tantrums and Laura's broodiness and forced them to remain close friends even when it seemed impossible. Kathy was their emotional center, with Ashley's impulsiveness balanced by Laura's conservatism. Laura had more fun when she was with Ashley, but she could talk to Kathy with greater intimacy.

"Hi, Laura. What's up?"

"I was thinking about driving over to Shawcut this afternoon. I need to buy a cell phone and some other things and there's nothing open around here. Do you want to come along?"

"Sure, a road trip. Sounds like fun. What time?"

"I can be at your place in ten minutes."

"Then I suppose I ought to get dressed. Are we just shopping or should I put on something sexy?"

"Just shopping," Laura answered firmly. "I want to be home before dark."

"Yeah, well shopping is fun, too. Just not as much."

The trip to Shawcut was uneventful, and Laura had no luck finding a cell phone. The small department store she remembered was still there, still opened on Sunday afternoons, and carried them, but they were out of stock. The clerk promised she could have one by Monday afternoon, but Laura thanked her and declined. They ate a plain but palatable lunch at a deli style sandwich shop and walked around town for a while, but Shawcut wasn't that much bigger than Dorrance and they started back earlier than Laura had expected.

Laura mentioned the possible break-in attempt at the farm and Ashley laughed shortly. "Nothing personal, Laura, but I can't imagine anyone actually wanting to get close to your mother. Maybe it was John Dill trying to find something he could use against her."

"Mother says the feud is pretty much over. Dill has gone out of his way to be nice to her lately."

"Maybe publicly. My dad's on the town council, remember? He says Dill really has it in for her and is always trying to find a way to piss her off. At least until his wife disappeared. Since then he's been walking around in a trance. Say what you will about the man, he was really in love with her. I hope I find a man like that someday."

"Did they ever find out why she took off?"

"Well, sort of. Dill insists they hadn't been fighting or anything. He tried to convince Chief Clay that she'd been kidnapped, but it looks more like she just did a bunk. Most of her clothes were gone, her makeup, some personal things. She cashed a big check the day before she disappeared and she gassed up her car at least once a long way from here. And she left a note."

"On her husband's computer. I heard about that. It doesn't prove anything."

"Maybe not, but it said she'd been unfaithful and that she was so ashamed she was going back to Ohio and asked him to forgive her."

Laura jerked the wheel slightly. "I hadn't heard that part. Colleen Dill unfaithful?"

"Well, she was certainly a looker, and a lot younger than her husband."

"Did she say who the man was?"

"No. Not according to my dad, anyway. Dill was devastated, though. Even your mother came by to say how sorry she was."

Laura's eyebrows went up. Apparently her mother was human after all. "They've been enemies ever since the Dills moved here. I think Mother got so used to running the town that she took it as a personal offense when the council hired an outsider after Ed Fallon died. Mr. Fallon was pretty much mother's creature. She even flirted with him a little bit," she hesitated, "back before my father left."

Ashley broke the uncomfortable silence. "You still haven't heard from him?"

Laura shook her head and her eyes were stinging. "I just don't understand it. I mean, I know things hadn't been great between them for a long time, but I thought they'd worked out some kind of peace. And then to just run off like that without a word. I don't even know if he's dead or alive." She didn't want to talk about this. "Isn't Dill's contract just about up?"

"It runs out some time next year if they don't extend it again.

If he decides to stay in town, they'll keep him. No offense meant, but your mother notwithstanding, he's done a good job here. He talked the state into finishing Moon Pond Road, for one thing. That brings some traffic into town and helps the local businesses."

Laura didn't share that opinion, but perhaps she had been overly influenced by her mother. "I heard he wanted to get rid of Sharp's Curve."

"Yeah, but your mother didn't want to give him the land and she got her way. Tommy Langston wrecked his car out there a few months later and killed his girlfriend. Now they're talking about extending Grisham Road so that they can make the turn more gradual."

"I dated Tommy's older brother a couple of times. Who was the girl?"

"Joyce Catterall. The lawyer's daughter."

Laura was stunned. "Joyce? I used to babysit for her sometimes. I was talking to her father just last week."

"That's her. Went through the windshield and died instantly. So how about a trip to the big city next weekend? I wouldn't want to live there again but I know where to shop."

"I'll think about it. Until I get a better job, my spending is going to be pretty limited."

"Who said anything about spending? I just like looking."

"Why'd you leave Buffalo, Ashley? I thought you wanted to get out of this town."

There was a short silence. "You want the truth, right?"

"That would be nice."

"Okay, then. I still want out. I got into some trouble in Buffalo, not all my fault. I met some of the people in my building and they introduced me to some others. There was nothing heavy at first—we drank a lot, did some pot, partied a little. Then things started to get out of hand and there was trouble with the cops and I nearly got busted a couple of times. I tried to drop out of the group, but I knew some stuff that could have gotten them into a lot of trouble and they started to get nervous when I said I didn't want to play anymore. And then I started to get nervous because they were watching me real close, and the job sucked anyway, so here I am."

It had all come out in a rush and Laura needed a few seconds to digest it. "So what are you going to do?"

"Save some money, hope they forget about me, and then try someplace else. I was thinking about going down south somewhere, maybe. I hate the cold weather. You should come with me. We can wait tables or run a register until we find something better."

Laura's first instinct was to dismiss the idea completely, but she hesitated. Maybe it wasn't such a bad plan. Returning to Dorrance had been a retreat; she was smart enough to recognize that. Maybe it was time to stop running away and start moving toward something, however nebulous. "Do your parents know?"

"Hell no, though Dad suspects something. Mom wouldn't notice if I'd arrived in a hail of bullets."

Laura wasn't so sure of that. Mrs. Sothern had always seemed calm and somehow above the concerns of the world, but she'd always suspected that it was a very clever act, and that she secretly saw deep into the souls of her daughter and her daughter's friends. "You're just full of surprises today. Anything else I should know?"

"Yeah, one thing."

"What's that?"

"You just missed our exit."

On Monday morning she unpacked the portable typewriter she'd bought in Vermont and started to type up her resume, but quickly grew discouraged when she realized how little she had to say. Her mother had never let her take a job in town because it would be too "undignified," and neither of the two jobs she'd held in Vermont had lasted very long. She'd been laid off from the first when the store cut back its operating hours, and the second had ended when Sean had tried to kill her, leading to everything that had followed. She was twenty-three years old, an indifferent high school graduate with no college, no serious job experience, and a recent history of emotional problems. She left the largely blank sheet of paper in the typewriter and decided to rearrange the two small closets instead.

That ended up taking most of the rest of the morning, but when she felt hungry and started chopping radishes to make tuna salad, she felt a twinge of loneliness. She had been by herself for most of the past year and hadn't felt that way. Her mother had driven to Vermont to visit her in the hospital two days after Sean's death, but Laura had hysterically refused to see her and Mary had taken the hint and gone home. They'd released her a few days later and her mother had called twice, suggesting on both occasions that she come home where she would feel safe again. Laura had been uncharacteristically hostile the second time and it had been almost a month before the third call, at which point Laura was seeing a therapist three times a week, oblivious to the speed with which her cash reserves were dwindling. When she felt well enough to cope, she stopped seeing the therapist, despite his objections. If the doctor suspected that she'd had more to do with Sean's death than she had admitted, he had never said so. Since the legal questions had been pretty much resolved by then, she sold everything that wouldn't fit in her car, and left Vermont.

She spent most of the early summer camping in state parks along the East Coast, cooking over a charcoal grill or wood fire or occasionally splurging at a cheap diner. When she couldn't find a free shower or swimming hole, she'd stay at an inexpensive motel for the night, and she had washed her clothes in so many Laundromats they all blurred in her memory. Summer found her in the Florida panhandle where she was arrested for sleeping on the beach one night and ordered to leave the Pensacola area.

Sobered by the experience, she rented a room in West Virginia and spent the rest of the summer cleaning house for a wealthy, two-career family named Welch and being paid under the table, something else that couldn't go on her resume. Then some money had disappeared and her services were no longer required. She suspected that the Welches would have filed a complaint with the police if they hadn't been afraid that her unconventional employment situation might not come out in the process. Laura hadn't taken the money, of course; she suspected the older of their two sons, who had expensive hobbies and a dirty mouth.

She had decided to return to southern New England for the autumn, and it was probably as spectacularly beautiful as ever, but for Laura, all the colors had been bleached out of the world, and all she could think of was that the changes in the trees were a warning of decay and death, just as the small changes in Sean's personality had been signs of what would eventually end their life together, and his life altogether. After that she had wandered aimlessly for a while, before realizing that she was moving by small increments back toward Dorrance.

But I learned something from all that, she told herself. I know that I can manage on my own. Life hit me with the worst thing imaginable and I survived. From here on, it should all be easy. Or at least easier.

Nevertheless, she felt lonely.

Dorrance had a total of two bars, three if you counted the one in Foster's. O'Brien's was a few miles east of the Dairy Stop, technically just outside the town line and on county land. Laura had never been in O'Brien's and didn't plan to change that now. It had a bad reputation, fights, gambling, even prostitution. Most of its patrons were either truckers taking a break or young farm laborers looking for some excitement. The Trading Post was a classier place, a block off Main Street, with tinted windows and a façade that was supposed to look vaguely frontier-like. Laura had gone there with Ashley and Kathy Peebles for her first legal drink; she was the youngest of the three and they'd been calling her "the child" ever since they both came of age during the same week a month earlier.

Laura parked on Main Street and walked the block to the Trading Post, where she discovered that it didn't open its doors until four o'clock. With almost an hour to wait, she decided to open a checking account at the bank and look for a cell phone while she was waiting. The bank took longer than she expected, almost an hour, mostly because she knew half the people working there and everyone wanted to welcome her back and find out how she was doing, tiptoeing around the questions they really wanted to ask. She finally escaped and went into Davenport's Hardware, but the clerk there—thankfully a stranger—told her that they didn't carry cell phones.

"Try Calloway's down the street. He has some electronics in the back."

But Calloway's didn't carry them, either, and Ethel Calloway was another practiced talker who wanted to welcome Laura back and tell her how glad she was to hear that she'd come through her troubles all right and what did she think had gotten into that young man anyway? Laura found it hard to escape because Ethel had come around the counter to grasp her by the arm, but eventually she either convinced the woman that she had a pressing engagement or more likely that she wasn't going to say anything that wasn't already public knowledge.

"Well, you just come back again when you have some time to talk."

Laura assured her that she would, mentally crossing her fingers, and left the store, glancing at her watch. To her astonishment, it was a few minutes after five o'clock. She should head back home and make supper, but she'd come into town to have a drink, and by God, she was going to have one.

It didn't look like the same place at all. There was a line of booths against the rear wall, where before there had been open floor covered with tables and chairs. The pool table had been replaced by a half dozen arcade games. The bar seemed untouched, but there was a new mirror, smaller than the original, flanked by pyramids of beer cans, no two alike. The bartender was unfamiliar as well. Jake Saunders had tended his own bar, day in and day out, since the first day it opened. If Jake was sick, the bar stayed closed until he was better.

The bartender now was about thirty years old, and his heavily muscled arms were covered with tattoos. He glanced up at her when she came in, his face neutral, and nodded before turning back to his current customer. Laura hesitated just inside the door, wondering if she'd made a mistake coming here. There were four people sitting at the bar, a young couple and two older men, one of whom she knew by sight but not by name. The rest were strangers. Half a dozen tables were occupied. The television over the bar was showing some kind of retrospective on the previous football season, but the volume was so low that no one could possibly be listening to it.

Just one drink, she told herself, and then I'll go.

She walked up to the bar and waited for the few seconds necessary before she was noticed. "Could I have a Tequila Sunrise, please?"

"Coming right up."

She took a bill from her purse while he was fixing the drink, left what she hoped was a reasonable tip, and took her drink over to a table halfway back, sitting so that she could watch the door. The drink was good, and strong, and she sipped at it tentatively. It had been a long time since she'd had anything stronger than beer.

Her drink was almost gone and she was thinking about getting up to go when suddenly someone was standing over her. When the shadow passed over her hand, she jumped as though she'd been physically touched, and the legs of her chair squealed slightly as she pushed herself away.

"Sorry! Didn't mean to startle you. I just wanted to say hello."

Laura glanced up at the young man standing to her left, didn't recognize him for the first few seconds. "Oh! Officer Sievert. I'm sorry, I didn't recognize you out of your uniform and you caught me by surprise."

He smiled pleasantly. "I'm more used to people jumping when I'm in uniform than when I'm out of it. And my name is Dan, remember?"

"Yes, it is. I'm sorry. You caught me by surprise. I take it you're off duty."

"According to Chief Clay, I'm never really off duty, but, yes, I am. May I buy you a drink?"

"Well, I don't know. I really shouldn't have more than one on an empty stomach."

"I can fix that. Hang on a second." He was gone before she could object, stood talking to the bartender in a low voice, then returned with two drinks on a small, round tray and a bowl full of cheese and crackers.

"May I?" He nodded toward the empty chair and she nodded back.

"Of course. Sorry, I should have offered." The cheese was

fresh and the crackers crisp. She looked at his glass. "Bloody Mary?"

"No, a Virgin Mary actually. I go on duty in a couple of hours."

"You're not from around here."

"No, I grew up in Rochester. When my uncle died he left everything to my brother and I, so we came out here and he took over the family business. I've never been very good at that sort of thing and there was an opening on the local police force so here I am."

"Dorrance must seem awfully small after Rochester."

"You'd be surprised how small-town Rochester is, but yes, I do notice the difference. I was a rent-a-cop there. Worked the front desk in a high-class apartment building for a while, things like that. I like it better when I can get out and around and not have to stay tied to one spot. How about you? Back here to stay?"

"I don't know yet. I'm still trying to decide what I want to be when I grow up, and where I want to be whatever that is." She frowned. "Did that make sense?"

"Not entirely, but I get the idea. It takes a while to find out who you really are."

"Particularly when you have a mother who wants you to be someone else." She closed her mouth with a snap. It must be the alcohol; she never spoke of personal things with strangers.

"Your mother has quite a reputation, all right, but you seem like the kind who can hold her own. How's the new home working out?"

"The cabin?" She was relieved by the switch to a neutral topic. "It's fine, in better shape than it should be considering how much it's been neglected. It doesn't have all the comforts, but I'm managing."

"I noticed you don't have telephone service."

"I'm going to get a cell phone at some point. I haven't had much luck finding one around here."

"Well, until you do, I'll make a point of checking your area more closely when I'm out that way. So if you see headlights pausing out on Moon Pond Road, don't automatically assume it's a prowler."

"Thanks, but I don't expect to have any problems. We're not a high–crime rate community, after all."

His face grew measurably more serious. "No, but we've had two break-ins, an attempted rape, and a handful of assaults this past year, plus the robbery at the Dairy Stop."

Laura's eyes flickered. "What robbery at the Dairy Stop? I work there nights."

Dan suddenly looked uncomfortable. "Sorry, I didn't know that. It's nothing to be alarmed about. The state troopers caught them the next day. Three joyriders just passing through. No one was hurt or anything. I don't want you to worry, Laura, just be cautious."

She was more angry than frightened. Wiegand should have told her. It wouldn't have affected her decision to take the job, but he should have told her, anyway.

Dan slowly stood up, his drink finished. "I have to get going. It was nice talking to you."

She looked up at him and smiled with what she hoped was friendly warmth and nothing more. "Same here. And thanks for the drink. I owe you one."

He bobbed his head, grinning. "Not really. I didn't pay for these. That ugly guy behind the bar is my brother. Jake Saunders was our uncle, so now we own the place."

Laura's mouth was still hanging open when he turned and walked through the door.

CHAPTER SEVEN

Despite the crackers and cheese, or perhaps because of her unusual work schedule, Laura felt very drowsy when she got back to the cabin. She knew that if she gave into it and went to bed, she'd wake up at eleven and be unable to get back to sleep before dawn. Initially she'd thought the graveyard shift could be ideal for her, but now she was beginning to discover the drawbacks. She'd have to remind Wiegand of his promise to see if he could move her to a different shift.

It was about seven o'clock when she thought she heard someone moving outside. The light was gone by then and it had clouded over again, so she could see very little when she looked out through the windows. There were no lights visible, and the trees hid even the faint distant glow of downtown Dorrance. It had sounded like booted feet in the snow and her first thought was that Dan Sievert had stopped by to see if she'd gotten home all right, a prospect that she found surprisingly pleasant. But surely he'd have carried a flashlight.

Just as she had decided that it must have been an animal or some other innocuous intruder, she heard a branch snap, followed by several sloshing footsteps, unmistakably human this time. She tried each window in turn without seeing anything. Laura wasn't frightened particularly. The things that had happened to her a year earlier were so much more terrifying that this seemed almost insignificant. Still, if someone was on her property, she wanted to know about it.

Laura put on a jacket and boots, but no gloves, and picked up the flashlight from its place on the shelf near the door. She had one hand on the doorknob when she hesitated, then returned to the stove and picked up the hatchet she'd used to make some kindling. It felt comfortable in her hand as she slipped through the door, locking it behind her. It was snowing lightly but blowing quite hard, stirring up the powdery snow that had already fallen and making it very difficult to see where she was going, even with the flashlight.

When she came around the side of the cabin, she moved the cone of light around slowly. Her car was already covered with fresh snow, and just beyond it was another lump, a second car, one she didn't recognize. A wisp of steam was rising from the hood where the falling snow landed on warm metal.

"Hello!" she shouted. "Who's out there?"

There was a muffled sound from the opposite side of the cabin. Laura tightened her grip on the hatchet and moved the light in that direction. "This is private property. Identify yourself immediately or I'll call the police." A thin threat, since she had no phone. She couldn't even drive off with the other car blocking the way.

The silence lasted only a few seconds, but it seemed like much longer. Then, just as she was beginning to get actively nervous, someone came around the corner of the cabin, a dark figure, tall and slender, one arm raised to shield his face.

"Who's there?" she called again.

"It's just me," came a strained male voice. "Ted Catterall. I thought the door was on the other side, and then I got disoriented in the snow." He was still coming forward, and Laura didn't relax until he was close enough that she could recognize him.

"Mr. Catterall? What are you doing out here?"

"I have some papers you need to sign." He raised a thin valise to illustrate his point. "Can we go inside? This will only take a minute."

Laura was more than slightly annoyed that he'd shown up uninvited, but there was nothing to be done about it now. "All right. It's this way."

She offered to make coffee but wasn't unhappy when the lawyer declined. "Sorry to barge in on you like this, but after your visit, I went through the files again and discovered the terms of the trust change if you actually take up residence in the cabin, which you obviously have. This gives you direct control over the monies rather than a maintenance allowance. I knew you were under some financial constraints, so I thought you would want to get the paperwork done as quickly as possible."

Laura's mood brightened and she decided to forgive Catterall's unannounced visit in view of the nature of his news. "I don't mean to sound mercenary, but just how much are we talking about?" He told her and she whistled. "I had no idea there was so much."

"The funds are currently in a cash management account, but you can change that if you wish. What we have here is the paperwork to give you access. It will take a couple of weeks to process and then they'll send you a checkbook and a monthly statement, unless you decide to close out the account and move the funds elsewhere. I should tell you that I also am authorized to dispense funds, but from this point forward I won't do so without your permission."

Laura felt a vague sense of unreality. The amount was enough to support her almost indefinitely so long as she continued her modest lifestyle. She could stop working at the Dairy Stop, maybe even replace the Chevy in the spring. "This is great news, Mr. Catterall, but you really didn't need to come all the way out here in this weather. I work nights so there's no reason why I couldn't have come by your office."

He looked uncomfortable for a few seconds, then recovered. "I would normally have called you and set up an appointment, but you don't have a phone listing and I thought this was too important to wait. I'm sorry if I've intruded."

"No," she protested, somewhat untruthfully. "I just meant that you shouldn't have inconvenienced yourself."

He smiled. "It wasn't a problem. You're only a few minutes from my office, after all." The papers were all signed and gathered and he closed them up in his briefcase. "If you don't have any more questions, I'll be on my way."

They rose together and she shook his hand. "Thank you again, Mr. Catterall. As soon as I get a cell phone, I'll call your office and leave my number." She walked him to the door and, just as he was stepping through, something else occurred to her. "Oh, I almost forgot. I was very sorry to hear about Joyce. She was a lovely girl."

He stopped but didn't turn back to face her. "Thank you. It was a stupid tragedy, of course. The boy was driving much too fast and that stretch of road has always had a bad reputation. They're finally going to do something about it, I understand. Good night, Miss Collier." And then he was off. His voice had become very bitter and Laura had had no idea how to respond to it.

Two things occurred to her after Catterall's visit and before she went to bed. The first was that her mother had made even more enemies in Dorrance than Laura had realized, and that Ted Catterall was almost certainly among their number. The second was renewed puzzlement about his visit. Sure, she had no telephone. But she had notified the post office of her address, and Catterall obviously knew where she was living. He could have sent a note asking her to make an appointment. Her finances were tight but not desperate. It was hard to believe that the attorney had made a house call, at night, in a snowstorm, at no charge, without some other motivation.

But what could it be?

The following day she had an unpleasant confrontation with Mason Cortway. There wasn't a cell phone to be had in Dorrance, but Calloway's was willing to order one for her. "I can have it shipped directly to you if you'd like."

Laura paid him, using one of the unnumbered checks that the bank had provided.

It was bright and cheery outside, despite the snow, which had changed over to freezing rain sometime during the night. The trees had been glassy when she'd left the cabin, and there had been a few slippery spots on Moon Pond Road, but once the sun had cleared the trees, the ice began to melt quickly even though the temperature hovered very close to the freezing mark. The streets had been plowed, even Moon Pond Road, either by the Public Works department or one of the farmers who had contracts with the township.

The sidewalks, however, could have used some work. A few merchants had shoveled but two out of three hadn't, and Laura slipped and fell hard enough to bruise her hip on one occasion. Limping slightly, she went into Slade's—whose sidewalk was completely clear—for a cup of coffee and a few minutes to recover. Surprisingly, she was the only customer, and if her hip hadn't been bothering her, she'd have taken one of the stools at the counter. Instead, she slipped into the second booth and told Kevin Slade that, yes, she would definitely like a cup. Her mother described Kevin as "not the brightest star in the sky" and he certainly wasn't quick, but he was good-natured, trustworthy, and quite clever when he actually grew interested in a problem. His solutions weren't always conventional, but they always worked.

Kevin was back in the kitchen with his mother when Mason came in. He glanced around, then came directly to Laura's booth and sat down opposite her without waiting for an invitation. "I thought that was you. I was across the street and saw you come in."

"Hello, Mason," Laura said evenly. "Why don't you sit down for a moment?"

He ignored her sarcasm, if he even noticed it. "I heard that you were dating again and wondered if we could get together this weekend. They opened one of those new cineplexes over in Nickleby."

"Who told you I was dating?" Laura wasn't offended, but was actively puzzled.

"Ned Blakely saw you drinking with some guy at the Trading Post. He said you two looked like real good friends."

"Well, then Ned Blakely needs glasses. I went there alone and one of the owners bought me a drink to welcome me to town." It was close to the truth, and more than Mason deserved as far as she was concerned. "I'm not dating anyone, Mason. Not for the foreseeable future. I'm sorry." She wasn't, actually. It astonished her that she'd ever gone out with Mason Cortway. He seemed incredibly immature to her now.

He'd been smiling and it slipped a little. His eyes were constantly moving though, nervously. "You shouldn't shut yourself away from people, Laura. It's not good for you. Listen, if you aren't interested in a movie, the Huston sisters are throwing a party in a few days. You could go as my guest if you don't want to call it a date. You need to get out and see your old friends, and you know they always show people a good time."

Laura could remember getting drunk on cheap wine at one of their parties when she was a sophomore. She had tried to tell her mother she had the flu the next day, but it hadn't worked.

"I don't think so, Mason. I'm just not in the mood for that sort of thing. Maybe some other time." She mentally kicked herself for encouraging him to ask again.

"What's your problem?" Mason sounded exasperated. "You're starting to act like your mother. Too good for the rest of us in Dorrance."

"That's not it at all, Mason. And lower your voice."

"Don't tell me what to do!" He leaned forward across the table and now his voice was uncomfortably loud.

Out of the corner of her eye, she saw Kevin come out of the kitchen, his face expressing concern. "I think you should go. I mean it."

"Oh, I'll go all right, but not before I have my say. You think you're better than the rest of us, but you're the one who married a crazy man who tried to kill you. Some of us tried to tell you that you were making a mistake, but you wouldn't listen. No, Laura Collier was going to make a better life for herself than living in a dull backwater town like Dorrance. Well, guess what? The rest of us grew up and took some responsibility for our lives. When we have problems, we work our way through them. We don't go off gallivanting around the country for a year and we don't hide in log cabins and ignore the rest of the world."

His outburst had shocked her into a brief silence, but now she protested. "I'm not hiding from the world, Mason. You have no idea what you're talking about." Her own voice had risen now and she was shaking with anger. "Please, just leave me alone."

Mason had made no move to rise and his glower was even more pronounced. He opened his mouth to say something more, but before he could, Kevin was standing beside the booth. "Could I get you some coffee, Mason?"

It was just enough to distract him. Mason looked back and forth between Kevin and Laura, then shrugged his shoulders and stood up. "What's the use? You're as pigheaded as your mother, and you'll end up just as alone and unpopular as she is. If the two of you disappeared tomorrow, all this town would do is breathe a great big sigh of relief."

He pushed past Kevin and then out the door without another word. Laura didn't watch him go, just leaned forward on her elbows and shook her head.

"My dad says Mason gets his bad temper from his mom." Kevin very slowly refilled her coffee cup. "The last time they were in here together, she slapped his face right in front of everybody."

Laura looked up at Kevin and smiled. "Thanks, Kevin. I know Mason's a jerk. He's just talk, though. Thanks for the rescue."

"My pleasure."

She could have quit her job right away, but the money didn't seem entirely real to her yet, and she felt as though she should give Wiegand some notice. It would be another job she couldn't list on her resume, of course, but the Dairy Stop was hardly the signpost for a promising career. Which raised the question of what she really wanted to do with herself, her future.

Laura could have gone to college. Her mother had wanted her to and would have paid for it without a moment's hesitation, although she made no secret of the fact that she expected her daughter to take over management of the farm in due course. It had tempted her. Her grades weren't spectacular, but they were high enough. Wherever she went would be at least as far as Buffalo, so she'd be out from under Mary Collier's thumb most of the time. But the tuition payments and support would just add another string to the many that held mother and daughter together, and Laura was more interested in severing them than adding to their number.

As a child she'd dreamed the usual dreams—actress, astronaut, lawyer—but they'd all passed quickly. She'd never demonstrated any particular aptitude or interest in any particular field. "I'm a generalist," she'd told her high school counselor, who suggested she look at a nice liberal arts college. Laura thought about teaching, but doubted she had the patience to deal with children, about business administration, and knew she lacked the patience for corporate politics, and finally announced that she was going to take a year off and travel.

The year had stretched to two years, and she'd never been farther away than New York City. Her mother had continued her allowance, which wasn't high enough to include such luxuries as a trip to Europe, or even a prolonged stay anywhere domestically. Then she'd met Sean Brennan and career plans had been the last thing she'd had in mind during the few months of their courtship.

Now she had money of her own, possibly even enough to attend college without being beholden to her mother. But she still didn't know what she wanted to do and she wasn't going to spend the money impulsively. It's my safety net, she told herself. It eliminates one whole set of worries so that I'm free to deal with the other ones.

She needed to talk with someone so she called Ashley on Tuesday evening and asked her out for a drink. Less than an hour later, the two of them walked into the Trading Post, which was somewhat more crowded and a great deal noisier than it had been during her first visit. They had their first drink standing at the bar, then grabbed a table that had just been vacated, conveniently located in the corner furthest from the jukebox. Laura had seen several familiar faces in the crowd, about half of whom she could put names to, including Ned Blakely, who would presumably be telling everyone tomorrow that she and Ashley were lesbians. She felt, and suppressed, an urge to play-act for his benefit. On the other hand, Dan Sievert wasn't there, and she felt a flash of disappointment.

The corner was quiet enough that they could talk without shouting, barely, and the drinks were good. The bartender, Dan's brother, had greeted them warmly and made them feel welcome, even though the rest of his patrons were male, or escorted by one. Laura hoped he wasn't assuming they were there to pick up men.

"I'm going to quit my job."

Ashley nodded, apparently unsurprised. "It's a shit job, Laura. I could have told you that."

"Actually, you did tell me that, and I agreed with you, but I was desperate."

"So you got a better offer?"

Laura shook her head. "No, no job."

"You're not going back to your mother already?" Ashley's eyes had widened in horror. "I'd talk Mom into letting you use the room over the garage before I'd let you do that."

"No, I'm not going . . . to the farm." She had almost said "home." "I came into some money unexpectedly, an inheritance."

"You're kidding! That's great." She hesitated and her face grew somber. "It wasn't, you know, your father, was it?"

Laura shook her head. "No. As far as I know he's still alive out there. Somewhere. It was my aunt." She explained briefly.

"Okay, then I'm back to that's great. So now you're a woman of leisure and you don't have to work."

"Only if I'm willing to live in a log cabin with no cable television, drive elderly used cars, and eat lots of pasta for the rest of my life, and only if the stock market doesn't go down again. Oh, Ashley, what am I going to do with myself? I've screwed things up so badly since high school, I'm almost afraid to try anything else."

"Hey, hold on there. You haven't done so badly. Yes, you chose the wrong guy to marry, but he wasn't like that then. Remember, I had the hots for him, too. He was a nice, charming, sexy guy. What happened to him afterward, well, that's a real tragedy, and it must have been terrible for you to go through it all, but you survived, and he's gone now, and none of it was your fault."

"You sound like my shrink."

"Hey, then maybe that's the career I should pick. I always was a good listener." She blinked her eyes rapidly and exaggeratedly. "But I'm a better talker."

"Don't go hanging out your shingle just yet. Besides, it's my career decision we're supposed to be talking about here." She noticed that her glass was empty but before she could act, Ashley was flagging down a harried looking waitress.

"This one's on me," she said. "To celebrate having you back."

"Thanks. I'm glad to be here." And to her surprise, she was telling the truth.

Ashley suddenly reached across the table and touched her lapel. "I love that pin."

Laura automatically craned her head downward. "Oh, that. I found it when I was cleaning the cabin. Mother must have dropped it there on one of her rare visits because it's not one of mine. It is rather pretty, isn't it?"

"Yeah. I've seen it before, or one really close. Give me a second." She squinched up her face, presumably to help her think, and Laura waited. Ashley had an encyclopedic memory of clothing and accessories and was no doubt running through her mental indexes. "Got it! Colleen Dill!"

"Mrs. Dill?" That was the last name she'd expected. "Mrs. Dill had a pin like this one?"

"She sure did. I remember seeing it when Dad made me go along as his date to the Founders' Day Dinner a couple of years ago. I remember it because she arranged the flowers for the hall and made some kind of joke about wearing it so that she could blend into the scenery."

"I can't think of any reason why Mrs. Dill would go out to my cabin. This can't be hers."

"No, it's probably not. Maybe your mother had one just like it and threw it out and it ended up there somehow. Lord knows, she dislikes John Dill enough that she might do something like that. Dad says a couple of times they almost came to blows during council meetings."

"That sounds like Mother. She always brings out the best in people."

"Sounds like it runs in the family."

"What?"

Ashley shook her head. "Sorry, I didn't mean it that way. I heard you had some issues with Mason Cortway today."

"How did you hear about that? No one heard us except Kevin Slade." She couldn't imagine Kevin gossiping about it.

"Mason is telling everyone he meets, probably trying to nail down his version as the truth before you get a chance to say otherwise."

"I don't understand. It wasn't that big a thing. He asked me for a date and I turned him down, and he got offended and walked off in a huff."

"That's not exactly the way he's telling it. Seems that he noticed you sitting alone and went in to keep you company, and you seemed depressed so he suggested that you might want to hang around with some of the old gang. You know, the Huston sisters, Merle Ridgeway, Bobbi Olsen, the crowd we pretended to like during high school. Anyway, you not only turned down his well-meant suggestion but unloaded on all your old friends as well."

"But that's not true! I never said anything about any of them!"

"Wait. It gets better. Then you told him that your mother was right back in high school when she tried to keep you away from them. When you started yelling at him like a crazy woman, he got scared because he thought maybe you'd caught insanity from Sean so he walked out while you stood there screaming at his back."

For a few seconds, Laura was absolutely horrified and terribly angry and she wanted to get up and drive over to the Cortway house immediately to tell Mason how utterly worthless a human being he really was. Then the absurdity of it all struck her, or perhaps the alcohol, and she started to laugh, and Ashley joined her, and for the next few minutes neither of them could manage an intelligible word.

When the fit passed, Laura sat back in her chair and sighed theatrically. "Well, there goes my chance of having a fantastic social life in this town."

"No one else has one. Why should you?" That set them off again, but they recovered more quickly and ordered another round of drinks.

"Remind me to thank Mason next time I see him. That's the first time I've laughed like that in a long time. It felt good." She rubbed her ribs. "Actually, it hurt a little, but I don't care. Are you going to be ostracized when it gets around that we're still friends?"

"When I first got back, I had something of a bad girl reputation, so I was pretty popular for about ten minutes. But then they caught on that if anything new and interesting had happened, I wasn't going to tell them about it, and I started getting accidentally left off party invitations. I think I made Kelly Huston nervous; she's always had the mystery woman title and I was her first real rival for the crown."

"Kelly was closemouthed and distant. There was no mystery about it. She never had anything worth saying and was at least smart enough to know it. The real reason she never had a steady boyfriend was because no one ever asked her."

The drinks arrived and they were silent for a while. "So what am I going to do, Ashley? Go back to school? Get a job? Become a hermit?"

"Look who you're asking. I'm working as a drugstore cashier after screwing up a not much better paying job in the big city. At least you're not still living at home. I love my parents, Laura, but as soon as I walk in that door, I swear I shed about four years of maturity. I can feel myself doing it but I can't make it stop."

"I know what you mean. And your mother is a lot easier to deal with than mine."

"You got me there. I was always a little bit afraid to come to your house, you know. I used to think your mother could read my thoughts with her eyes."

"If she can, that's one family trait she didn't pass down to me." She reached for her glass and bumped the table with her elbow. Some of her drink splashed over the rim onto the table. "Okay, that's it. I've had enough. I'm just sober enough to drive you back and then go home. Are you about finished?"

"Sure." Ashley tossed down the last of her drink, and then her voice, though slurred, became serious. "Laura, you don't have to rush into anything. Take your time and think things through. I'm the one who makes decisions on the spur of the moment and we both know how well I've been doing. You'll work it out."

"I hope so, Ashley. I really do. Because most of the time now I just feel lost."

CHAPTER EIGHT

Quitting her job was both harder and easier than Laura had expected.

Although she could have called Wiegand right away, she procrastinated until Thursday and went to work without having said anything. There were actually several customers in the store when she arrived, and she was busy for a while, but only one grungy-looking trucker showed up during the next hour, and then there was the usual long gap before business picked up again at four in the morning.

Things were busier than usual right up until six, and she was feeling rather harried when her relief showed up. Most of the time she cheated and disposed of the trash during her regular hours, but she'd done some restocking just before the rush started and there were about a dozen boxes to toss into the Dumpster. She was just finishing up when Bud Wiegand drove up, parked illegally at the side of the building, and came around to see her rather than go inside.

Under normal circumstances, Laura would have been displeased, but it felt better to give him the news in person rather than over the telephone. She didn't like conversations where she couldn't see the face of the other party, even scruffy, unshaven, and vaguely belligerent faces like this one.

"Good morning, Mr. Wiegand." She heaved the last of the trash up over the lip of the Dumpster and brushed her palms together to clean them before reaching into her pocket for her gloves.

"Came down to see how you were doing." His eyes roved briefly around the pavement, as though he was looking for trash she'd missed, then came back to her, not quite high enough to be looking at her face.

Laura was amused rather than offended. He couldn't possibly find anything sexy through her heavy quilted jacket and sweater, but that didn't stop him from trying. It seemed almost instinctive with the man, or perhaps obsessive. "I'm afraid I have some bad news."

His eyes snapped up to her face and his jaw clenched. "What kind of bad news?"

"I'm going to have to give you two weeks' notice."

"You're quitting?"

She nodded. "I'm afraid so. I'm sorry, but I'm having too much trouble sleeping on this funny schedule." The lie came quickly and without pre-thought.

"Told you I'd move you to another shift as soon as I could." He sounded belligerent and puzzled at the same time.

Laura shook her head. "No, I really need to find something else. Something full time. I'm sorry for the inconvenience, and I can stay a few days longer if you have trouble getting a replacement."

"What's the matter? Too good to work for a living?" Wiegand's fists had clenched at his sides and his voice was deeper and uneven.

"I beg your pardon?" She felt a flash of anger of her own.

"You Rustins always thought you was too good for the rest of us. I shouldn't be surprised you couldn't stick it out."

"I'm a Collier, not a Rustin." Actually, she was still a Brennan right now, she supposed. "And my family has nothing to do with this."

111

"Gonna live off your mother, I suppose. Might as well. You don't seem to be good for anything else anyway. Drove your man so crazy he killed himself."

Laura opened her mouth to respond, then clamped it shut. He's not worth it, she told herself. You don't have to explain anything to him. He has no idea what he's talking about and he just said that to make you upset, so don't let him get away with it. Stay calm and in control.

"I don't think we need to talk about this anymore, Mr. Wiegand. Two weeks, like I said."

"No, damn it! No two weeks!" He raised his fists and for a second she thought he might actually attack her. She glanced around quickly, looking for an escape route, or a weapon. "You get out of here right now! You're fired, you hear me? I don't ever want to see you in here again! You buy your stuff somewhere else!"

Laura was certain that if she'd been closer she would have felt his spittle on her face. In a matter of seconds he had worked himself up into a rage.

"I'll do that, Mr. Wiegand. You have my address. You can send my last paycheck there." She turned away, hoping to cut off any response, but Wiegand began to follow her, still shouting.

"Damned if I will! Sue me if you want to, but you won't get a single penny from me otherwise! Damned little stuck-up bitch!"

She forced herself to walk at a normal pace, shutting out his words, reached her car and got inside. Her hands were shaking so badly that it took three tries to get the key into the ignition, but then she was pulling out onto the road, with Bud Wiegand still standing there, waving one fist impotently and shouting imprecations she couldn't hear.

Halfway home, she felt her muscles begin to relax and shook her head. "Well, that could have gone better."

She was too upset to take her usual mid-morning nap so she went for a walk instead. It had warmed up a bit, enough that the snow was retreating slowly, relinquishing its grip on the trees first, then fading away in those areas where the sun most easily penetrated the canopy of branches overhead. Although she wasn't following any preset path, there was no chance of her getting lost. Laura had played in these woods so many times as a child that some of the trees seemed like close friends. She could have been blindfolded and set down at random anywhere within a couple of square miles and would have oriented herself within a few minutes, at least during daylight.

Little had changed since her last visit. The trees were slightly larger and some of the underbrush had thickened. One elderly pine tree had fallen over and lay at a forty-five degree angle, cradled in the embrace of its younger competitors. She found a couple of pieces of trash, probably windborne, and stuffed them into her jacket pocket. Eventually she turned toward Moon Pond itself, bypassing the now frozen swamp along its eastern edge. There was probably more trash here, because this was one of the spots where local teens came to drink, but it was buried under the snow and out of sight.

She stood at the shoreline and looked out across an expanse of dark, peaceful water. Moon Pond wasn't particularly impressive if measured by surface area, but it threaded its way through the wooded countryside for over a mile. There were several cabins at the opposite end, mostly rentals owned by people from Toucan Township. Occasionally someone would try putting a speedboat in the water, but never for long. There were too many shallow spots and underwater obstructions on that side. More than one boat had foundered, and she remembered one overbearing tourist who tore the bottom out of his boat on a submerged rock during the summer of her sophomore year. The idiot had nearly drowned before another tourist had cautiously approached to rescue him. A few people canoed, either romancing or fishing, but they were usually quiet enough.

Her walk took longer than she realized, and it was well into the afternoon by the time she returned. Her stomach was growling and she'd been mentally reviewing the contents of her thinly stocked larder, trying to decide what would be the quickest to fix, when she noticed that she'd had a visitor.

A line of footsteps, quickly melting, almost completely encircled the house, as though whoever had arrived had been looking for a way in. That thought struck her as mildly paranoid, but she still hadn't shaken off the sense of menace she'd felt during her confrontation with Bud Wiegand. There was no way to identify the visitor. Whoever it was must have arrived shortly after she'd left, because the melting snow had almost completely erased the evidence. She following the tracks back to the unpaved driveway, but lost them there. The sun had been so efficient here that she couldn't even tell if her visitor had driven up or walked in from outside the property.

It's probably nothing, she told herself. Maybe Ashley or even her mother had come by for some reason. She still didn't have a phone so there was no way to call ahead. Her car was in plain sight, so it would have seemed obvious that she was home. The visitor had probably knocked on the door, received no response, then walked around the house to see if there was any sign of life before leaving.

It made sense and it seemed innocuous, but when Laura went inside, she locked the door behind her.

The two days that followed were peaceful, but Laura was surprised to discover that she was bored. She had spent most of the past year keeping her own company, with nothing in particular to do except reflect on what was past and try to reconcile things in her mind. No one but she really knew everything that had happened during that last day with Sean, not the authorities, not her mother, not even the psychiatrist she'd been seeing. Laura told herself it didn't matter, that everyone believed Sean had killed himself at the end, falling on the blade of the knife he'd meant to use on her when he stumbled on the stairs. It wasn't the truth, but the truth wouldn't help anyone, and it would have made things so much more complicated that she'd concealed the details and then confirmed the story the police had innocently suggested to her. The truth would not have brought him back, or erased anything that he'd done, nor would it have made her feel any better.

That part of her trauma she'd had to heal without help, and it had left a scar she thought she'd carry around, invisibly, forever. It had preoccupied her so much that when she realized that she was actually monumentally bored, that fact actually cheered her, gave her hope that she was finally starting to let go of all the bad stuff.

Other than a single trip to town for groceries and to learn that her cell phone had been back ordered, she stayed at the cabin for most of the following week. Walking down to the shore of Moon Pond became a daily habit. When the last of the snow had vanished by Friday morning, she carried down several plastic grocery bags and methodically picked up all the trash, even used a stick to maneuver sunken objects out of the nearby shallows. When she was done, it took three trips to carry all the debris back to the cabin and deposit it in the large drum she was using to collect empty cans and other waste. There was no garbage service out here, but she planned to borrow the pickup truck from the farm and cart her trash to the town dump.

She made herself a sandwich for lunch and walked back down to the shoreline to enjoy the results of the morning's work. The sun was almost warm and she was sweating under her heavy clothing, so she climbed up onto an enormous bald rock under the shade of two pine trees and sat in the shadows. At the far end of the lake, she could see some sort of activity at one of the private docks, but it was too distant for her to make out any details. Her eyelids drooped and she leaned back against the tree and closed them, and either daydreamed or actually dozed off for a while, because her head suddenly snapped up and she felt disoriented and vaguely uneasy.

Laura stood up carefully on the uneven surface, half convinced that she had been wakened by some unusual sound but unable to remember exactly what it might have been. She was about to climb down the rock when she heard an odd popping somewhere in the distance and then a sharp crack. A spray of dust rose up from below and she jumped back, suddenly frightened.

Someone just shot at me, she thought.

She shrank back against the tree and crouched, trying to make as small a target as possible. There was no sound, no repetition of the shot, no movement that she could see other than the slight swaying of the branches as a gentle breeze played with them. Although she'd been relatively warm a short while ago, now she felt terribly cold and her forehead throbbed with a sudden headache. Laura turned her head slowly, trying to peer through the evergreen branches, but she couldn't see anything out of the ordinary. Of course, it was so overgrown here that a dozen people could have lurked within a stone's throw without giving themselves away.

Moving as slowly and silently as possible, she backed around the tree trunk. It wouldn't be as easy to descend on this side; trees and vines had grown up to and across the rock surface here, making her path awkward and treacherous. She was also going to get quite dirty. Her descent took a quarter of an hour. Each bit of footing had to be tested to make certain it would support her weight, and on several occasions her clothing got snagged on the end of a branch. But she managed to get down to ground level without anything too disastrous, a shallow scratch across the back of one hand and a bruise on the side of one knee, but otherwise intact.

She kept to cover as much as possible on her way back to the cabin, but sprinted the last few yards. There had been no repetition of the shot, no shouting, nothing to indicate that the shooter was after her or even still in the vicinity. But she was in the cabin only long enough to get her keys, and she broke the speed limit on her way to town.

Chief Clay came personally, possibly because she was the daughter of Mary Collier, but more likely because he was bored and welcomed the excuse to get out of his office and away from his paperwork. He took another man with him, Paul Schuyler, whom Laura remembered from the many times he'd chaperoned dances at the high school. They told her to stay at the cabin while they investigated, and she did so for almost half an hour before the suspense grew so great that she couldn't stand it. They were already walking back up from the pond and she met them halfway.

"There doesn't seem to be anyone around anymore, and the ground's frozen too hard to tell us much. Too bad the snow melted. Can you show us the exact spot where it happened?"

"I certainly can." They spent several minutes, the Chief examining the impact mark on the rock while Schuyler searched unsuccessfully for the round.

"There was only the single shot?"

She nodded and gathered her arms around herself. The sun was dropping now and the air was growing decidedly cooler.

"And you didn't hear anything else? No shouting? No one running off?"

"Not a thing."

"Well, Miss Collier. I've no doubt that what you've told me is true, and it's a serious thing all right, but I'd guess what we have here is a careless city person out hunting illegally and not watching where he's firing." He gestured toward the other end of the pond. "There's a few of them rented cabins over there, and Ted Bixby told me some of them brought along firearms of one sort or another. They're not technically in my jurisdiction, but I'm going to have a talk with Cal Sharpton over in Toucan and see if he'll stop by and bring them up to date about our laws here. I wouldn't be too worried about it, but if I were you I'd make sure I was wearing something bright when I was out walking, and I wouldn't spend too much time in the shadows."

It sounded plausible, but Laura had almost died because she had spent so much time interpreting Sean's increasingly bizarre behavior as simple idiosyncrasies and overwork. She wasn't going to repeat that mistake. But it wouldn't help her case to make too big a point of it to Chief Clay. Once he had someone pigeonholed, it was hard to make him change his evaluation, and she didn't want to be labeled and dismissed as an hysterical female.

"That's probably it. Thank you for coming by, Chief. I'm sorry if it was all for nothing."

"Not at all. It's too pretty a day to spend in the office anyway. Just for safety's sake, I'd make sure I bolted the door at night if I were you. And I understand you don't have a phone yet?"

"No. I have a cell phone ordered, but they keep changing the delivery date."

"Well, I'd appreciate it if you'd call the station when you get it and let us know the number. And I'll have Officer Sievert stop by and check up on you for a while if you don't mind."

"No, not at all. Thanks again." Her mood brightened slightly. At least one good thing had come of this. She'd get to see Dan Sievert again. The pleasure she felt at the prospect quite surprised her.

But she still wasn't willing to accept at face value that the shot had been fired by a careless hunter. It might be true, probably was in fact, but she wasn't going to take any chances. As soon as the chief was gone, she got into the Chevy and drove to the farm.

Laura knocked, then let herself in. Her mother was in the house, lying on the couch with her feet up.

"Since when do you loaf during the day?" Laura sat down in a chair opposite.

"Since my feet started to swell up when I spent a lot of time on them. I may be stubborn but I'm not stupid. When my body tells me to take a rest, I do what I'm told."

"I'm shocked. I thought Rustin women weren't supposed to have any weaknesses." She hoped her tone was light enough that her mother wouldn't take offense.

"No, we have our weaknesses. We just do our best to keep them to ourselves."

"Any word on your prowler?"

"No. Nathan Clay's useless. I told people it was a mistake to give him that job, but no one would listen. We haven't had any more trouble out here, thank heaven. I've asked Del to keep a watchful eye and he says he's doing it, but you know how he is about anything he thinks is a waste of time. Your father wanted me to fire him a couple of times for insubordination."

"Why didn't you? He's not the most agreeable man I've ever met, and I think behind that sullen, thoughtful silence he's hiding a sulking, thoughtless mind."

Mary actually laughed. "You won't get any argument from me about that. But he's a hard worker, he's good with machinery, and he follows orders—mostly. Very few of the other farmhands around here can claim more than one of those virtues."

Laura's thoughts had already moved elsewhere. "Do you ever miss him?" She saw her mother's puzzled expression and explained. "Dad, I mean. Not Del."

Mary settled back into the cushions and crossed her arms on her chest. "I don't know, Laura. Sometimes I think I do, but it's no secret that the romance had gone out of our marriage long before your father left. I suppose I've changed with the years, but I've never doubted my core beliefs. Your father was different. He was a brilliant man when we first met; he managed this farm as well as anyone could have. Even grandfather would have been pleased. But something happened along the way. He lost interest, lost his edge, began making bad decisions, then started retreating from making decisions altogether. When I stepped in, he resented it, but he wouldn't make the hard choices himself."

"I don't remember you fighting very much."

"No, at first we tried to keep our troubles hidden, and then your father just stopped trying. It was like having another farmhand around. He wouldn't even make suggestions unless I really pushed."

"Do you think he was seeing someone else?"

Mary laughed again. "No, never. Oh, I don't think I'm such a prize that he wouldn't have been tempted, but I'll say one thing for your father. He had a sense of honor second to none. He would never have cheated on me."

But he would abandon his only daughter without a word, Laura thought to herself. "If he came back, would you take him?"

"Oh, that's too big a question to answer easily. It would depend, I suppose. In some ways, he's still here, you know. I see him in you, and every once in a while I get the impression that he's around, watching, keeping track of things. I'm sorry he left, but I'm sorry mostly for your sake. But a little bit for myself as well. So anyway, will you stay for dinner?"

"Sure, but I didn't come by to cadge a meal. I want to take my old hunting rifle."

"The twenty-two? I think it's locked up with your father's guns. Why in the world would you want that?"

Laura didn't want to say anything about the shooting incident, although it would reach her mother eventually. There wasn't much that remained secret in Dorrance for any length of time. "I think I saw some of your rats near the cabin. I was a pretty good shot a few years ago."

"I remember you and your father going out to practice. He was an excellent marksman. Whenever he and the boys went out to hunt, he always came back with something, maybe just a squirrel or a rabbit, but he'd have something when the others were all bare-handed."

"I seem to recall that you were pretty handy with firearms yourself."

"Oh, I can pretty much hit what I aim at, but I don't get much practice nowadays. Although there have been times when I considered taking a shot at John Dill."

"Do you have the key?"

"The key? Oh, the key! It's in one of the drawers in the desk over there." She pointed to the rolltop desk in the corner. "The top one, I think."

The key was mixed in with some loose change in the top drawer. Laura carried it into the den and turned on the overhead light. The gun closet was on the far wall, completely enclosed in heavy mahogany. The lock turned easily and she opened the doors, revealing almost a dozen weapons; two shotguns, several low-caliber hunting rifles, and a single handgun. One slot was empty, but her old .22 was right in its place. She unhooked it and lifted it down and it felt reassuringly solid, although even a brief look told her it would have to be cleaned and oiled before it could be used. She took a box of ammunition, then relocked the cabinet, carried the rifle out into the front room and leaned it against the wall beside the door so she wouldn't forget it.

Her mother came in from the kitchen, wiping her hands on a dish towel. "Find what you were looking for?"

"Yes, I did. One of Dad's hunting rifles is missing."

Mary nodded. "Del came by two days ago and borrowed it."

"Del? Has he taken up hunting?"

"No, of course not. Wrong time of year anyway. He says he saw some rats when he was working on the equipment out in the barn and took it so he could shoot them if they came back."

Laura's brow furrowed. "Why didn't he just use the pellet gun like he always used to? Or laid traps."

Her mother shrugged. "He doesn't like to admit it, but Del's eyesight's not nearly as good as it used to be."

Laura had one more surprise that day, this one delivered during supper. They were having spaghetti, which was fine, but Mary had drenched the accompanying salad with far more dressing than Laura preferred. Each bite had dripped cholesterol.

"While I'm thinking of it, I should tell you that I'll be away tomorrow night, and possibly the night after. I'm going out of town for a day or two."

"What? You? Away from home?" Mary Collier had rarely spent a night away from the farm since she and Ben had returned from their honeymoon. They never even took a proper vacation when Laura was a child, despite her father's intermittent campaign in favor of a trip to the Southwest to see the Grand Canyon. "What's the catastrophe?"

"It actually is a bit of an emergency or I wouldn't be going. Lydia Hallworth's husband is having a triple bypass and I offered to stay with her until he's out of danger."

Laura was pleasantly surprised by her mother's uncharacteristic generosity. "I didn't know you were still in touch with Lydia. She moved away, what, almost ten years ago?"

"Twelve. And it's only one night, or two at most. I may not be particularly demonstrative about my friendships, Laura, but that doesn't mean I don't feel them just as strongly as everyone else." She looked around again and wrinkled her nose. "I don't suppose I could induce you to house-sit for me? I'd feel better knowing there was someone here while I was gone."

"The house will be fine. I'm sure you've already told Del to watch over it."

"Yes, but he'll walk around it once or twice during the evening and then again first thing in the morning and that will be it. If someone sneaks in late at night, they could loot the whole place or set it on fire and he wouldn't know until the sirens woke him up."

"I'll drive by myself and look in on things both nights, but that's as far as I go. I'm comfortable in my cabin, believe it or not, and that's where I plan to sleep nights for the foreseeable future."

There was a flicker of disappointment, even anger, in her mother's expression, but it was gone almost immediately. "All right, I guess I'm just being silly, and silliness is not one of the Rustin family traits."

"No, it most definitely is not. People might call you a lot of things, Mother, but silly is not one of them."

And despite their disagreement, Laura went home that evening feeling closer to her mother than she had in years.

CHAPTER NINE

Laura took her usual walk on Saturday morning. She didn't bring along her freshly cleaned and presently loaded rifle, but she was wary, stayed out of the shadows, and her eyes searched ahead as she moved. She hated the way she felt, resented the theft of something that she'd found pleasurable, but she had no intention of changing her habits because of a stupid accident. If it was an accident.

There was a note from Ted Catterall in the mail that day. The paperwork had been processed and a cashier's check was supposedly en route. That cheered her up enough that she went into town to buy a few things she'd been putting off, including shoes, two sweaters, and a new pair of gloves. The local selection wasn't very appealing and it was a nice, sunny day so she got onto the highway and drove all the way to the mall in Nickleby. She had such a good time that it was dark before she knew it, so she ate in the food court before starting the long ride back.

Traffic was heavier than usual but she was in no hurry, and when she reached Dorrance she decided to make a quick run by the farm just so she could tell her mother that she had done so. The porch light was on as well as one in the upstairs hall, but the farm was otherwise dark and silent. Laura parked directly in front of the house, telling herself that she would only be a minute.

Something felt wrong the moment she stepped inside. She

froze in the front hallway, straining with all of her senses to pick up whatever was subliminally warning her of danger.

There was a very slight sound from her right, from the small front room that served as the farm office. It might have just been the settling of the house, but her nerves were so on edge that she immediately interpreted it in the worst possible terms. Her first inclination was to back out of the house, run to the car, and drive to the nearest telephone for help, but perhaps some of her mother's stubbornness had bred true because instead she lunged suddenly through the doorway and stabbed at the switch, flooding the room with pale light.

Del Huggins was standing in the far corner, near the filing cabinets.

"Del! What the hell are you doing standing there in the dark? I thought you were Mother's prowler."

His face was expressionless and he met her eyes without flinching. "Thought the same about you. She told me to keep a watch on the place while she was gone, so that's what I was doing. What are you doing here, anyway?" He took a step forward, his voice becoming mildly belligerent.

"She asked me to stop by and check on things. I guess she figured two sets of eyes were better than one." Laura didn't think it would be a good idea to pass on her mother's doubts about Del. "Since you're here, I'll assume everything's all right and be on my way." But she stayed where she was, feeling that there was something wrong about the situation but not knowing what it was.

"There's no need for you to come up here. Your mother and I have things under control. We got along without you for better than two years, so I guess we can manage for two nights."

Laura was tempted to snap back at him, but suppressed it, although some of her anger must have shown in her voice. "What's bothering you, Del? I know we were never good friends when I lived here, but we were civil to one another, most of the time, anyway. Mother and I have had our differences, but we've moved past them. Have I done something to offend you? If so, I'd like to know what it is."

He was silent for so long that Laura didn't think he was going to answer. "I'm sure you would, Miss. You and your mother always want to know things, whether or not they concern you. Well, what I feel and why are matters I keep to myself." Del sounded disproportionately angry, but he remained motionless and Laura felt more puzzled than menaced. "I may have to take orders from your mother but I don't have to take them from you."

"I wasn't trying to give you orders, Del. I just hoped things could be more pleasant between us."

He didn't answer this time, and when Laura realized he didn't intend to, she gave it up as a wasted effort. "All right, I'm going. But I may stop by again tomorrow night, so don't be surprised if you see me." She turned and left quickly, resisting the temptation to slam the door behind her.

She was at the foot of Taggart Hill before she realized what had been bothering her. The overhead light hadn't illuminated the room all that well, and she hadn't been paying particular attention to anything except Del, but now that she had leisure to play back her memories, she realized that one of the filing cabinet drawers had been wide open. Her mother would never have left it like that, so there was only one possible conclusion. Del had been searching for something when she arrived, had probably turned off the office lights when he saw her turn into the driveway. If her mother hadn't gone out of town, if she hadn't chosen that moment to stop by, no one would ever have known about it.

Was this something she should tell her mother? It might be perfectly innocuous, after all. There were few things about the farm that Del wouldn't already have known. She didn't want to get Del into trouble unnecessarily despite his belligerent attitude. She shook her head impatiently and dismissed it for the time being. There would be time enough to decide once her mother was home again.

Ashley was supposed to meet her at the Trading Post on Monday evening. The Sievert brothers had decided to add a limited menu of sandwiches to their offering in an effort to build trade. It had been Ashley's suggestion that they go, but Laura had been secretly enthusiastic. She hadn't seen Dan Sievert all week, but she'd been keeping such unusual hours that it was quite possible he'd been stopping by the cabin to check on her just as Chief Clay had promised.

Laura was aware of her tendency to arrive early, but today she had an actual reason for doing so. The moment she walked in, her eyes were searching for Dan Sievert, although it didn't take long to discover that he was nowhere in sight. The bar, in fact, was quiet, with a single customer sitting near the back. She hesitated just inside the door, disconcerted by its emptiness.

"Hello there. Come right in." It was the bartender, Dan's brother, looking more cordial than previously. "What can I get you?"

Laura walked over to the bar and took one of the stools. "Just a class of white wine. I'm meeting someone."

"Coming right up. You're Laura Collier, aren't you?"

"Yes," she said firmly. Maybe not legally, but she'd talk to Ted Catterall next week and arrange to have it changed back. It was definitely time to put Sean Brennan behind her and move on.

"I'm Paul Sievert. My brother and I are the new owners of this palatial establishment." He gestured with his arms to encompass the entire bar.

"So Dan told me. I was hoping to buy him the drink I owe him."

"Have to be another time. He got called in for extra duty this afternoon. Somebody's down with the flu." He set a glass of wine in front of her and she put a twenty-dollar bill next to it. Sievert never even glanced at the money. "Dan's not really the businessman type and he's not a heavy drinker, so he doesn't spend a lot of time in here."

"I thought he moved to Dorrance because the two of you inherited the business together."

"Well, technically we did, but I'm buying his share out of the profits, such as they are."

She sipped at her wine, wondering how much she could ask without sounding too inquisitive. "Is he planning to leave town then?"

Paul shrugged. "You never can tell what Dan is going to do next. I don't think he even knows. Dan and I never understood one another when we were kids, and we aren't doing much better as adults. But we get along."

"You don't even look like brothers, if you don't mind my saying so." It was true. Dan was sandy haired, clean shaven, with a slightly athletic build and a fair complexion. Paul had a thick, dark beard, and his hair was almost black; he was tall and thin and his elbows jutted out awkwardly when he folded his arms.

"I don't mind, and it's no surprise. Dan was adopted when he was a baby." Her face must have changed because he went on hastily, "Oh, it's no secret. Our parents told us both as soon as he was old enough to understand it. Uncle Jake helped arrange it. All we know about Dan's mother is that she was from somewhere around here. I think that's why Dan came along with me. He's hoping to find out something about her, although as far as I know he's come up empty so far. He's been asking around pretty openly so I'm not telling you anything you couldn't have heard elsewhere."

"His mother was from Dorrance?" She guessed Dan to be three or four years older than she was, which meant it was quite possible that she'd gone to school with one of his siblings, if he had any.

"Or hereabouts. Uncle Jake probably knew, but he didn't tell any of us. Said he was doing a favor to pay an old debt and that Dan's mother insisted that no one be told her identity. They had to clear it through the state, so I imagine there's a record there, but it would be sealed."

Two couples entered the bar just then and Paul excused himself to wait on them. There was a slow but steady stream after that, and she never had a chance to talk to him again before Ashley arrived.

"Boy, do I have something interesting to tell you!"

"Interesting good or interesting bad?"

"Just interesting. But first I need a drink."

It took them a while because there was a steady influx of new customers, a few of whom Laura knew slightly. She said hello to people she hadn't spoken to in years, and felt awkward because they were obviously avoiding any reference to her marriage or the way it had ended. A few pretended not to have seen her, and the rest made a hasty departure to one of the tables as quickly as they could manage. By the time Ashley finally got her drink, and Laura had a refill, there were no longer any empty seats at the tables. They did manage to get the end stools at the bar, which provided some privacy, but not much. A few people were ordering from the new sandwich menus and Laura took one and glanced through it, without being greatly impressed.

"So what's your big news?" she asked at last.

"First, you have to promise to keep this to yourself. My dad doesn't know I heard him talking about this and he'd have a fit if I said anything. For one thing, that cabin of yours might be worth a lot more than you think it is."

"What are you talking about?"

"You own all the way to the waterline, don't you?"

"Yes, I think so. And about twelve acres of land. But it's all woods. Even if I had it cleared, it wouldn't be first-rate farmland, and you know as well as I do that farming isn't paying all that well around here lately."

"No, but something else might." Ashley lifted her glass and her eyes twinkled mischievously.

"Are you going to tell me or are we going to play games all night?"

"I'm telling you. Just give me time. I haven't had a secret this good in a long time. You know about the lodges down at the other end of Moon Pond?"

"Sure. I can see them from my property."

"Well, the pond is too shallow at that end to develop properly, and they can't expand because they're right flush up against the reservation."

"So?" But she was starting to see what this was leading up to.

"So your end of the pond is deeper and the land, your land and the lots to either side of you, don't have any restrictions against development and they're not even close to the reservation. Now that Moon Pond Road runs right up to the highway, there's easy access, and Dorrance could sure use a new source of revenue."

Laura shook her head. "This all seems pretty far-fetched to me. It would cost a lot of money to develop that area, and it would be a big risk as well."

"Well, someone thinks that it's worth the gamble. Do you know who owns the property around you?"

"Sure. Townside of me are two big plots of land, one owned by the Olsen sisters and the other by Mason Cortway's parents. On the other side are three parcels. One belongs to the Calloways, one to the Taylors, and one to Russell Steiger, if he's still alive."

"He's not. He died last year and the property went to his brother-in-law, Bud Wiegand."

Laura grimaced. "Not my first choice for a neighbor."

"Oh, it gets better. The Calloways and Taylors both sold their property within the last year to a holding company called Moon Pond Investments, and the Olsens sold theirs to the Cortways the year before."

"Moon Pond Investments? I never heard of them."

"You wouldn't have. They were formed for the express purpose of buying that property. All of this is in the public record. What we're not supposed to know is that my father found out who's behind Moon Pond Investments."

"And you're going to tell me, of course."

"Of course. There are two equal partners. One is Bryant Wiegand, better known to us as 'Bud.' The other partner is Cortway's, Inc. So with the exception of your lot, every bit of property on this side of Moon Pond is owned by either Bud Wiegand or the Cortway family, singly or jointly. Interesting, isn't it?"

"Very interesting. And Bud Wiegand tried to get my mother to sell him the cabin while I was gone, but she couldn't do it because I'm the sole owner."

"It sounds like you could make a lot of money out of this."

"Yes," Laura answered thoughtfully. "Or find myself in a lot of trouble. I don't want to sell, and I've already managed to get Mason and Wiegand both mad at me. This just makes it more complicated."

"Well, you could just sell to them and move someplace else. You did say you weren't planning to stay in Dorrance permanently."

"Yes, I did say that. But I'm going to be the one who decides when it's time to go, not Bud Wiegand or Mason Cortway or even my mother."

Laura really didn't want to drive out to the farm after dropping Ashley off later that night, but she felt obligated to make at least a token visit. With her luck, she'd skip it and find out in the morning that the house had been stripped of all its valuables. Although she'd stuck to wine throughout the evening, she was feeling mildly light-headed and drove with exaggerated caution and left the heater off.

This time she sat in the car for a full minute before entering the house, and made as much noise as possible without being obvious about it. She turned on all the lights and checked each room, assuring herself that the house was in fact empty and that there were no obvious signs of uninvited entry. All of the filing cabinet drawers were closed but she checked the office more carefully. The files that Del had been looking through were old financial records for the farm, none of them less than ten years old. That puzzled her more than ever. The previous night's encounter seemed trivial now, and she told herself to forget about it.

She stumbled over the rug in the living room and twisted her ankle slightly, sat down on the couch to rub it and realized that she was incredibly sleepy. Well, her mother had wanted her to house-sit, hadn't she? This really wasn't what she had planned, but there was no real reason why she had to go back to the cabin tonight. She slipped off her jacket and sweater and dropped them on a chair, trying to remember if she'd left a robe or anything else useful in her closet upstairs. But climbing the steps seemed like too arduous a task right at the moment and the house was cozily warm, so she slipped off her shoes and put her feet up and was asleep almost immediately.

It was a little past one when she woke up, cramped, disoriented, and needing to use the bathroom. She went upstairs barefooted and feeling a bit shaky. There was aspirin in the medicine cabinet and she took three in anticipation of the headache she felt looming on the horizon, then walked to the far end of the hall and leaned forward, pressing her nose up against the window pane. In the distance, she could just make out the lights out past Sharp's Curve. As she stood there, two vehicles drove past, both headed toward town, which was particularly interesting since the only building for miles in that direction was Del Huggins' place and she'd never known him to entertain visitors.

But it wasn't any of her business and she was too tired to worry about it. She went into her old bedroom and burrowed under the covers and was asleep again within minutes.

Laura slept quite late the following morning, but her mother still hadn't gotten home by the time she left. Despite the aspirin, her head ached and she stopped at Slade's for breakfast rather than risk her own cooking. The food made her mild nausea briefly worse, then much better, and she was feeling pretty chipper by the time she arrived at the cabin. She made herself a pot of coffee and decided it was time for a thorough cleaning, then spent most of the morning scrubbing, polishing, and reorganizing things in the cupboards and on the shelves. She was also giving serious thought to what Ashley had told her.

What would she do if Bud Wiegand or Mason Cortway, or some anonymous third party representing them, made a good offer for the property? It was easy enough to say she'd have no part of it, that she wanted the property to remain untouched, and it was even true up to a point. On the other hand, now that she knew what was going on behind the scenes, she could probably hold out for a much better price, perhaps even a part ownership in the resort. It was possible that she could come out of this quite well off. Neither Mason nor Wiegand were ideal business partners, but she wouldn't be interested in the details of the project anyway. She could pay someone more knowledgeable to protect her interests, or just sell her share to some other third party.

On the other hand, both men had had ample opportunity to make an offer already, and neither had. Nor had she been approached by anyone acting as their agent. That puzzled her. Could Ashley have gotten the story wrong?

The mail came early and, much to her delight, there was a small package that was indeed her cell phone. It took over an hour for her to understand the instructions well enough to activate it, but when she was done, she called her mother's house and got a ring, though no answer.

She tried the Sothern house and left her number on their answering machine, and the police department, and Ted Catterall's office. His secretary took down her number. "Did you need anything else? I'm afraid Mr. Catterall has been out of town for the past two days, although I'm expecting him back sometime today."

"No, I just wanted him to know how to reach me. Thanks."

She drove into town in the middle of the afternoon, planning to pick up some groceries, but as she was parking the car, she saw Mason Cortway walk into the market. The prospect of meeting him even casually was so distasteful that she decided she could do without fresh bread for another day, and she eased out of the lot. She went to the car wash instead, then stopped at the drugstore, but Ashley wasn't there. Despite Wiegand's insistence that she stay away from the Dairy Stop, she walked across the street and bought a package of rolls from another teenager, a young girl this time, one who actually seemed pleasant and helpful.

It was late afternoon when she called the farm again, and this time her mother picked up the phone so quickly she must have been standing right beside it.

"Hello, Mother? It's me, Laura."

"Oh, hello, Laura." Mary sounded mildly disappointed, as though she'd been hoping it was someone else.

"How was the trip?"

"Oh, about what you'd expect. Exhausting. Everything seems to be all right now, though. I'm rather tired and my feet hurt again, so I'm going to take a long bath and a nap."

"I slept at the house last night. No sign of your prowler. And Del was keeping an eye out as well." She decided not to tell her mother about Del's mysterious activities inside the house, at least not over the phone.

"I guess I was just being silly, but you can't be too careful nowadays. I've just had this feeling lately that someone has been watching the farm. It's probably just my imagination."

"Don't underestimate your imagination. Sometimes it picks up on things we can't see with our eyes. You be careful. I'll leave you to your bath and your nap. Have you got a pencil? I'll give you my number."

The afternoon turned bitterly cold and as dusk approached, the wind rose until it was screaming through the woods. The cabin was solid and tight but Laura felt the hint of drafts for the first time since she'd moved in. She spent some time walking around, trying to pinpoint them, but they were too elusive, so she put extra wood on the fire and changed into her heaviest sweater before settling down to read the first in the stack of paperbacks she'd picked up earlier at the tiny used bookstore near the Trading Post.

She became so engrossed that she didn't hear the car drive up, or perhaps the wailing wind would have masked it, anyway. For whichever reason, she was so startled when someone rapped on the door that she dropped her book and immediately lost her place.

"Damn!" She stood up and started for the door. Who might it be? If it was her mother, she should have called first, to make sure she was home if not to warn her of an impending visit. Ashley didn't have a car and certainly wouldn't have walked this far in bad weather. She hesitated just inside the door.

"Who is it?"

"It's Dan Sievert, Miss Collier. I just wanted to make sure everything was all right. Sorry to have disturbed you."

"No, wait!" She opened the door quickly. He was hunched up just outside, obviously cold, despite the heavy parka. "Come in for a moment."

He didn't hesitate, and she noticed that his eyes moved systematically around the interior. "Is something wrong?"

"No, nothing at all. I just didn't want to let the heat out. Can I get you some coffee?"

"I wouldn't want to bother you."

"No bother. I just bought myself a new coffeemaker but it's so big that I never manage to finish the whole pot. You look half frozen."

He visibly relaxed, though he still seemed vaguely uneasy. "It is a cold one out there all right. And it's starting to snow again."

"We almost always have a big accumulation. I can remember missing school for a whole week at least twice when I was growing up here." She found two mismatched mugs and set them down on the table. "Sit, please. You're making me nervous. I feel like I should be saluting you or something."

His smile was more relaxed this time. "Yes, Ma'am." He slid into one of the wickerback chairs and put one arm down on the table while he watched her.

She retrieved the coffee and poured two cups. "There's sugar in that little bowl. I don't have cream but there's milk."

He shook his head. "Black is fine. This is a pretty nice place. You've really brightened things up in here since the first time I came by."

"My aunt lived here by herself for many years, although it turned out she had quite a bit of money tucked away."

"Did she have any kids?"

"No, never married, either. My father says she came close once, back before I was born, but nothing ever came of it. I hardly remember her. She died when I was four, but for some reason she left everything to me."

"So are you planning to follow in her footsteps?" His face twitched. "Sorry, I shouldn't have asked that."

"No, it's all right. Well, obviously it's too late for me to avoid marriage, although that didn't work out very well. But I haven't sworn off romance, if that's what you mean. And I don't plan to spend my life here, pleasant though it may be. It's a comfortable refuge, but it's a temporary one. How about you? Is Dorrance what you expected?"

"Pretty much. It's quite a change from Rochester, more relaxed, slower paced, but it's hard to get to know people here. There's a story they tell about Maine, that a traveler stopped to ask directions to the house of a friend of his who'd moved there twenty years earlier. No one recognized the friend's name until one person suddenly had an inspiration. 'Oh, you mean the new people.' "

Laura laughed. "Yes, that's Dorrance all right. My mother thinks people should have to live here ten years before they can vote for council members, and she's probably one of the town's moderates."

"Most people don't describe her quite that way." He grimaced. "Sorry again. I'm not usually this careless about what I say."

"No apology necessary. Believe me, I've heard plenty of criticism of my mother, and I even agree with some of it. She was raised in a tradition that's not popular anymore, and she's strong willed enough to refuse to change with the times."

Dan finished his coffee and set the cup down. "Well, thanks again for the coffee, Miss Collier."

"Laura," she reminded him.

"Laura," he nodded. "But I have to get back on the road. If you don't mind, could I use your . . ." He hesitated.

"The bathroom is right over there." She pointed.

"Thank you kindly."

CHAPTER TEN

She found hairs in the bathroom sink in the morning. Not her own artificially auburn hair, but black ones, truncated, the remnants of a man's untidy shaving. There weren't many and she wouldn't have noticed them if the light had been dimmer, but it was enough to send her reeling out into the main room, light-headed and nauseated. Sean had littered the sink in that way every day of their marriage, a minor but persistent annoyance to which she'd grown accustomed. Seeing them here was like a flashback to their life together, and that sent a chill through her body that had nothing to do with the temperature.

Once her heart had stopped racing, she tried to consider the situation logically. She'd cleaned the bathroom very thoroughly the previous morning and refused to believe that she could have missed them. Could it have been an hallucination? Slowly, unsteadily, she walked back into the closet-like room and bent over the sink. They were still there, at least a dozen of them. She dropped to her knees beside the toilet, her stomach churning, convinced she was going to vomit. But she didn't, and as she crouched, shivering, the rolling turmoil settled and she began to think again.

Sean is dead. That's the first thing she told herself. Whatever the explanation, these aren't his hairs. So whose are they? The only man who'd been in the cabin recently was Dan Sievert, and Dan had used the bathroom the night before. But surely he hadn't shaved? No, she told herself, but he had done so earlier in the day. A few hairs must have stuck to his clothing, and maybe he brushed at himself while standing over the sink. Or possibly her earlier cleaning had disturbed some hairs trapped in the drain or in some other hidden place and one of the mild drafts had been just strong enough to lift them into view.

Yes, it had to be something like that, an explanation so prosaic that she laughed at herself and her fears. Or tried to. She was still unsteady as she made breakfast and couldn't even begin to relax until she'd gone back to the bathroom and cleaned it thoroughly.

"That's that," she said aloud, running the faucet full blast to ensure that the drain was completely clean. She heard the distant rumble as the pump under the cabin began refilling her tank. Laura told herself that the incident was over, but she had brief periods of mild panic on and off for the rest of the day.

Laura made her belated shopping trip late on Wednesday morning, after a boring but necessary trip to the Laundromat. She went through the aisles rapidly, not bothering to compare prices but just selecting the staples she needed as quickly as possible. The disinterested cashier was no one she knew, but at least two of the other shoppers wore familiar faces. One was the mother of a boy she had dated briefly in school, the other a retired teacher. Neither of them seemed to recognize her, but she avoided them anyway.

Her luck didn't hold for long, but it was good luck when it did change. She had just packed the three plastic bags into the rear seat of the Chevy when someone called her name.

"Laura? Laura Collier? Is that you?"

The voice was familiar, but it wasn't until she turned that she recognized the young woman approaching her. "Kathy Peebles?"

"It is you! Mother told me that you were back." She threw her arms around Laura who returned the embrace warmly.

"But it's not Peebles anymore. It's Cronyn."

"Well, congratulations. I didn't think you'd ever meet a man who measured up to your standards."

"Hold the congrats. I didn't. We're separated pending the divorce even as we speak."

"Oh." Laura blinked, uncertain how to proceed. "Sorry to hear that."

"I'm not." Kathy's face grew serious. "I heard about your husband. Sounds like you had a tough time of it. Are you okay now?"

Laura had rehearsed scores of glib answers, and had used some of them, but when the moment came to talk about it with Kathy, she couldn't recall a single one. Instead, to her horror, she burst into tears, unable to speak.

"Oh God, now I've done it." Kathy put her arm around Laura and waited patiently until her friend was back in control of herself. "I'm really sorry I said anything, Laura. Can I help?"

Laura shook her head, wiped her eyes with the back of her hand. "No, I'll be all right. Really. In fact, I feel a lot better now. I haven't been able to cry about it . . . for a while."

"Still miss him?"

Laura surprised her friend with a short, ugly laugh. "Miss him? Not for a second. Not after what he turned into."

Kathy nodded. "Another prick, huh? Maybe it's just as well for you that he killed himself."

"He didn't kill himself, Kathy. I stabbed him. I had to." And then the tears were back.

She recovered more quickly this time, perhaps responding to Kathy's look of stunned disbelief. "Sorry, I didn't mean to hit you with that so suddenly. Sean was sick, mentally ill, almost from the first day we arrived in Vermont. I kept making excuses for him, told myself he was under a lot of stress, that kind of thing, and never realized how bad he was. Last Christmas, things got much worse, out of control. His commissions had been dropping for months, but I couldn't get him to cut back on his spending, and he started blaming me for it. Told me I was hiding the money, lying to him. Then when he lost his job, it got even uglier."

Kathy stirred uncomfortably. "You don't have to talk about this if you don't want to, Laura."

"No, but I want to. I need to. I've never told anyone what really happened, not even the police, and everything's been building up inside me."

Kathy looked around nervously. "Okay, but let's go sit in my van where we're at least out of the wind." She led Laura to the opposite end of the small parking lot and the two of them climbed into the front of the vehicle.

Kathy started the engine and the heater while Laura gathered her wits. She knew it was unfair to dump this on Kathy so abruptly, but it had always been Kathy she'd gone to with troubles in the past, and her sudden appearance seemed to have magically transported her backwards to a time when talking to her would make everything feel better.

"Toward the end, I started getting angry, maybe a little crazy myself. When he started making sarcastic remarks about what presents I ought to be buying him for Christmas, I just blew up. I filled boxes with dirt, stones, trash, anything I could find, wrapped them all, and put them under the tree. Christmas morning, he was awake before me, and he opened every single one of them without saying a word. Then, when I came down to make breakfast, I saw that he'd cut every single ornament off the tree. He'd killed our cat, cut it open, and it was hanging from one of the branches. And then he came after me with that sheath knife of his, the one he always took when he went hunting. He chased me through the house, cornered me upstairs, but I've always been pretty strong, and I don't think he was expecting me to fight back."

The silence that followed stretched for over a minute before Kathy reached over and patted Laura on the knee. "Sounds pretty terrible." Her voice was strained.

"It was." Laura threw her head back and tried to smile. "We struggled for a long time, before he slipped and fell at the top of the staircase. I had a dozen cuts by then, a couple of them pretty deep, and I was terrified. But I was also angry and when I saw my chance, I took it. I kicked him in the face and he started to lose his balance, so I rushed forward and grabbed his arm and pushed it back at him as hard as I could. He just stared at me for a second with those blazing eyes of his and then he toppled over and fell all the way down to the bottom. I told the police he lost his footing while he was chasing me and they believed my story. Or at least they pretended to. I know it was self-defense but the fact remains that I killed him." She stopped then, and Kathy sat silently, staring out through the windshield. Her tears had stopped and she felt as though she'd just emerged from a shadow she hadn't known was there. "So what's new in your life?"

Kathy looked startled for a second, then burst into laughter. "Well, comparatively speaking, not much."

"You staying in Dorrance or just visiting?"

"A little of both. I told Ed he could keep the house and I took some cash, my clothes, and a few other things, and came home. Since Dad died, Mom's living alone," she gestured toward the residential neighborhood behind the market, "and I'm using the guest room for a couple of months while I figure out what's next."

"You know Ashley's back, right?"

"Yeah, so I heard." Kathy sounded less than enthused. "I thought she had finally abandoned us for the big city."

"It didn't work out. She had a pretty bad time, actually. The three of us need to get together."

"Where? There's not much going on here in Dorrance."

"The Trading Post has new owners. It's actually kind of nice. C'mon, we can compare notes about how all of us messed up our lives."

"That sounds like fun. Okay, you're on. When?"

"I'll have to call Ashley first."

"Great! I assume you still remember the number at my mom's house."

"It's engraved on my soul."

When she got back to the cabin, the Jeep was parked in the driveway. Her mother had a key so she was sitting inside when Laura came through the door, her arms full of grocery bags. "Hello, Mother." She crossed to the table and set the bags down. "I wasn't expecting you."

"I was out and I thought I'd stop and see how you were making out here. I came by earlier, in fact, but no one was home so I ran some errands. I'd just about given up waiting this time as well."

"Yes, Mother, I was out. I didn't come here to hide, you know." Or maybe she had, but it didn't seem to be working that way. "You could have called first."

Mary ignored the implied admonition. "There was a police car backing out of the driveway the first time I came by."

"Oh?" That was interesting. Dan Sievert, dropping by for more coffee? She hoped so, then flushed at the thought, turned away so her mother couldn't see her face. "Probably just checking things over. I told you about the hunting accident."

"I'm still not convinced that it was an accident. People have been stirring up trouble behind my back, and I wouldn't put it past them to try to get at me through you. Throw a scare into you hoping I'll take it as a warning."

"If you think that, you should tell the police."

"Incompetent busybodies. Ever since Chief Dowdell died, the police in town have been more interested in public relations than in doing their job. John Dill picked Nathan Clay, you know. I thought we needed someone with more experience."

Laura remembered her mother complaining about Bill Dowdell's investigation into Ben Collier's disappearance but wisely decided not to mention the past. "I ran into Kathy Peebles today."

"Back to visit her mother, I imagine."

"So I gather. She and her husband are splitting up."

"Why am I not surprised? I never understood what you saw in her, Laura. She's not an unpleasant girl, Lord knows, but she has less personality than a barn cat. I don't remember her ever expressing an opinion on any subject other than the latest fashion or which movie star was the dreamiest. She just wasn't very bright."

"Kathy was an honor student, Mother."

"Which tells you something about standards in schools these days. All right, I won't criticize your friends anymore. I suppose there's not a lot to choose from in Dorrance, and you could certainly associate with worse. At least you're not hanging around with the Huston twins. Have you caught up with Mason yet?"

So there were some things that happened in Dorrance that didn't get back to her mother after all. "Yes, twice in fact."

"Did he ask you out?"

"Yes, he did, but no, I didn't accept. I'm not ready to date anyone yet, and I don't think I'll ever be ready to date Mason Cortway again. He seems younger now than when I left."

"Maybe you're right. He'd be easy to manage, but clay won't do when you need steel."

"So what do you think?" Laura raised her arms to indicate

she was soliciting an opinion of her redecorating, such as it was.

"I think you've done a marvelous job, under the circumstances. But I also think you'd be better off, more comfortable, and safer living at home."

"You never give up, do you?"

"Rustins never quit." She had the grace to smile. "I know that you're a grown woman now and need to make your own life in your own way. And I know that I have a tendency to overmanage people. Even allowing for that, don't you think you'd be better off moving back? It's a big house; we can avoid each other if we need to. You never seemed to have any trouble getting around me when you were younger, and I'm considerably less formidable now than I was then."

"No, Mother, you're as formidable as ever." Laura laughed as she said it, taking the sting out. "And I admit that I sometimes miss the luxuries, particularly a bathtub instead of a shower stall. But I really need the space just now. Besides, I have enough Rustin in me that I don't plan to be run off my property just because someone takes a shot in my direction, accidental or otherwise."

"All right, I give up." She picked up her oversized purse from the floor beside the chair and stood up. "I have to get back to the farm to listen to Del's latest list of disasters in the making. Why don't you come out for supper tonight?"

"How about tomorrow night? I'm having dinner with Kathy and Ashley."

"Tomorrow night then. And if you're still pining for a real bath, you can have one of those while you're there."

"I just might take you up on that."

Laura picked up Ashley, grumbling when her friend wasn't ready at the agreed time. Ashley was either oblivious to her complaints or pretended to be, and it was several minutes more before Laura finally got her into the Chevy. The Trading Post was already doing a brisk business when they arrived, but there were a few empty tables and they managed to grab one in a relatively private spot. A harried-looking waitress was taking their order when Kathy arrived, and they waved to attract her attention.

"So I guess none of us made it out of here," said Ashley, pointedly looking in Kathy's direction.

"Well, some of us came back voluntarily," she responded without heat. "And some of us aren't planning to stay."

"Hey guys, no fighting on the first drink." Laura was sitting in the middle, predictably, and she put her hands on the nearest arms of her friends and squeezed. "If we're comparing bad stories, I'm the clear winner."

"I had to get at least one crack in," complained Ashley. "It's a tradition."

"Tonight we're not going to snipe at each other, and we're only going to think happy thoughts."

"Does that mean we can snipe at other people?" asked Kathy.

"I suppose. Did you have anyone in particular in mind?"

"Have you seen Mason Cortway recently? He's going bald."

"Actually, I have seen him, but I wasn't paying much attention to his hairline."

"Mason asked her out," explained Ashley. "And he got pissed when she turned him down."

"Why? He should be used to it by now."

The waitress returned and took Kathy's order. They spent the next hour comparing life in Buffalo, Vermont, and Albany, deciding that any of the three were preferable to Dorrance despite their numerous shortcomings, and that they had all returned at the will of unfriendly fate.

Dan Sievert didn't come in while they were there, and Laura was tempted to ask about him, but she decided against it. She still wasn't sure that she wanted to get involved, even informally, with another man just yet. But she had to admit that she liked it when he was around.

Kathy loosened up after her second drink and ordered a plate of munchies. "If I drink on an empty stomach, I get heartburn."

"They have sandwiches, you know." Ashley waved the single sheet menu.

"I don't think I'm up to anything that complicated. I'm your basic snack person. I'm going to grow old and fat in front of the television."

Laura doubted that. Kathy didn't look as though she'd gained a pound since high school, and she wasn't soft, either. She was a little too tall to be a great gymnast, but short enough to be a very good one, and probably had a membership in a fancy health club in Albany.

They talked together amiably for two hours, eventually ordering sandwiches despite Kathy's token objection. The sandwiches were good, though not outstanding, and Laura felt better with something solid in her stomach. She let the other two do most of the talking, drinking in the tacky gossip as an antidote to the poisons she'd been carrying around with her for the past year. Sometimes her thoughts drifted and she only half followed the conversation, letting the familiar voices and themes take her back through time to an era when none of the bad stuff had happened yet.

Then something triggered a reaction and she looked back and forth between Ashley and Kathy, blinking. "I'm sorry, guys. I was daydreaming. What was that about Tommy Langston?"

Ashley gave her a dirty look. "Get with it, girl. Gossiping is a fine art and we're not supposed to have to repeat ourselves. Rumor has it that he was drunk the night he had his accident on all too appropriately named Sharp's Curve. Rumor also has it that the reason he was drunk was because he spent the afternoon at O'Brien's Bar flashing more big bills than he had any right to be carrying. He's still working on the family farm, and people around here were surprised when he came up with enough money to finance that muscle car he was driving."

Kathy wrinkled her nose. "I never thought much of Tommy. He was always more show than go. And remember how he dumped Paula Fenton right in the middle of the cafeteria? No class at all."

"I'm kind of surprised that Joyce even dated him. She seemed like a pretty savvy kid, although I suppose a lot could change in a couple of years. She was what, nineteen?"

"Eighteen," said Ashley. "And just. She skipped third grade. And actually, I heard that they weren't dating at all."

"Then why was she out riding in his car at one in the morning?" Kathy picked up her glass, noted that it was empty, and looked around for the waitress.

"Tommy says she asked him for a ride and then dared him to speed up at the curve."

Laura snorted in disbelief. "I find that hard to believe."

"So did Chief Clay, but there wasn't much he could do about it. He already had Tommy for manslaughter. He's lucky not to be in jail, even with his uncle pulling strings behind the scenes. As it is, he's on probation for the next five years and they pulled his license."

"I'd pull more than that," Kathy mumbled almost inaudibly. "She was a good kid."

"Yes, she was," said Laura. "And I still wonder what she was doing in his car."

They stopped after five rounds and ordered coffee, but Ashley was obviously having trouble staying awake, and Kathy always became very quiet when she'd had a few, so Laura suggested that they call it a night, and get together again in a few days.

Ashley and Kathy actually hugged when they parted, which made Laura a little bit teary eyed, and she drove Ashley home with exaggerated care, feeling sober but fully aware of the fact that legally she probably was not.

Back at the cabin, Laura fell asleep the moment she went to bed but was wakened less than an hour later by an intrusive, tapping sound.

She sat up, disoriented for the first few seconds, then reached over to turn on the lamp beside her bed. There had been a strange sound, she was quite certain, but the only thing she could hear now was the clicking of the space heater, a very faint crackling from the woodstove, and the muffled moaning of the wind outside.

Laura got up, wrapped herself in a robe, fumbled for slippers. The glow from the woodstove was faint, draping the outer room with silvered shadows. There was no sign of anything amiss; the door was closed, the latch thrown. None of the appliances had been left on and she'd closed the curtains to cover all the windows.

Something tapped against glass, once, twice, a third time. It was the window on the wall opposite the porch, facing toward Moon Pond Road. A branch? There were several trees theoretically close enough but she didn't think any of the branches were actually within reach of the window. Some night bird perhaps, misinterpreting its own shadow as food.

She crossed directly to the window, pressed her face against the glass and peered outside. There was barely enough light to look around and it took several seconds before her eyes adjusted. She saw nothing out of the ordinary, at least, not at first. A very light snow was falling and accumulating on the ground, but not heavily enough to significantly obscure her vision. The figure standing between two trees was so motionless that initially she mistook it for just a deeper shadow than those around it. Then the moon came out from behind a cloud and, as her eyes adjusted, she saw more clearly.

Someone was standing out there, perhaps ten meters from the house. Whoever it was wore dark clothing and had a hood pulled up over his or her head.

Laura's first instinct was to call the police, and she grabbed her purse and pulled out the cell phone. There was no reason to panic. The door was locked, the windows latched, and she had her rifle.

The very thought of violence sickened her, but she had dealt with it before and survived, and she was determined to survive again if it came to that. Moving as quietly as possible, she retreated from the window and took the rifle from its resting place, leaning against the wall, then selected a knife from her limited supply of cutlery. A treacherous board squeaked ominously under her weight and she wondered if the sound was audible outside. With one weapon in each hand, she returned to the window, only to find that the mysterious figure was gone.

Laura didn't call the police, although she was tempted. She and her mother had both complained of trespassers recently, and Chief Clay had been proper and polite and clearly unconcerned. He would most likely dismiss a fresh complaint as the lingering effects of a nightmare brought on by too much drinking.

Laura did, however, spend most of the rest of the night awake, sitting in front of a freshly built fire, jumping at every sound, rifle and boning knife near at hand, finally nodding off just as the sun began to add tint to the sky.

Laura woke stiff and sore. In the bright daylight, she wondered if she'd dreamed the entire thing, but only until she dressed and went outside and found the freshly broken snow, footprints where she hadn't walked, leading up to the window and then away. Feeling a bit foolish, she nonetheless went back for her rifle and carried it with her when she followed them, back through the trees, then along the line of brush that stretched toward the road. The same place she'd seen an animal lurking the night she'd moved in.

Or had it been an animal after all? Was someone lurking outside the cabin on a regular basis? There were an awful lot of tracks at the spot where she'd seen the mysterious figure, as though whoever had been there had paced back and forth for a considerable length of time. There could only be one explanation.

Someone was watching her.

The trail disappeared at the roadway, which had been plowed down to the blacktop. She found some marks that might indicate where a vehicle had been pulled off the road, but falling and drifting snow had rendered the tire marks, if that's what they were, unidentifiable.

She was just about to return to the cabin, wondering whether or not she should call the police, when she was saved the trouble. A patrol car appeared in the distance and slowed abruptly as it came closer, finally pulling to the side of the road right beside her. Dan Sievert leaned over to the passenger side and rolled down the window.

"Good morning! You're not hunting out of season, are you?"

Laura blinked, then realized she was holding the rifle in plain view. "Oh, no. Sorry, nothing like that." She realized she was sounding as confused as she felt. "I think someone was on my property last night, watching the cabin."

"Okay, let me back up and pull off the road."

She waited as he parked, then took him back along the path she'd followed.

"They sure look like tracks all right, but I don't see anything clear enough for us to get even a partial footprint. Where was he standing when you caught him watching the cabin?"

She showed him that as well, but even to her untrained eye, it was obvious that it was too late. Even the partial prints she'd seen earlier had already softened to mush as the morning sun touched them.

"Well, the good news is that you don't seem to be in any immediate danger. Your mysterious visitor didn't try to break into the cabin."

"He tapped at the window, though. Or she. It could have been a woman."

"I'm going to make an official report and see if I can convince Chief Clay to increase the coverage out here." He looked away uncomfortably. "But, off the record, I'm going to tell you that's unlikely. We're shorthanded even when everyone's fit for duty and we have two officers down with the flu and one on leave."

"And Chief Clay is going to consider this just another case of an hysterical female overreacting to an inadvertent trespass."

He looked even more uncomfortable. "Actually, he's more likely to say that Mary Collier's daughter is as spoiled and neurotic as her mother and is just wasting everyone's time."

"He wouldn't!"

Dan just looked at her.

"He didn't!"

There was just the slightest hint of a nod. "I'll file the report, and I'll tell him that I saw clear evidence that you weren't imagining things. I'll also stop by a little more often for the next few nights, just in case. But don't expect a crime scene unit to show up with lots of expensive equipment."

"All right, I understand. Thanks for doing as much as you can. And if I'm here when you come by, there's almost always coffee ready."

"I'll keep that in mind, Laura."

CHAPTER ELEVEN

Laura lost track of time and almost forgot her dinner date with her mother. She drove directly to the farm, bending the local speeding laws in the process, and arrived only about ten minutes late. Mary Collier was clearly not in a good mood, aggravated by Laura's tardiness, and she had hardly let her daughter get settled before she told her the reason.

"The Trading Post is not a proper place for a young woman to go without an escort. You know what people will think if you walk in there alone."

"I wasn't alone, Mother. I was with Ashley and Kathy, remember? I told you we were going out together." Laura wondered how her mother had found out. None of her cronies had been there, at least none that Laura had noticed.

"You said you were going out to eat together, not drink."

"We did eat. They serve sandwiches now. One of the owners is a policeman and the other seems very pleasant. It's not a dive."

"This was Ashley's idea, I presume." A dramatic sigh prefaced the predictable words that followed. "I should have known she hadn't changed since her high school days. Wasn't it Ashley who got you drunk that night back in your junior year?"

Actually, it had been Laura who'd arranged and paid for the bottle of gin that had made both of them quite sick. Kathy had sipped some, made a face, and declined, and ultimately she had been the one who had helped the other two get home after the inevitable spell of vomiting in the bushes. Mary had always assumed that Ashley was the bad influence, and at the time, Laura had been perfectly willing to let her cherish that illusion.

"We're all grown up now and we didn't get drunk. We talked about old times mostly."

But once her mother had judged a situation, she was unwilling to discuss it further or consider new evidence. They ate in relative silence, an uncomfortable hour after which Laura declined the chance for a bath that she'd actually been looking forward to and said that she was so tired she just wanted to go to bed. Although her mother almost certainly saw through the lie, she didn't argue the point.

The disagreement, muted though it had been, still bothered her the following morning. In an attempt to brighten her mood, she brought the tree in from the back. Her brand-new tree stand fitted perfectly and she had cleared a space for it in the corner farthest from the woodstove.

It was shorter than she'd realized, the topmost branch just level with her forehead. Laura retrieved the small box of delicate ornaments she'd brought with her from Vermont, each carefully restrung with black thread. Most of her collection had been damaged when Sean cut them loose from the tree that last night together, but she'd recovered and repaired the survivors once the police had given permission.

She took her time, fussing over each placement.

The following week went by very quickly. Laura received the check from her inheritance on Monday. It was the first time she'd seen a check with six figures to the left of the decimal, and she spent several minutes just staring at it, trying to convince herself that it was real. Then she drove into town and deposited it in her checking account, fending off the efforts by an earnest young woman to have her divert most of it into a short-term certificate of deposit.

"I'll be doing something with the money shortly, but for the moment I just want it safe here in the bank."

"I should tell you that the FDIC only insures accounts up to a hundred thousand dollars." The woman seemed quite alarmed on her behalf.

"I'll keep that in mind." She had, however, upgraded her account and applied for a credit card to accompany the debit card she'd already received. Dorrance had only one cash machine, and it was in the lobby of the bank, but it felt good to know she didn't have to carry a lot of cash with her any longer.

Despite Ed Burgess' ministrations, the generator refused to start on Tuesday morning. The cabin did have commercial electrical power so she wasn't in any real difficulty, but she knew she'd feel better if the generator was operational. Ice storms were common at this time of year, and the power lines routinely went down at least once or twice each winter.

Burgess came out himself late that morning, apologizing profusely, even after he identified the problem as a defective part and replaced it. Laura felt duty bound to stand out in the cold with him throughout the process, and went inside only to periodically refill their coffee mugs. Most of the time Burgess confined his conversation to grunts and whispered curses, but he said one thing that Laura found very interesting.

"Heard you and Bud Wiegand had words."

"Most of the words were his, actually. I was working out at the Dairy Stop and tried to give him two weeks' notice, but he blew his top and ordered me off the property."

"Sounds like Bud. Back when we were kids together, he used to mouth off to the teachers all the time. I think he spent more time in the principal's office than in class. You might want to steer clear of him for a while, though. He'll forget about it in time, but he's got a bad temper."

"I'm not afraid of him."

Burgess had momentarily stopped what he was doing and turned his head to catch her eyes. "Maybe you should be. I don't mean to frighten you, Miss Collier, but Bud's gotten meaner and stupider as he got older. Chief Clay's had him locked up a couple of times, though no one ever pressed charges. He and Del Huggins got into it one night, and Del bloodied his nose for him. The next day all the windows on Del's shack were broken and someone had tossed in some fresh manure. You might want to keep an eye on things and make sure your doors are locked at night."

Burgess was the third person who'd cautioned her to lock her doors since she'd returned to Dorrance. Whoever had said that you couldn't go home again had been right.

On Wednesday she took laundry into town and visited the Laundromat despite the open invitation from her mother to use her laundry room. To do so would have risked another lecture. It would be nice to have her own washing machine and dryer in the cabin, but there really wasn't room for them. She splurged and had lunch at Foster's, although from force of habit rather than necessity she chose one of the least expensive meals. Thursday she took the car to Ed's Garage for a tune-up and spent most of the afternoon sitting in what passed for a waiting room, finishing the novel she'd been reading and starting a new one.

Kathy and her family had been away most of the week visiting family, but they were due back Thursday night, and she was supposed to meet Laura and Ashley at the Trading Post for a reprise of their previous week's get together. The hours seemed to drag by on Friday, and Laura couldn't concentrate enough to read for more than a few minutes at a time. She realized now how starved for company she'd been during the past year, and how much she was looking forward to pretending that things were normal and that nothing extraordinary had happened in her life. The change had started when she'd told Kathy the truth about Sean's death, the first time she'd ever said it aloud. Nor had they spoken of it again. If Kathy was curious about details, she was restraining herself until Laura was ready to provide them.

Ashley was surprisingly early and the three of them entered together this time. The Trading Post wasn't quite packed to capacity, but it was appreciably busier than the last time they'd come, and the table they grabbed wasn't nearly as private as the one they'd had before. They were playing the what-would-I-do-if-I-won-the-lottery game when a male voice spoke up behind them.

"Could I buy you ladies a drink?"

Laura didn't react at first because it came so unexpectedly, but she saw the look of wakening interest on Kathy's face, and craned her head backward. "Oh, hi, Dan. I didn't know you were here. These are my friends Kathy and Ashley. Guys, this is Dan Sievert."

She pretended not to see the disappointment on Kathy's face when she realized that Dan was, at least for the moment, off limits.

Before Laura could say anything, Ashley had invited him to join them and he had accepted. "But only for one drink. I'm playing the sociable host this evening."

He settled into his chair and put a half finished mug of beer on the table. The waitress had already responded to his gesture and was off to fetch another round.

Laura felt suddenly shy and couldn't think of anything to say, but Kathy filled in for her. "You're new here in Dorrance, aren't you?"

"It's been almost two years now. I was in Rochester before that."

"Isn't this pretty dull after the big city?"

"Sometimes dullness isn't all that bad. Particularly if you're a cop. I'd be perfectly happy if nothing worth mentioning happened between now and retirement."

They exchanged small talk for a while, Dan stayed just long enough to be polite and divided his conversation evenly among the three women, which left Laura feeling mildly jealous and confused about her feelings. Then he made his excuses and left, moving off to the next table of customers.

"Seems like a nice guy," was Kathy's final opinion. "And he's not bad to look at, either."

Ashley had been unusually quiet. "I still get nervous around cops. Sorry. Making allowances for that, I liked him, though. Do you think he's interested, Laura?"

"I don't know." She laughed nervously. "He comes by the cabin a lot, but Chief Clay told him to after the shooting incident. I don't think it's just a sense of duty, but he hasn't said or done anything to make me think otherwise."

"Come on, girl. He couldn't keep his eyes off you just now."

"No way. He was just playing tavernkeeper or whatever. You have to be nice to your customers if you expect them to come back."

"Trust me on this. He wasn't just being polite. Play your cards right and he'll ask you out."

Laura pointedly changed the subject but she kept watching for Dan during the next two hours. He nodded in her direction once when she caught his eye, and she blushed and lost track of the conversation for a while. They ordered sandwiches, which were slightly better this time, or she was hungrier. When she next looked for Dan, he was gone and she never saw him again that evening.

They were thinking about calling it a night when the waitress showed up with a tray of drinks.

"We didn't order these," Kathy protested. "You've got the wrong table."

The waitress checked her slip. "You're drinking one Black Russian, one Tequila Sunrise, and one Margarita, right?"

They all exchanged looks. "That's what we're drinking, but we didn't order another round."

"Well, ladies, they're paid for already, so either you drink them or I pour them out. What's it going to be?"

"Oh, what the hell, leave 'em." Ashley shrugged, waited while the waitress set them down one at a time, and a fourth drink in front of the empty chair.

"What's that?" Laura spoke this time, and her throat was tight, because she thought she knew the answer already.

"The order called for four drinks, so that's what I brought." She sounded tired and irritable, but as she turned to leave, Laura half stood up and called after her.

"Wait! What is it? What is that drink?" She was gripping the edge of the table so tightly her knuckles had turned white.

The waitress sighed. "It's a Scotch Sour."

"Who paid for the drinks?" Laura's eyes darted around the room and her voice crackled with tension.

"Sorry, Miss, but I have no idea. Ask Paul at the bar. He took the order."

"What's going on?" Kathy's voice was crisp and businesslike.

Laura had to try three times before she could get the words out. "That's what Sean drank all the time, Scotch Sours. Excuse me a minute."

But Paul Sievert couldn't tell her anything useful. "Someone left an envelope on the bar with a twenty-dollar bill and a note saying it was to buy a round for Laura Collier's party and to add a Scotch Sour. I figured someone was meeting you or trying to meet you. I told Tina to let me know when you looked about dry and made up the order. Is there a problem?"

"No," she said untruthfully. "No problem. Thanks."

The liquor or the shock, or both, caught up to Laura on the way back and she drove with exaggerated caution until she reached the Sothern house.

"Are you going to be all right?" They were sitting in the car in her driveway, the engine running, but Ashley had made no move to get out.

"Sure. I'll be fine. I'm sorry, it was probably just some stupid mistake, but it caught me by surprise. I'll call you in a couple of days. Maybe next weekend we'll all drive up to Nickleby."

It seemed to take forever to get back to the cabin, and she had a pounding headache that had little to do with the amount of alcohol she'd consumed. Once inside, she remembered to lock the door, but then everything else faded into a blur as she stumbled to the bed and collapsed across it, kicking off her shoes but otherwise without bothering to undress.

When she woke the following morning, her head was still throbbing, her stomach was queasy, and she had a sour taste in her mouth. Barefoot despite the chill, she stumbled out into the main room and headed for the bathroom, intent upon relieving her bladder and taking a shower that lasted as long as her store of hot water.

Halfway there, she almost lost her footing when something sharp and hard bit painfully into the ball of her left foot.

She had stepped on a Christmas ornament, one of many lying scattered across the floor. Each had been detached from the tree by having its thin black thread neatly severed, and almost every one of them was broken.

Dan must have been off duty because it was a different patrolman who answered the call this time, a dark, quiet man named Enfield who was either skeptical, uninterested, or both. He was a couple of years older than she was and looked vaguely familiar, so she assumed they'd been in high school together.

"You say you're sure you locked the front door last night, Ma'am?"

"Yes, and it was locked when I got home. But I forgot to throw the bolt on the porch door when I went out yesterday, and the lock on that one is so primitive even I could pick it. When I checked this morning, it wasn't locked."

"But you didn't notice anything when you came in?"

"I wasn't feeling well. The only light was from that little one over the sink that I keep on all the time, and I went straight to bed."

"And you'd been out drinking until . . ." he looked at his notes ". . . almost midnight?"

"I hadn't had that much, maybe five drinks over five hours. Look, someone got in here somehow, either while I was out or after I got home."

"And nothing else has been disturbed? There's nothing missing or out of place?"

"Not that I can think of."

"Well, I'll file this report and someone will get back to you in due course. I understand you've had a previous incident."

"Two of them." She wondered belatedly if Dan had filed a report about her prowler.

Officer Enfield flipped his notebook closed, glanced toward the porch door, obviously eager to be gone. "If I were you, I'd get a heavier deadbolt for the door and a new lock and maybe find another place to sleep for a few nights. It's the kind of prank that kids'll pull and they probably won't risk coming back, but you'll feel better if you aren't alone for a while."

Laura opened her mouth to protest but gave it up as a waste

of time. She was most certainly not going to be driven out of her home, and she didn't for one moment think that mischievous children had broken into her house and trashed her Christmas tree ornaments. What really unnerved her was the possibility that she hadn't missed the wreckage because of her exhaustion the night before. It was entirely possible that the break-in had taken place after she had returned. The ornaments wouldn't have made much noise when they shattered and she was a notoriously sound sleeper. "All right. Thank you for coming out, Officer."

"It's my job, Ma'am." And a few minutes later he was gone.

She called the local locksmith and made an appointment, then drove up to the farm. Laura had hoped her mother was over her earlier snit, but if anything she was more distant than ever.

"I understand you and your friends put on quite a show last night."

"Show?" Laura's head still hurt and she poured herself a fresh cup of tea that she really didn't want. "We had a few drinks, talked a little, that's all."

"I heard that you had a man at your table and that you were flirting with him quite shamelessly."

"Nothing much gets past you in this town, does it, Mother?"

"Nothing important."

Mary's tone was distinctly unfriendly, and Laura felt herself sliding into the old conciliatory strategy she'd used throughout high school. Felt it and consciously willed herself out of the pattern. She was an adult now. If her mother didn't like the way she conducted her social life, that was her mother's problem, not hers. "As a matter of fact, he was there long enough for one drink, he's a police officer, and we were most definitely not flirting."

"That's not what Tina said."

"Tina?"

"Your waitress, Tina Brougham. You remember, Emily's daughter."

"That was Tina Brougham? I guess her acne cleared up."

"That's right. She owed me a favor so I asked her to keep an eye on you. She also said you made quite a scene just before you left."

Laura sighed. "I got a little upset about a stupid mistake is all." A thought occurred to her. "You didn't ask her to buy us a round of drinks, did you?"

"Of course not! You know what I think about drinking in public places."

"You know, I could get really mad about this, you spying on me."

"I wasn't spying, just looking out for your interests. I've lost you once before, you know, and I won't stand for it again."

There was more along the same lines and when Laura left, the rift was larger, not smaller.

Thursday evening, Dan Sievert knocked on her door.

"Dan! Hi! Come on in. I'll make us some coffee."

He stepped in but he wasn't smiling. "I'll take a raincheck on the coffee if you don't mind. This is an official visit."

"Oh?" There was something unsettling about the way he carried himself this evening. "Am I in trouble about something?"

"No, not that I'm aware of. I apologize for asking this question, but you were in fact married to Sean Brennan of 110 Riverrun Drive in Cobblestone, Vermont, were you not?"

"Yes. Yes, I was." Laura felt a chill of fear run through her body.

"Your husband . . . your late husband died on December 25 of last year?"

"Yes." She breathed the word so low he could barely have

164

heard it. What was this about? She wanted desperately to know. She wanted desperately not to know.

"And he was buried in Mountainview Cemetery?"

"That's correct." Her voice had returned but it sounded alien to her. "What's this all about, Dan? Or is it Officer Sievert?"

"A little of both, I guess. Look, Laura, maybe you should sit down. This is going to come as a bit of a shock."

"No, I'm fine." But she pressed her hands together, interlocking the fingers. "Tell me what's going on."

"Your husband's body is missing. The grave is in a remote part of the graveyard and they've had a lot of bad weather there the past several days so no one knew about it until this morning when a groundskeeper happened out that way almost by accident. The local police are investigating, but at the moment they haven't the faintest idea where . . . where the body is. They called the department about an hour ago and Chief Clay thought maybe someone should come tell you in person, and I volunteered."

It was strange how the world seemed to recede from her, as though suddenly everything around her had been wrapped in gauze.

"When did this happen?"

"Apparently they don't know for certain. At least a week ago, maybe more. The ground was pretty well frozen, so whoever dug him up worked pretty damned hard to get it done. The coffin's still there, and they found some marks where a vehicle had been pulled up almost to the grave site, but not enough to identify it. There was a sudden thaw and the ground turned to mush. No one reported seeing anything."

"I've been there. I'm not surprised. They put him way in the back, near the woods. There isn't a building within half a mile and it's heavily overgrown."

"There's no reason to believe this is anything more than a

165

prank and your husband's body might have been chosen at random."

Laura nodded, but she didn't believe it. No one went to that much trouble for a prank. "I understand. Is there more? Is there something I need to do?"

"Not unless you have any idea who might have done this? Or why?"

"No, no idea at all. My husband's family died years ago, he had no friends, and as far as I know he didn't have any enemies, either. There's no reason I can think of for anyone to do something like this."

There was a little more, but not much, and Laura got through it in the same fashion she'd gotten through the aftermath of Sean's death, by cutting herself off from her emotions, answering Dan's questions mechanically, trying not to think about what had happened.

Trying not to imagine that Sean had come back for her.

The locksmith showed up on schedule, complaining about the weather, the state of the wood on her door, the shoddy workmanship of the previous metalwork. He put on a sturdy new key lock and replaced her bolt and chain with a newer and heavier one, and Laura paid him with the very first of her new personalized checks, which had arrived that very day.

Del came by and picked up her trash later that morning. Her mother might be mad at her, but Rustins didn't live in a trash heap and they looked out for each other. Del didn't come to the door and Laura felt no urge to speak to him so she stayed inside. It only took five minutes for him to lift the trash barrel into the back of the pickup and replace it with an empty one.

She drove into town and parked in front of the police station while she ran a few errands. Chief Clay nodded to her when he passed by but his look struck her as unfriendly, as though he was annoyed with her for being the focus of so much trouble lately, however minor. That made her mildly angry, which helped a bit, but she was still on edge. She walked to the package store and bought herself a bottle of brandy, then went to Foster's and had a very expensive steak for lunch.

When she got back to the cabin, she took the rifle and an empty can down to the edge of Moon Pond. She set it on a fallen log as a target, backed up a reasonable distance, and raised the weapon to her shoulder. As a teenager, she'd been a good shot, had a natural talent for it. Sighting carefully, she softly squeezed the trigger.

Nothing happened.

Frowning, she tried again. Same result. Bad ammunition? It was at least a few years old, but that shouldn't have made any difference. She tried a third time, not bothering to aim, and there was another dull click. Frowning, she lowered the rifle and then methodically began to disassemble it.

It only took a few seconds for her to discover that the firing pin was missing.

CHAPTER TWELVE

The snow held off for two straight weeks other than some mild flurries that didn't stick, and Laura and her mother remained untroubled by prowlers. Dan stopped by during the evening every three or four days, sometimes accepting a cup of coffee, sometimes leaving as soon as he was sure there was nothing wrong. He was always quite professional, but Laura thought she noticed him watching her with more interest as the days passed, and once she even thought he was going to ask her out. His belt radio had crackled at just the wrong moment and the chance was gone, but she was reasonably sure she hadn't misinterpreted.

She also knew that she would have agreed without hesitation, and that realization alone was worth a month of therapy.

Relations with her mother had their ups and downs. Mary still seemed convinced that Laura would not be able to stick it out through the holidays, but as the days rolled by with nothing to indicate she was going to get her way, she became increasingly irritable. Laura made a point of stopping by the farm every couple of days, and ate there at least once a week, and she had also promised to spend Christmas day with her mother, but these small concessions blunted without turning Mary's displeasure.

The weekend get-together at the Trading Post had quickly become a ritual, and Laura was amused to observe that the three of them had fallen back into their old interpersonal habits. Ashley proposed wild plans including a midnight raid on Bud

Wiegand's house, and Kathy countered with suggestions of shopping trips and movies. Laura negotiated compromises, which resulted in a vaguely obscene poem about Wiegand being posted on the message board at the Dairy Stop and a trip to the mall during which she spent entirely too much money.

She was actually feeling quite good about herself and her prospects until the third Monday in December.

It was a bright, clear morning, chilly but not bitter. Laura had gotten up late and was eating breakfast when the cell phone buzzed.

"Hello, Laura? This is Edith Sothern. Is my daughter with you by any chance?"

"Ashley? No, I haven't seen her since Friday night. Is something wrong?"

"I hope not, but she didn't come home last night. It isn't the first time, but she's usually pretty good about calling and telling us not to expect her."

"Maybe she went straight to work." Laura tactfully avoided suggesting a call to Calvin Reese's house. Ashley insisted she wasn't seriously interested in Calvin, but they'd been out together at least four or five times and Calvin lived by himself now that his mother had moved to a managed care facility.

"No, I called there and they said she hadn't come in yet. She's going to lose that job, too, if she isn't careful."

"Well, I'm sure she'll show up eventually. If I run into her, I'll make sure she calls home."

"Thanks, dear, I appreciate it. I'm sorry to have bothered you so early."

Laura went back to breakfast, telling herself not to worry, that Ashley would turn up again just as she always did.

But this time she didn't.

Technically it was too soon to file a missing person's report, but

Chief Clay wasn't a stickler for the rules, particularly when the father of the missing person was a member of the town council. It was Officer Enfield who came out to ask Laura about Ashley, but she couldn't add anything to what she'd told Mrs. Sothern.

"We've already checked with Calvin Reese. He says he hasn't seen her since Saturday night. Had they been fighting, do you know?"

Laura shook her head. "I don't think Ashley cared about him enough to fight with him. It was a pretty casual thing for her."

Enfield wouldn't say much more, but Dan stopped by later that same day and was slightly more forthcoming. "She left home shortly after noon on Saturday. Told her mother she had some errands to run in town. Mrs. Talbot saw her walk past her place around one o'clock, and several local merchants remember her being in their stores. She made only one purchase that we know of, some stockings and lipstick, and that was just after three o'clock. That's when the rain started."

They'd had a mixture of freezing rain and sleet for about two hours on Saturday afternoon. Laura remembered the soft clicking as it landed on the roof while she lay in bed reading.

"And no one saw her after that?"

"Apparently not. We've been all over the road between town and her parents' house. There are a couple of ditches, but there was no sign of her or of any accident. It sounds like she was heading home, got caught by the weather, tried to shelter somewhere off the road, and then something happened. Maybe she slipped and hit her head. But we've looked everywhere we can think of and there's absolutely no sign of her."

Laura was supposed to have supper at the farm that evening, but she was tempted to call and cancel. The prospect of the argument that would inevitably follow dissuaded her, and she showed up half an hour early to punish herself for thinking unkind thoughts about her mother.

"Why so quiet?"

Laura was sitting in the kitchen, watching her mother finish making an elaborate salad topped with cheese and hard-boiled eggs. "I thought you knew. Ashley has disappeared. No one has any idea where she is."

"Well, it's hardly the first time, is it?"

"Mother! That's very unfair."

"I beg your pardon. Isn't this the same Ashley Sothern who ran away from home three times in elementary school, and four times in high school? The same Ashley Sothern who moved to Buffalo after telling her parents it was just a visit? The same Ashley Sothern who couldn't hold a summer job because she missed so many days of work? We are talking about the same person here."

"That was different. The police are involved this time. She was walking home from town and never got there. All of her things are at the house. This time she didn't just skip out because she got bored or had a sudden impulse. Something has happened to her, an accident of some kind, or worse."

"She always did lead a rather dangerous lifestyle." Her mother chopped up some freshly cooked bacon strips and sprinkled them across the top of the salad. "Maybe she finally got into trouble with some boy she was dating."

"The only person she was seeing lately was Calvin Reese and he's not the Charles Manson type." He was actually rather dull unless he'd changed considerably since high school. "And he was working with Ed Burgess all day Saturday so he has an alibi."

"What time did this great mystery take place?"

Laura shrugged. "Between three and four o'clock."

"Take this into the dining room, will you?" Mary indicated the salad bowl. "I'll bring in the fish."

They were seated and filling their plates before Mary spoke again. "Doesn't the bus to Buffalo come through town at just about four o'clock on Saturday?"

"Yes, but the police checked with the driver. No one of her description got on the bus Saturday."

"Didn't you tell me Ashley had gotten in with a bad crowd while she was living in Buffalo?"

"Yes." She hadn't given her mother the details, which would have led to another heated argument given Mary Collier's absolute horror of drugs and those who used them, but she had mentioned that Ashley had come home to get away from trouble.

"Well, perhaps the trouble followed her here. I know this sounds all Old Testament to you, but sometimes we reap what we sow."

Her first impulse was to argue, but she hesitated. Ashley probably hadn't covered her tracks at all, let alone very thoroughly. It would have been ridiculously simple to find out where her family lived, and it was entirely possible that her problems in Buffalo had indeed followed her home. The possibility that she'd been abducted by drug dealers from the big city had its ludicrous aspect, but she couldn't deny the possibility. And she had no better suggestion to make.

The rest of the meal passed in relative silence.

Two days went by and then a third and there was no sign of Ashley. Laura passed on her mother's theory to Dan Sievert and visited the Sothern's almost daily. Ashley's mother seemed to be holding up quite well, but Mr. Sothern went around looking like a zombie. They'd weathered several disappearances by their daughter in the past, but it was obvious that this time was different. This time it hadn't been by Ashley's choice.

An investigator from the state police showed up on Thursday and asked Laura the same questions she'd already answered for

Office Enfield, plus some additional ones about Ashley's stay in Buffalo. She answered as best she could, knowing that it wasn't going to be of any use to him, but the investigator nodded and took notes and told her she'd been very helpful.

She and Kathy talked on the phone several times, but they made no effort to get together, as if by doing so they would be forced to acknowledge that one of the threesome was missing. Laura even drove up and down the various routes Ashley might have taken to go home, as though she might notice a clue that the police had missed.

When Friday came, Laura had trouble concentrating and spent most of the day cleaning the cabin even though it didn't need her attention. When her cell phone buzzed in the middle of the afternoon, she literally jumped to her feet and picked it up with a hand that shook visibly.

"Hello?" Let it be Ashley, she thought. Or good news about her.

But it was Kathy, wanting to know if they were going to meet at the Trading Post. Laura thought about it, almost called it off again, but then set her lips and nodded her head, even though Kathy couldn't have seen the gesture. "Yes, why don't we? I'm tired of moping around here waiting for news."

But if anything, the contrast was more depressing. Ashley was loud, boisterous, brash, and enthusiastic; her high spirits needed to be kept in check, but things were never dull when she was around. The friendship between Laura and Kathy was quieter, less dependent upon conversation, and they spent minutes at a time staring at their drinks, trying not to stare at the empty chairs at their table. She brightened a little, but not much, when Dan Sievert came by briefly, but he seemed to sense their mood and declined an invitation to sit down for a drink.

On balance, the evening was a failure, but at the same time it was a necessary first step for both of them. If the worst had happened, if Ashley was gone forever, then they would go on from here, just as they had gone on from one bad and one horrible marriage.

But they called it a night sooner than usual, and neither of them felt the usual euphoria that followed a night at the Post.

The ride home didn't improve her spirits. There was another storm coming and although it wasn't snowing yet, it had dropped at least ten degrees while she was at the Trading Post and the wind was blustery. She had to struggle to stay in her lane a couple of times when a gust caught her by surprise, and there was enough airborne debris to reduce her visibility. The ten-minute drive took more than twice as long as usual, and she reached the cabin tense and headachy.

The wind tore the car door out of her hands as she was getting out and it grazed her knee hard enough to bring tears to her eyes. She locked the car, then turned and leaned into the wind, which was growing stronger by the minute. The front door seemed impossibly far away, but eventually she reached it, fumbling for her keys with fingers that were already numb with cold despite her gloves. A moment later, she slammed the door behind her, throwing the bolt immediately, and started to relax in the comparative warmth of the cabin.

But it wasn't very warm. The fire in the woodstove had long since died down to embers, and the two space heaters she had turned on were not able to make any headway against the stream of cold air that came in through the shattered window on the far wall. Laura stared at the spray of broken glass disbelievingly, unable at first to comprehend what could have happened. It was the sheltered side of the house, so the inflow wasn't as violent as it might have been, but it was still strong enough to have moved all of the loose papers and magazines and to have knocked over more than a few items.

Her first priority was to cover the window, which meant she

had to stand on a chair and use duct tape and a large flat metal tray as a temporary measure. Once it was sealed tightly enough that she couldn't feel a draft, she started a fresh fire in the woodstove and surveyed the damage.

Nothing major or obvious was broken, although her tree leaned at a dangerous angle. She hadn't bought fresh ornaments yet and had been considering taking it down anyway. She found one broken cup that she'd left on the table; it had shattered when it hit the floor. Most of the rest of the mess was just annoying, sales receipts blown under furniture, the bookmark missing from the book she'd been reading. After the worst of it was taken care of she checked the stove, which was radiating heat quite nicely now, and made herself a cup of coffee.

It was late, she was exhausted physically and mentally wrung out. A shower might help, but she didn't have the energy and the air was still cool enough that she decided against facing the shock of emerging into it still wet and steamy. She washed out her cup and checked the locks on both doors and the security of her tape job on the broken window. In the morning she would have to figure out how that happened. There was an aging pine tree on that side of the house. Possibly a branch had broken free in the wind. That seemed the most likely explanation.

She changed into her woolen pajamas as quickly as possible and put on a brand-new pair of slippers for the dash across the cold floor to the bathroom. Laura pulled the cord on the overhead light and turned toward the toilet, but then her head snapped back to the writing on her mirror.

"Ashley says good-bye," it read. "And don't worry, I'll be home for Xmas." It was signed "Sean."

Officer Enfield and another officer she didn't know answered her emergency call. They examined the window and the writing on the mirror and asked her a few questions, then told her to lock up securely for the night. "Or maybe it'd be better if you stayed someplace else."

Over the worst of her shock, Laura shook her head. "I'll stay here. I have a gun." She'd taken it to the hardware store and replaced the firing pin.

The following morning more police arrived, including a rather abrupt detective named Hopper. He asked her a few questions, most of them the same ones she'd been asked before, while technicians took photographs of the writing, dusted for fingerprints, and conducted various other mysterious tests no one bothered to explain to her. Dan was there, but he stood to one side, not saying anything, and deferred to Hopper. Laura didn't like the detective; he was brusque and sarcastic and kept staring at her during the interview, and at one point even implied she had written the message herself.

"There's one thing I don't understand, Miss Collier. If someone wanted to break in here, why would they pick the most difficult window to climb through?" He pointed to her makeshift repairs. "I suppose if he was tall enough, he could scramble up the outside wall and get in that way, but why not break the porch window? It's bigger and a child could climb through it."

"You're asking the wrong person. Maybe whoever it was thought that side of the house was better hidden from the road." She knew even as she said it that this made no sense. The porch was at the rear, completely out of sight; the broken window was on the side, concealed well enough but with nothing to make it preferable.

"Well, we know one person who certainly wasn't responsible. Your intruder was not Sean Brennan, Miss Collier. He is well and truly dead according to the police back in Vermont."

"I know that." She'd killed him after all, although sometimes, when it was very dark and she was all by herself, she thought something of Sean had lingered. There was a part of him inside her now that would never die.

"So who would be pissed off enough to do something like this? Or are you one of those people who have no enemies?"

"None sick enough to do this." But she wasn't so sure. It didn't seem like Mason Cortway's style. He was mean enough, but his rare infractions had tended to be impulsive and poorly planned. He was too lazy to go to this much work just to annoy her. Or was he? Two years had passed and people can change a lot in less time than that. Sean had taught her that lesson. Bud Wiegand was a more likely candidate, but she knew with absolute certainty that he could not have pulled his bulky body in through the broken window. Del Huggins? He might just possibly have fit through the window and he was obviously not on her cheering squad, but whatever the reason for the animosity between them, it couldn't be sufficient to have resulted in this. Nor did she think that Del had the imagination to conceive such a thing. He'd always been irritable and unfriendly, but she had never known him to be cruel.

"Well, someone certainly was." He gave her a hard look as though he suspected she knew more than she was saying, but he didn't have any more questions, and less than half an hour later the police cars were pulling out of her driveway.

All except one. Dan Sievert had quietly remained behind.

"Are you all right, Laura?" He walked over to stand beside her as she watched the other three vehicles turn onto Moon Pond Road.

"I think so. What's going on, Dan? First Ashley, and now this!" He didn't answer and they stood within arm's reach of one another for a few seconds. "Want to come in for a cup of coffee?"

"I thought you'd never ask."

"You won't get into trouble?" She glanced back toward the road.

"Nope. As of twenty minutes ago, I'm off duty."

"Well then, how about some breakfast to go with that coffee?"

Their conversation was much more personal that morning than it had ever been before. Dan talked about growing up in Rochester and seemed not at all uncomfortable about having been an orphan. "That's part of the reason I came here. My mother was from this area. I'm not on a great quest to discover my roots or anything like that, but I have been asking around. It's become a hobby, I guess."

"Any luck?"

"Not a whole lot, and most of it negative. People don't gossip here, at least with outsiders."

"Definitely not with outsiders, but we gossip with the best of them."

"I have a list of possibilities, and I've winnowed it down some. You know, the right age group, no children close to the same age. There are almost a hundred names left, about half married, half widowed or single. I even had your mother on the list for a while, but I couldn't understand why she'd abandon me and then keep you two years later."

"She might be willing to trade right now. She's not entirely pleased with me."

He ignored her. "About ten percent of the names are deceased, and a handful more have relocated. Dorrance has a pretty stable population, though. I've actually managed to meet most of the women I consider high-probability, usually in the line of duty. Sometimes their husbands as well. If any of them are relatives, there sure isn't any obvious physical resemblance. I look more like my uncle than most of them."

Laura almost joked that he was much too good looking to

178

have relatives in the area, but she had second thoughts at the last moment. Things were going too well to take a chance and spoil the mood.

"So how was it to grow up here?"

Laura told him how she'd felt stifled and resentful during high school, how hurt she'd been when her father abandoned her without a word, how she'd only been close to a handful of people in her entire life. That made her think of Ashley and she was abruptly silent and moody.

"Maybe I should go." He stirred restlessly and she realized that neither of them had spoken for an uncomfortably long period of time.

"No, please stay. I'm sorry. I got caught up in old memories for a moment there. Can I get you some more coffee?"

Dan stayed until mid-morning before insisting that he needed a shower and a change of clothing. Laura was reluctant to let him go, but as soon as he was out the door she realized how exhausted she was. She decided to take a nap, replenished the wood in the stove, and then stumbled to her bed.

It was late afternoon before she woke up.

Ed Burgess wasn't home but his wife took the message. "I'm sure he'll come out as soon as he gets back, dear. We don't want you to freeze to death out there."

"Don't make him come out if he's busy, Mrs. Burgess. I have the window covered. I just want to have it fixed before the next storm comes up and blows it in again." She hadn't said anything about the circumstances under which the window had been broken, but she knew that in Dorrance it was only a matter of days, if not hours, before information like that was common knowledge.

She'd managed to disrupt her normal sleep cycle once again, and when dusk arrived Laura felt dislocated in time. Ed Burgess called after seven and offered to come out, but she told him Monday would be fine. "I'll be over tomorrow afternoon," he insisted. "How about two o'clock?"

Laura knew better than to argue further. "That's fine. Thanks again, Mr. B."

He arrived right on schedule, had the ladder off the back of his truck before she'd had time to put on her coat and go out to meet him. It had turned surprisingly warm and almost pleasant, although she knew that another big storm front was supposed to arrive by midweek.

Laura stayed close to Burgess, offering to hand him things as he stood on the ladder, clearing away the broken glass from inside the frame. "How the hell did this get broken anyway?" He glanced up at the branches over his head. "I don't see anything big enough or close enough to break a double-paned glass like this one was."

"Someone broke into the cabin yesterday, Mr. B. Kids maybe, playing a prank." She knew it wasn't kids.

So did he. "Too much work for a prank. Kids would've gone in through one of the porch windows. We've got a couple of young hellions that just might do such a thing, but one of them's in Florida with his parents and the other's not brave enough to do this on his own." He stopped what he was doing and looked down at her. "Your mother has some people seriously mad at her, you know."

"I can't remember a time when people weren't seriously mad at Mother."

He chuckled. "That's true, sure enough. Mary Rustin fancied herself lady of the manor when she was young and marrying Ben Collier didn't thin her blood any." His face grew solemn. "But it's worse now. The town is ailing, Miss Collier. Prices are down and costs are up, there's not enough jobs for the young people, and too many of us old farts lingering on and taking up space. It was the beginning of the end when the highway bypassed us. We've got half a dozen stores closed up now and more to come."

"That's not Mother's fault."

"No, it isn't. Since when did people around here need a good reason for hating someone? All they need to see is someone making out fine while they struggle to get by."

Laura didn't tell him that even Rustin Farm was barely breaking even. "I'm sure Mother can take care of herself."

"Wouldn't surprise me. I was more concerned with her little girl. There's people mean enough that they might want to get at her through her daughter." He sounded uncomfortable suddenly and turned back to his work. "I don't know anything, mind you, but I've lived here all my life and I can feel things I can't rightly describe, like back currents in a stream that you don't notice unless you concentrate real hard. Be careful, Miss Collier. That's all I'm saying."

It didn't take long to replace the window. Laura wrote him a check and Burgess stuck it in his pocket without a glance. "Anything else you need, you just give us a call, you hear?"

"I'll do that, Mr. B. Thanks again."

Chapter Thirteen

Laura didn't exactly ignore Ed Burgess' warning, but it ended up at the bottom of the basement stairs of her mind, not out of sight exactly, but not in the way, either. The implied threat seemed almost unreal, and trivial compared to Ashley's unexplained disappearance.

She was also growing increasingly bored. At first it had been refreshing and rewarding to sit in her own place, reading by a warm fire, cooking her own meals, occasionally listening to music on her new CD player. Laura had never been a big fan of television, not even as a child, and she didn't miss it here. The radio provided weather reports, she picked up the weekly *Courier* for local news, and for more in-depth reporting she only had to call her mother and ask.

Although she had the wherewithal to live as a woman of comparative leisure, it was not as pleasant a prospect as she'd expected. Sooner, rather than later, she was going to have to find something to do with her life. She thought about going to college or perhaps a business school, but not knowing what she wanted to do afterwards discouraged her from investigating what could well be a waste of time. For most of one painful afternoon she considered trying to write about Sean's deterioration and ultimate breakdown; she'd always been fluent and had actually considered going into journalism during her junior year. The memories were still too painful, though, and there was the additional problem that she couldn't tell the truth about his death without causing the authorities back in Vermont to want answers to a whole new array of questions.

Her mother would be happy to involve her in managing the farm, but Laura knew what that involvement would consist of. Her suggestions would be greeted either with tolerant skepticism or sarcastic rejection, and she would never be able to change anything significant no matter how well reasoned. The Rustin Farm would be run the way the Rustin Farm had always been run, and that was that. She might be given a small plot of land in which to experiment with different crops or techniques, but even if she grew corn the size of watermelons and peas the size of cabbages, her innovations would be dismissed as "interesting but impractical." And for that matter, she found farming itself incredibly dull.

No, it would have to be something else. Perhaps she could write children's books, or get a license as a realtor. Laura started to make a list of every profession she could think of, then crossed off the ones that were completely impractical, put check marks next to those that were just unlikely, crosses next to those that sounded interesting, and left blank the ones she didn't know enough about to judge. The last was the largest category.

Late Wednesday morning she was returning from the grocery store when she saw the mail truck pulling away from her driveway. She paused next to the mailbox, managed to extract the handful of envelopes without getting out of her car, and dropped them into one of the plastic bags before driving up to the cabin.

Most of the mail she'd received since moving back to Dorrance had consisted of bills and advertising circulars, so she set today's batch aside to be looked through later. Once the groceries were dispersed to their assigned places, she drove back into town and met Kathy for lunch at Slade's.

They exchanged their lack of news about Ashley, which left

both of them feeling unhappy and untalkative. "I heard someone broke into your place."

"Someone with a sick sense of humor." The police had told her not to talk about the details, but this was Kathy, after all. "They left me a note and signed Sean's name to it."

"Sickos all right. I'm guessing Bud Wiegand. He's mean enough."

Laura shook her head. "I don't think so. It didn't feel like something he'd do. I thought about Mason Cortway."

"Mason? But he's always had a crush on you."

"He's always had a crush on himself, and he thinks being seen with me would help his career." She sighed. "Oh, I don't know. It's not really his kind of thing, is it? Maybe I'm just being a bitch. But I can't think of anyone else who would have any reason to do something like that."

They both ate quickly and Kathy excused herself from having dessert. "I have to lose a couple of pounds again, and besides I promised Mom I'd take her to Shawcut."

"Be careful on the roads. We're supposed to get a storm tonight."

"That's why we're going early. Are we on for Saturday?"

Laura nodded determinedly. "Who knows? Maybe Ashley will walk in on us, all surprised that we were worried about her."

"That would be typical." But Kathy didn't smile and Laura felt more depressed than ever as she drove back to the house.

What with one thing and another, it was dusk when she finally sorted through the stack of envelopes. The bills went one way, the circulars into the trash, but one plain envelope was in a group all by itself. Her name and address was typed neatly; there was a local postmark but no return address. Curious, she tore open the envelope and removed a single folded piece of white paper. It was typed as well.

"Laura, this is Ashley. I'm sorry if you've been worried but it wasn't my fault. Someone tried to kill me, and they almost succeeded. He chased me up to Wilson's Ravine and I slipped and fell. Banged up my hand so bad I can't write with it, but otherwise I'm all right. He must've thought I was dead because he didn't come down to check on me or anything, and I've been staying out of sight since. But if he knows I'm alive, he'll come after me. I'm sure of it."

Laura paused after the first paragraph, went back and reread it before continuing. "You can't tell anyone about this, not even my parents. If you do, it'll put them in danger as well. And not the police, either. I know this must sound crazy, but I'll explain everything if you meet me Friday night, seven o'clock, down at Moon Pond, where the pier used to be. Come by yourself but be very careful, Laura, because he must be after you, too. It's Sean, Laura, Sean Brennan. I don't know how, but he's back. He's not dead after all. I'm scared, and you're the only person I can trust. Meet me and I'll tell you everything and then we can decide what to do next. I'm relying on you, Laura. Don't let me down."

Ashley's name was typed at the bottom.

Laura read the entire message again, and then again, and then still one more time. The paper fell to the tabletop and she stared at the opposite wall, not seeing anything, not even able to think coherently for the first few minutes. What in the world could Ashley have gotten herself into? Sean was dead. There was no question about that. She had seen his body, broken and lifeless. He had been embalmed and buried and she'd been to his grave site. But so had someone else. His body was missing. What did that mean? What was going on?

She stood up and began pacing back and forth. Twice she picked up her cell phone to call someone. But who could she call? Ashley had expressly forbidden her to call the Sotherns or the police. Maybe she could tell Kathy. She actually started to press the numbers, then stopped. Even if Kathy was back from Shawcut, which was unlikely, this wasn't something Laura could tell her over the phone. Instead she returned to the table and read the note one more time, then folded it, slipped it into its envelope, and set it aside.

Sean was dead, but Ashley thought he was alive, thought he'd chased her and nearly killed her, and that he would kill her if he had the chance. Obviously, she had to be mistaken. It wasn't Sean she'd seen. But who was it? Someone who looked like Sean, enough that he could pass for him in bad weather and at long range? That was the only possibility she could think of. And why would Sean be after Ashley in any case? It would be Laura he had a grudge against. No, it had to be one of Ashley's Buffalo acquaintances, someone who had followed her to Dorrance. And if that was the case, it probably was best that she play dead for a while, at least long enough for the stranger to believe he'd done what he'd intended and leave town.

But where was Ashley hiding out? Laura couldn't think of any place she could run to. Obviously she had shelter, and a typewriter, so she wasn't living in a cave somewhere. She grabbed the envelope, pulled out the letter, and read it again. Friday, two nights from now. Laura would wait until she could talk to her friend, urge her to go to the police, force the issue if necessary.

She knew from experience that it was not a good idea to simply hope things would get better.

There were several times on Thursday when Laura came close to calling the police. If Dan Sievert had happened by, she would almost certainly have confided in him, even if that meant he would insist upon telling Chief Clay. But she didn't see him at all that day and when she finally called the station on Friday, they told her he was out sick and wasn't expected in.

"Is there something I can help you with, Miss Collier?"

"No," she answered unhappily. "It's nothing. I'm sorry to have bothered you."

Laura spent the afternoon making preparations. She took the rifle out and test fired it a couple of times, then cleaned and reloaded it. She recharged the battery on her cell phone and opened a new package of batteries for her flashlight. At three o'clock she walked down to Moon Pond and along the shore until she spotted the rotting posts that had formerly supported a rickety pier. There was nothing visible that seemed wrong or out of place, but she was dismayed to discover how dramatically the area had become overgrown in recent years. She wished that Ashley had picked someplace out in the open, where they could see anyone who approached them.

Although she had little appetite, she ate a light supper back at the cabin. At half past six, she dressed warmly and put on her overcoat with the deepest pockets. The cell phone went into one along with the flashlight. A box of cartridges went into the other. She locked the door behind her and set off to the rendezvous with her rifle held at port arms in front of her and the hairs on the back of her neck standing at attention.

The unseasonable warmth had long since moved away to the east, but the chill she felt had little to do with the weather. The moon and clouds were invisible, hidden behind the advance pickets of the stormy army scheduled to hit sometime between midnight and dawn. She followed a circuitous route to her destination, not out of any specific fear but just to be unpredictable. Ashley couldn't be right about the identity of whoever had attacked her, but that didn't make the person any less dangerous. Laura gripped her weapon more tightly and concentrated on listening to the night around her. She knew these woods as well as anyone alive, and would take whatever advantage that knowledge might provide.

She stopped within sight of her destination and waited until it was time for Ashley to appear. It was so dark that she couldn't see much, so reluctantly she stepped out into the open and turned on the flashlight, playing the cone of illumination in a rapid circle all around, then a second circuit, much slower and more methodical this time. There was no sign of anyone else, either by sight nor sound.

Laura found a spot where she could press her back against a broad tree trunk and still watch the entire area, then flicked the light off. Although she was tempted to call out Ashley's name, she refrained. For whatever reason, Ashley wanted this meeting to be private, and although they were about as isolated here as was possible in Dorrance, sounds traveled long distances at night, particularly over the open water. So she settled back, shivered a little, and waited.

And waited.

And then waited some more.

After half an hour, she was annoyed as well as cold, worry mixed with irritation. But then she remembered that Ashley was always late, and she settled back and told herself to be patient. Another fifteen minutes crawled by, followed by another that moved at glacial speed. After an hour of waiting, she was stiff with cold, her feet hurt, her nose was running, and she had the beginning of a really fine headache. Laura decided to take a chance and called out her friend's name, low at first, then louder when there was no response.

Nothing. No answering cry, no rustling in the brush. It was as if she was alone out here. But she wasn't. Laura had absolutely no idea how she knew, but she was absolutely certain that someone else was present. Her first impulse was happiness, because she thought it must be Ashley. But when there was no response to her call, and the night remained still and silent, her mood turned to worry and then anxiety. If she was right and someone else was here, then it wasn't Ashley.

She shifted her weapon slightly and was startled to discover how stiff and cold her fingers were despite the thermal gloves she was wearing. The frigid air and the prolonged inactivity were getting to her. If she was going to do something, she'd have to do it soon. She put the stock of the rifle into her right armpit, her finger ready on the trigger, and used her free hand to lift the flashlight. Then, impulsively, she stepped out into the open, playing the light around once more, and walked directly to the ruined pier.

Nothing rushed out of the shadows toward her. No one cried out a greeting, a warning, or a threat. Nothing at all happened and after a few moments Laura knew by that same subliminal magic that she was alone now, that whoever had lurked nearby a few minutes earlier had silently departed. And she also knew that wherever Ashley had gone, she was not going to keep their rendezvous tonight.

"That's it. I'm going back." She whispered the words and they seemed unnaturally loud in the darkness. Reluctant to abandon the chance to find out what happened to Ashley, she took one last look around and had almost turned to go when she noticed something anomalous about the post nearest to shore.

It was within arm's reach so she could just touch it without putting her feet in the water. Something seemed to be stuck to the top of the post, and her fingers brushed across rough fabric. The flashlight revealed it to be some kind of cloth, wound horizontally around the splintered wood. Laura carefully unwound it, taking in the slack so that it wouldn't dip into the water. Even with the flashlight, she couldn't be positive, but she felt certain that she knew what it was.

Once it was completely unwound, she gathered it into a ball and went directly back to the cabin, the brisk exercise helping dispel some of the chill in her muscles. She walked around the cabin once before going inside, just to assure herself that all was well, then unlocked the door and stepped gratefully into the warm interior.

She raised her hand and looked at her prize and recognized it instantly. It was Ashley's scarf, the one Laura had given her on her eighteenth birthday.

Laura was sitting in the cabin, staring at the strip of gaily colored material, trying to decide whether or not to call the police when the matter was essentially taken out of her hands. Someone knocked on the door.

Cautiously, and only after picking up her weapon, she crossed the room. "Who is it?"

"It's me, Dan Sievert. Is everything all right?"

"Oh thank God!" She unlocked the door immediately.

Dan's eyes took in her expression and the rifle in her hand and he stepped quickly inside. "What's wrong?"

She told him everything, the note, her feeling that she wasn't alone, the scarf. He listened closely and without reacting. "Do you still have the note?"

"Yes, I'll get it." She started to turn but he hastily blocked her way.

"No, I don't want you to touch it. Do you have something I can put it in, a file folder or something like that?"

"Yes, of course." She took one from the cardboard file box where she kept all of her important papers.

"How about a pair of tweezers?"

She provided that as well, then pointed out where she'd put the single typed page. He picked it up with the tweezers and placed it in the folder. "You really should have called us right away, you know? Do you have the envelope?"

"It's in the trash. Outside."

"We'll have to find it."

She held the light while he explored the trash with her tweezers, eventually finding the envelope. He added it to the folder. "I'll have to take these back to the station. The state police will want them."

"All right. Dan, do you think something has happened to her?"

"Well, obviously something has happened. I wouldn't want to speculate about how serious it might be." He hesitated. "Your husband really is dead, isn't he?"

"Of course he is! I don't know what or who Ashley saw, but it wasn't Sean."

"All right. I don't suppose I could talk you into moving back to your mother's place, at least for a few days while we sort this all out."

Her jaw set. "I'm not running home to mother just because it's scary out."

He smiled. "I didn't think so, but I had to ask. I'm going to take this in now and call the Chief. My guess is he won't send anyone out until first light, but with the outside interest and all, he might fool me. I want you to lock the door as soon as I'm gone and don't open up unless you know who's there." He hesitated. "And even if you know who it is, you might want to be cautious."

Laura nodded. "Do you think she's in the pond?"

His eyes skittered away from hers. "I don't think anything yet."

The state police mobile lab arrived just before dawn, as did Detective Hopper, a contingent of technicians, and Chief Clay himself. Clay was quiet and irritable and avoided Hopper's presence. Hopper delivered a predictable lecture about withholding information from the police to which Laura responded with appropriate though not entirely genuine regret.

More police showed up in a small launch from the opposite end of Moon Pond, two of them in diving suits. Laura stood on the shore watching them bob up and down as they systematically examined the bottom of Moon Pond, and was quietly relieved when they eventually abandoned the search without finding anything. She pointed out the spot where she'd stood the night before, and gave as accurate a recounting as possible of her movements, both then and during her earlier visit.

"Could the scarf have been there when you came down in the afternoon?"

She shook her head. "No. It's very bright and distinctive and I walked right to the edge of the water. If it had been there, I would have seen it."

There were more questions, many more questions, the same ones repeated, sometimes phrased differently, but obviously designed to catch her in a contradiction. She endured it all quietly and cooperated as best she could, but not without deepening her dislike of Detective Hopper. Chief Clay had left early in the morning without saying a word, and Laura noticed that the two local policemen who remained were posted to prevent anyone from interfering with the personnel from the state and were otherwise not involved in the investigation.

Not that anyone tried to interfere or even showed up to gawk. It was cold and the air was damp. The storm had held off, or bypassed them, but not by far. The sky was leaden gray and grew darker as the day grew longer.

It was late afternoon before Hopper told his men to pack up and return to wherever it was they'd come from. "We'll let you know if we find anything, Miss Collier. I want to stress again that you need to call my office immediately if you receive any further communications from Miss Sothern or any information about her whereabouts."

"Yes, I realize that now. I'm sorry. I was just trying to do what was best for Ashley."

"Ashley's best chance is with us. You have my card?"

It was in her wallet. She nodded and thanked him and felt an enormous sense of relief when he finally pulled out onto Moon Pond Road and drove off.

Laura almost called Kathy and cancelled for the evening, but the cabin suddenly seemed very close and confining and she was desperate to get away for a while. She showered and changed clothing and felt marginally better. It was snowing when she started the Chevy but not heavily. According to the weather report she'd heard on the radio an hour earlier, the storm had veered southward unexpectedly, and Dorrance was only faced with a projected accumulation of less than six inches. That was almost a non-event.

She was early, as always, but by such a wide margin this time that she decided to run an errand before heading over to the Trading Post. The weather was foul enough that she didn't want to walk any more than was necessary, so she drove to the center of town and parked on one of the side streets. She was about to get out of her car when another vehicle seemed to come out of nowhere and she flinched back. Although she'd only had a second to look, she was quite sure that the vehicle had been Del Huggins' Land Rover. What was even more surprising was that his passenger had looked a lot like Tommy Langston.

The night that Joyce Catterall had died at Sharp's Curve, Tommy had insisted they were just going for a joy ride. The only buildings for the next several miles were Del Huggin's cottage and a handful of utility buildings servicing the local farms. Tommy's story seemed perfectly plausible, but now Laura wondered if maybe he hadn't had a definite destination in mind.

But why would Tommy Langston and Joyce Catterall want to visit Del Huggins? It made no sense. Laura put the matter out of her mind. It was one of the many questions in life for which she had no answer, and it wasn't any of her business anyway. She got out of the car and went to buy some fresh batteries.

Detective Hopper had told her not to discuss the previous night's events with anyone, but of course that couldn't include Kathy. They were barely seated before Laura was telling her everything, although she did keep her voice low enough that it wouldn't carry and extracted a promise that it would go no further. Kathy solemnly crossed her heart and listened without interrupting until Laura finally ran out of breath.

"You know, this is beginning to sound like something out of a bad horror movie."

Laura nodded. "I think it's deliberate. Stealing Sean's body, then impersonating him, the message on my mirror. Someone's trying to convince me he's back from the dead."

"Did Sean have any family?"

"A couple of cousins, but he lost track of them years ago. His parents are dead and he was an only child."

"Could there have been a twin brother?"

Laura shook her head. "That's too Hollywood, Kathy. I can't believe in a mysterious twin reappearing for revenge any more than I can believe Sean is a zombie risen from the grave."

"Then who did Ashley see? She obviously thought, I mean, thinks that it was Sean."

"I don't know. She's not the superstitious type. I can't imagine how she could have been fooled that way. It just doesn't seem like her. There's got to be more, something we don't know yet. And we won't know it until we find Ashley and talk to her."

There was a long, awkward silence. "You think she's alive, then?" Kathy's voice was uneven.

"I hope so. I have to keep thinking she's alive because I can't deal with the alternative just now. There's been too much death around me recently, death and loss. First my father, then Sean, now Ashley. Look, let's talk about something else for a while. What's new with you?"

"The divorce papers came in the mail today. It was all remarkably civilized if I do say so. It's so much nicer when you fall out of love simultaneously."

"So what's next for Kathy Peebles?"

"Oh, it's still Cronyn. I like it better and my luggage is all monogrammed. I'm staying here through the holidays, but I'll probably split before spring. I wrote to Northeastern and they'll readmit me."

Laura's spirits dropped. She had been hoping Kathy's return to Dorrance would be more or less permanent. But then, she didn't know how much longer she'd be staying herself. She still hadn't decided what she wanted to be when she grew up, and she was growing up fast.

"How about you? Going to take over Rustin Farm and put your mother in a rest home?"

"God, she'd be running the whole place within thirty days. No, she was born on the farm and she'll die on the farm. Fertilizer runs in her veins. She wants to groom me to take over, but I just don't feel the same way about the land. If she died tomorrow, I'd have the place up for sale by the first of the year. Don't ever tell her I said that, though. She'd have a stroke and disown me."

"Then what are you going to do? You can't just live in that cabin by yourself for the rest of your life."

"My aunt did. But you're right, I can't hold up that family tradition, either. I don't know, Kathy. Maybe I should go back to school for a while, learn a profession. But right now I honestly can't think of anything I want to do with my life."

"Well, you're only twenty-three. It's not as though you have a deadline hanging over your head."

"No, but something's hanging over my head, Kathy. I don't know what it is, but I can feel it. It's big and dark and one of these days it's going to fall and I don't know if I'm going to be able to get out from under it in time."

CHAPTER FOURTEEN

A week passed with no further word from Ashley, and no progress on the part of the authorities in finding out what had happened to her. Detective Hopper personally assured the Sotherns that the case would remain active, but he and his staff left Dorrance the following day, and Dan told Laura off the record that the active investigation was probably over.

"Unless something new turns up, there's really nothing more they can do. I'm sorry, Laura, but that's the way it is. I know Ashley is important to you and to her family, but in the greater scheme of things, she's just another missing person in a world that has no shortage of them."

On the other hand, Laura actually earned some money on her own that week. She'd been shopping in the Thrift Market when she came across a half-finished sign advertising handheld, solar power calculators. "Solar" was spelled "solor" and whoever had started it hadn't left enough room for the entire word "calculator." It was probably Old Man Taylor, who'd been running the store since she was a child, and who was notorious for his bad spelling and illegible signs. Impulsively, she turned the placard over and rewrote it legibly and completely, even added a tiny stylized calculator as an embellishment.

"That's pretty good."

She jumped, dropping the marker, feeling ridiculous and guilty simultaneously. "Oh, Mr. Calloway. I didn't see you there."

He smiled and glanced back at her handiwork. "That's nice work. I don't suppose I could talk you into doing the signs for us at the store."

Laura assumed he was joking and laughed nervously. "I always got an 'A' for penmanship. I write the world's neatest checks."

"Can't read my own handwriting, most of the time, and the kids I hire are careless and sloppy. I couldn't pay you much and it would only be a couple of hours every week or so, but you could pretty much pick your own time to come in."

She blinked at him. "Are you serious, Mr. Calloway?"

"Of course I am. When have you ever known me to joke?" Tom Calloway was famous for his practical jokes, and his eyes twinkled as he spoke, but Laura suddenly realized he was in earnest.

"Sure. That would be great. When would you like me to start? My calendar is pretty much a blank piece of paper right now."

"How about tomorrow morning? Around ten?"

"I'll be there. And thanks, Mr. Calloway."

They eventually agreed that Laura would work a half day every two weeks. In addition to lettering the signs, she would take care of a few other minor chores as time allowed. The pay was not terrific but at least it made her feel a little less like a social outcast. And Calloway openly hinted that she could have a full-time job in the spring if she wanted it. "Bess over there is going off to college in Albany and Skip is talking about working for Ed Burgess, so I'll be looking for reliable help."

She mentioned her prospects to her mother the next time they got together, with predictable results. "You're too smart a girl to work as a sales clerk, Laura. If you won't come help manage the farm, maybe you could go to school. A two-year degree in business management would certainly be helpful."

"It's only temporary, Mother. It's not as though I need the

money." She managed to change the subject fairly quickly.

Christmas was imminent. The town had its decorations up, but they seemed less grand and extensive than she remembered. Laura couldn't tell whether it was just the change in her perspective or whether the town actually had scaled back, but the streets at night seemed darker and more sinister.

Laura had been stopping to see the Sotherns every two or three days, but it became more of a struggle as the days passed without any further news. Ashley's father had become increasingly moody and uncommunicative, and even Mrs. Sothern seemed to have lost most of the bounce from her step and most of the spirit from her voice.

On the last Friday before Christmas, Laura and Kathy met at the Trading Post, and managed to snag their favorite table in the back corner. Tina served them their drinks with her usual frosty smile. She had never been more than minimally polite to them despite the fact that they always left a respectable tip. Laura thought it was just bad chemistry, but Kathy thought it was because they were both interested in the same guy.

"Watch her some time when he's here. That is, if you can tear your eyes away from him for a minute. She's definitely got a thing for the boss."

Dan wasn't there that evening, so she wasn't able to test it empirically, but Laura thought Kathy might be right. "Hey, I've got an idea. Once the holiday madness is over with, why don't you and I go down to New York City for a weekend? Maybe we could get tickets to a show or something. I haven't even seen a movie since I left Vermont."

Kathy's face fell slightly. "I'm sorry, I can't. I've been meaning to tell you. I'm going to Boston right after Christmas. I'll be staying with a couple of friends while I look for an apartment and investigate the job market. I'm going to be there at least a couple of weeks, maybe more." She hesitated. "If things work out, I might just stay until classes start in the spring. But you could come out and visit me. We could drive down to Providence or take the train to New York."

"Sure. Sounds great." But the prospect of life in Dorrance with both Ashley and Kathy gone took most of the pleasure out of idea, and she was moody for the rest of the evening.

Then things started to get worse.

Just when Laura was starting to think about going home, Mason Cortway walked into the Trading Post. His companion was a short, thin young woman with a pinched face, blonde hair teased beyond distraction, and too much makeup. Laura didn't recognize her but Kathy did. "Gail Shaw. She was a year behind us. Big glasses, long dark hair covering her face, baggy clothes. She missed most of our senior year while she was being treated for anorexia."

"Doesn't look like the cure worked."

Mason made his way to the bar with Gail following in his wake. She looked extremely uncomfortable and flinched whenever the noise level spiked. "I don't think I've ever seen him in here before."

"O'Brien's is more his style, I think. How about one more before we call it a night?" Kathy looked around for Tina, who hadn't come by for at least a half hour.

"I never thought of Mason as a drinker."

"He didn't dare when he was underage, but it's a different story now." Kathy abruptly stood up and waved her arm vigorously. "That got her attention."

Laura glanced at her wristwatch. "It's getting late."

"Just one more. What with Christmas and all, we won't be able to do this next weekend, and then there's New Year's and then I'm gone."

"Don't remind me. You're abandoning me in the wilderness, you know."

"So come with me. You can find something in Boston."

Laura shook her head. "I'm not ready yet. But thanks for the offer."

She was suddenly aware of someone standing close behind her and turned in her chair. It was Mason, swaying slightly, his date standing a step behind him with her eyes downcast and her expression anxious.

"So look who's here!" His voice was louder than it needed to be, as if he was deliberately trying to attract attention. "The princess is out slumming with the common people. Who'd have thought it?"

"Hello, Mason," Laura said evenly.

"Good night, Mason," Kathy added.

He took a step back in exaggerated shock. "Oh, excuse me. Am I intruding? Wait, I get it. Now I understand why the princess here didn't want to be seen with me. She's found her true love after all." He looked back and forth between the two of them.

Laura's reaction was weary disgust. "Just go away, Mason, before you make an even bigger fool of yourself than you have already."

But surprisingly it was Kathy who stood up and leaned across the table, staring directly into Mason's face. "That sounds pretty funny coming from a guy who always preferred skinny-dipping with the other guys to dating, Mason. Is that why you dumped Susie Conway out of your car when she got drunk and tried to come on to you at the Halloween dance?"

Mason's mouth moved, and his eyes flickered, but he didn't say anything. His date put her hand on his arm. "Mason, I don't like it here. Why don't we go someplace else?" Her voice was high-pitched and squeaky and Laura belatedly recognized her.

He shrugged her off. "I kind of figured the princess played

the guy, but maybe I had it wrong." His voice wasn't as loud now, and it quavered uncertainly.

Kathy laughed and sat back down in her chair, shaking her head in wonderment.

Laura finally found her voice. "Mason, you were a nasty little boy and a sneaky teenager and now you're just a stupid, small-minded man. Go away before you hurt yourself."

For a few seconds, it looked like he was going to respond, but then he spun on his heel and stalked off, without even looking to see if Gail was following. She gave Laura and Kathy a quick apologetic look and then set off in his wake.

"Well, that was different." Kathy had stopped laughing the instant Mason was gone.

Laura didn't feel like laughing. She felt like crying, not for Mason and what he had said, but because of what had become of her childhood. It wasn't supposed to turn out like this. "I have to go, Kathy. I'm sorry."

"Sure, no problem. It looks like Tina forgot about us again anyway. You still going to your mother's for Christmas?"

"Yes. It was never a big thing, even when I was a kid, but Mother believes in observing all the proprieties, and families are supposed to be together for Christmas so that's what we'll do."

"You want to stop by afterward? I made mincemeat pies."

"I'll try, but I'm not promising anything. I'll call and let you know when I find out what Mother has planned."

"Great. Call even if it's late. We can at least have pie and eggnog together."

A wave of frustration and weariness hit her when she got into the Chevy and she sat there for several minutes with her head leaning forward against the wheel, recovering herself. Freezing rain glistened on every visible surface and streetlights made strange patterns as they were reflected at unusual angles. Then the cold began to penetrate and she hastily turned the key and pulled away from the curb.

There was a sudden screech of brakes and something flashed past her. The other vehicle narrowly missed hers as it turned to avoid her, the wheels locking on the icy pavement so that it spun a quarter circle, straddling both lanes. Laura slammed her foot down as well and the Chevy jerked and stalled. There was no movement from the other vehicle, which she now recognized as a station wagon, so she opened the door and got out.

John Dill was sitting behind the wheel, looking stunned. The station wagon's engine was still thrumming. He rolled the window down when Laura took off her gloves and rapped her knuckles against it.

"Mr. Dill, are you all right? I'm so sorry. I should have looked."

"Laura Collier?" He sounded distracted and confused. "Is that you? I heard you were back in town. I should have stopped by to see you but I've been very busy."

He spoke in a monotone and Laura wondered if he'd hit his head, if he was in shock. "Did you hit your head, Mr. Dill? You don't sound too good."

He hesitated, and when he spoke again his voice was almost normal. "No, I'm fine. Just a bit shaken is all. Are you all right?"

"Yes I am. Is there anything I can do?"

"No, we're fine. No harm done. I was very sorry to hear about your husband, Miss Collier. It must have been a terrible time for you."

"Yes, it was. And I was very sorry to hear about your troubles, Mr. Dill."

"My troubles? Oh, you mean Colleen. They think she left me, you know." His speech was slurred and the possibility of a concussion occurred to her until she leaned slightly forward and smelled the alcohol. "It's not true. Colleen and I loved each other. I don't know what happened and I don't know where she is, but I know she didn't leave me."

Dill sounded as though he was on the verge of tears and Laura felt more uncomfortable than ever. "We need to stop blocking the street, Mr. Dill, before someone else comes this way."

He glanced back toward her car. "If you could back up a little bit, I think I can manage."

"Sure. Give me a second." She started to run back to the Chevy, but the footing was too uncertain. Once behind the wheel, she was relieved to find that the engine started smoothly; she was afraid it might have flooded. As soon as she reversed back into her parking space, Dill backed around to face in the direction he'd originally been traveling. Laura opened her door, intending to speak to him again, but he switched gears and drove off immediately, leaving her with one foot inside and one out.

"Now that was strange," she told herself.

The strangeness didn't end there. Her route back to Main Street took her past the Catterall house. The road conditions forced her to keep her speed down and she had plenty of time to recognize the aging, badly maintained Buick in Catterall's driveway. It belonged to Bud Wiegand. It was entirely possible that Wiegand was one of Ted Catterall's clients, since there was only one other attorney practicing in Dorrance, but why in the world would he need to see his lawyer at home late on a Friday night in bad weather?

The freezing rain increased in intensity while Laura was still on the road. The ice coated her windshield as fast as her struggling defroster could melt it, and she was reduced to a crawl. Main Street had been freshly sanded, but she was only on it for a couple of blocks before she turned onto Moon Pond Road, and that hadn't been touched yet. As careful as she was, she lost control briefly three times before reaching her turn off, and she made a mental note to have Ed Burgess replace her tires. They hadn't been new when she'd left Vermont, and they were probably balding after all the driving she'd done since.

She parked under a tree, hoping for some shelter, but she knew the Chevy would be encased in ice by morning. Well, she didn't have to be anywhere. She locked the car, then picked her way across the uncertain ground to the door. The lock was stiff with the cold and coated with ice, and for an awful few seconds she thought she might not be able to get it open, but then it clicked and she pushed the door inward.

The first thing that struck her as wrong was that the cabin was far too warm. The woodstove had been nice and toasty when she left for the Trading Post, but it should have cooled down by now. The cabin wasn't well insulated and cooled quickly, and she had decided not to leave the electric space heaters running when she wasn't home. Puzzled, she removed her gloves and dropped them on a chair, rubbing her hands together as she approached the stove.

The fire was strong and hot. Someone had put new wood on it since she'd left.

Laura retreated a step, then glanced toward the corner where she kept her rifle. It was still there, apparently untouched, although she couldn't be certain of that. Then her eyes flicked across the room to the window Ed Burgess had replaced, but it was intact. Another half turn and she was staring at the porch door. It was closed, but even in the dim light she could see that something was wrong with the lock.

The hasp was hanging down rather than horizontal. Someone had forced the door.

From where she was standing she could see the entire interior of the cabin, with two exceptions, and not counting the closets, which were too small to conceal anything other than a very small child. The bathroom was behind her and to the right, the door closed. Her sleeping area was ahead and to the left, hidden by the spare blanket she'd hung from the ceiling to give her some additional privacy and deflect the drafts.

If someone was hiding in either place, they knew she was out here. Laura slowly stepped to the side until she could reach the rifle, scooped it up, broke it open. It was loaded, just as she had left it. Feeling slightly more comfortable, she backed along the wall, then moved quickly to the bathroom door. It opened inward until it hit the sink, and the only space beyond was the shower stall. Taking a deep breath, and with the rifle held ready to use as a club, she turned the knob and pushed the door quickly open, her heart racing and her breath a heavy staccato.

Nothing was out of place. She glanced at the mirror, but nothing had been written there.

She started toward her bedroom, eyes sweeping quickly back and forth. Nothing else in the cabin seemed out of place or missing. Someone had broken in and they must have had a reason, but what? She had nothing here worth stealing.

Laura paused a few steps from the hanging blanket. Just beyond it was the set of bunk beds, a small carpenter's table, a plain wooden chair, and a space heater. She could see the space heater and the foot of the bed around the corner of the blanket. As with the rest of the cabin, nothing seemed amiss. She felt a strange reluctance to move forward, and then impatience with herself for prolonging the moment. Before she had time to vacillate any further, she reached out, grasped the corner of the blanket, and pulled it to the side.

Her bed was empty and neatly made up, just the way she had left it. On the table sat a reading lamp, turned off at the moment, the paperback she was currently reading, a box of salted nuts, and a hair brush. To the right of the table was the wooden chair.

And sitting in the wooden chair was the half frozen body of Ashley Sothern.

For the first time in her life, Laura Collier fainted.

It took the local police a long time to respond to her call. The ice storm had continued to intensify and Moon Pond Road was like a skating rink. Laura sat huddled by the stove with her back to the bedroom while she waited, shivering despite the heat, her thoughts as frozen as the trees outside her windows. Dan Sievert was the first to arrive, and he had to call her name and knock repeatedly before she roused herself to let him in. He took one look at the body without approaching, then let the blanket fall back.

"Are you all right?"

Laura wanted to cry, to scream, in fact, but her mouth and eyes were equally dry. "No, I'm not all right," she said at last. "I'll never be all right."

He put his hands on her shoulders and guided her back to her chair. "Just sit here by the fire for the time being. I'd offer to make coffee but I'm not sure we should touch anything."

Another patrol car showed up fifteen minutes later. One of the officers tried to take a statement but Dan waved him off. "Give her a few minutes."

It was two hours before the state police arrived, two cars, in one of which rode Detective Hopper. He took Laura's statement personally after examining the body.

"May I assume that you've had no further communications from Miss Sothern since the one we know about?"

She shook her head. "No, nothing."

"We'll have an ambulance here soon for the body, but my people will need to go over everything here pretty carefully. Do you have someplace else you could stay tonight, and possibly tomorrow night as well?"

"Yes, I can stay at my mother's house."

"That's right. I'd forgotten you're from Rustin Farm. In view of everything that's happened, maybe it would be best if you moved back there more or less permanently. Someone doesn't like you or your friends very much, Miss Collier, and you'd probably be safer if you weren't living alone, at least until we get this all sorted out."

"This is my home, Detective," she said quietly. "But I'll get out of your way for a couple of days."

"It might be better if you didn't drive yourself."

Dan had been standing nearby and he stepped forward. "I'll see that she gets there safely."

Hopper didn't even glance in his direction. "The sooner the better, Officer."

"I need to call first, let my mother know we're coming." Laura fumbled for her purse and found the cell phone.

Hopper turned to talk to one of the technicians while she made the call. Unlike Laura, her mother was a light sleeper, always woke instantly alert, and this was no exception. "Mother, I need to come to the farm for the night. There's been another incident. I'll be there in just a few minutes."

"All right. I'll make tea."

Dan refused the offer of tea and left Laura at the door. "I need to get back. Try to get some sleep and I'll call you later and let you know what we've found out. Or at least as much as I'm allowed to say," he added apologetically.

"Thanks, Dan." She closed the door behind him.

Her mother's expression was a blend of concern and curiosity. "I'm not sure it's a good thing to be on a first-name basis with the local police, except socially, of course. Now what's happened?"

Laura told her, using short, blunt sentences. It still didn't seem real to her and her emotions were still locked away just as they had been in the hours immediately following Sean's attempt to kill her and the struggle that had claimed his life instead. Mary Collier looked surprised, shocked, and concerned in rapid succession, and gave her brandy from a bottle that had probably first been opened by her father. Laura managed to drink only a little before she pleaded exhaustion and went up to bed, and the pillow was damp with tears moments after her head touched it.

Dan stopped by shortly before lunch. Laura had only been up for an hour, was dressed in an old pair of jeans she'd found in the back of her bedroom closet and one of her mother's thick sweaters. She invited him inside, and he accepted but insisted he could only stay for a moment.

"How are you feeling?"

Laura shrugged. "How do you think? But I'm okay, or I'll be okay. What happened to her, Dan?"

He twisted uncomfortably. "There's some stuff I'm not supposed to tell anyone, you understand, and there's a lot we don't know yet, anyway. She's been dead for a while, but we won't know how long until the medical examiner gets done with her. And maybe not then, either. When a body is frozen like that, it's hard to tell just how much time has passed."

"How was she killed?"

"We don't know the cause of death yet." He wouldn't meet her eyes. "Not for sure. There was no evidence of a gunshot, no blood, nothing like that. I'm not a detective, Laura, but I listened while the state techs were talking. There were no obvious signs of a struggle, but there was some damage to the back of her head. Too soon to know if that was what killed her."

"Why was she in my cabin?" She meant the question rhetorically but he answered it anyway.

"We don't know that, either, but given everything else that's happened, it's not too surprising. Look, Laura, someone is trying to make you think Sean is still alive. That's pretty obvious, even if we didn't have the notes. The reason for all this is there somewhere, someone who knew him and maybe blames you for his death."

"There's no one, Dan. Sean was all alone when he came to Dorrance. He didn't make friends when we got to Vermont, at first because we were newlyweds, and then I guess because of his sickness." She paused, remembering something that had seemed wrong. "What did you mean when you said 'notes'? There was only one note."

If he'd looked uncomfortable before, he looked agonized now. "Damn it, I knew I was going to let that slip. I'm sorry, Laura. I really can't talk about it."

She stepped forward, so close that she could feel his breath on her face. "You have to tell me, Dan. I have to know what's happening."

He hesitated and cleared his throat, but he didn't retreat and she knew she had him. She waited, and he dropped his eyes. "I can't tell you the details. Please don't ask me to. But there was a typewritten note pinned to her shoulder. It was addressed to you and it was signed 'Sean Brennan.' That's all I can say and I shouldn't have said anything at all."

Laura actually felt almost relieved. In a way, it was what she had expected, and now that she knew, she felt calmer and her voice was almost normal. "Thank you, Dan. I appreciate that. I won't tell anyone, I promise."

"Well, okay. If there's nothing else, I really need to get back to the station and sign out for the night. Is there anything else you need?"

"No, I'm fine." But she wasn't.

CHAPTER FIFTEEN

Oddly enough, Laura slept well when she finally went to bed, and if she dreamed, the images were innocuous and she couldn't remember them when she got up early in the afternoon. She did feel disoriented and took a long bath, scrubbing her skin until it was red and sore in spots. When she got back to her room, some of her clothing was lying on the bed. She put it on and went downstairs, found her mother sitting in the kitchen.

"Where did these come from? You didn't go to the cabin, did you?"

"Your dashing young policeman dropped them off. Apparently he rescued them from the state police just as they were about to be tagged and dusted. Tea?"

"Yes, please." She slid into a seat opposite her mother. "That was nice of him."

"He seems a polite young man. Not particularly ambitious, though. I understand he left a job with the Rochester Police to come here. Not the wisest career decision he could have made."

"Not everyone feels the urge to compete." She brought herself up short. "I can't believe we're talking about this, Mother. Ashley's dead." Her voice trembled.

"I know that, Laura. But I'm more interested in you just now. This shock, coming after everything you've gone through, well, it must be terrible. I don't know whether it's better to try to keep your mind off it or to bring it out in the open and deal with it."

"I'll be fine. I'm stronger than you think." Laura tried to smile but failed. "Maybe I have more Rustin blood in me than I thought."

She drank down her tea quickly and nodded when Mary offered a refill, wishing that it was coffee instead.

"Officer Sievert didn't know how soon you'd be able to reclaim the rest of your clothing and personal items. If there's anything you need, I can pick it up in town for you when I go to the bank later."

"Has it been on the news?"

"The radio? Yes, it has, but they're not saying much, just that she was found dead in the vicinity of Moon Pond and that the cause of death is unknown."

"I should call her parents."

"Yes, but not now. Tomorrow will be soon enough."

"Mother, who could be doing this? Ashley was a flake but she never hurt anyone."

"I know that, dear. I think she was just in the wrong place at the wrong time. Someone is trying to hurt us, either you directly, or indirectly to get to me."

"But why?" Laura was on the verge of tears, struggled to hold them back. "What did either of us do that was so horrible that Ashley deserved to die?"

"I don't have any idea, Laura. Nowadays it seems like reasons don't have the same importance they used to. Maybe someone doesn't like the way you drive, or resented something you said in high school. Maybe one of the farmhands I've fired over the years has decided he was treated badly. The Rustins have made a lot of enemies in their time." She leaned forward and her eyes were intense. "But we've always gotten the best of them in the past and they won't beat us this time, either."

Dan Sievert stopped by later in the day. He was driving a brown Ford and wearing civilian clothing.

"Hi. How are you feeling?"

Laura had answered the door and invited him inside. "A little rocky but I'll survive. Thanks for bringing by the clothing."

"No problem."

He accepted the offer of a cup of coffee from the pot Laura had made the moment her mother had left on an errand. They were sitting in the living room when the Jeep pulled into the yard and Mary came into the house, carrying a small bag of groceries.

"And how is your investigation going, young man? And do sit back down, please, you're making me nervous."

Dan sat, but he didn't look nearly as comfortable as he had a moment before. "I was just telling your daughter that they found four sets of recent prints in the cabin. Laura's were the most common, of course, and I had touched a few things. We're pretty sure the third set is yours, Mrs. Collier. If you don't mind, we're going to send someone out to take impressions to confirm that."

"Of course, anything to help. You said four sets. Who's the fourth?"

Dan shifted in obvious discomfort and let his eyes drop. "We found a match right away. According to the state police, those prints were made by Sean Brennan."

"That's impossible! He's dead, I tell you!" Laura was suddenly standing, almost shouting the words, and Dan stood as well.

Mary grabbed her daughter by the arm and gently pushed her back down into the chair. "Of course he is, Laura. This is some kind of mistake. They must be old prints from before. Sean is dead and gone and he's not coming back."

Laura fought for control. "I never took Sean out to the cabin. I don't understand what's happening and I don't know how to act or react."

Dan looked more uncomfortable than ever. "They'll be done with your place late this afternoon, but I think you should stay here with your mother, at least for a while. Or better yet, get out of Dorrance and don't tell anyone except the police where you're going. Take a vacation."

She thought about it, wavering, but her anger was greater than her terror. "No, Dan, I'm not going to do that. I've spent the last year running away from a dead man, and I'm not going to do it anymore. Whoever is doing this will just follow me or wait for me to come back. And I won't be run out of my own home! I won't let someone ruin it for me!"

Dan and her mother exchanged glances as Laura struggled to calm herself. When she felt confident she could control her voice, she apologized for the outburst. "I know you can't say much about the investigation, Dan, but are they going to find the killer?"

He nodded, but it seemed more through choice than conviction. "Hopper's thorough and has a good reputation. He'll figure this out eventually. We'll just have to be patient."

Laura nodded, reading the uncertainty that lay behind the words.

"I really should go." Dan got to his feet.

Laura stood up slowly. "Thank you for coming by to tell me all this, Dan. I appreciate it." She followed him to the door, her feet moving mechanically.

He turned and took a small piece of paper from his pocket and handed it to her.

"What's this?"

"It's my phone number. My home phone number. Just in case you need something unofficially." He fidgeted awkwardly and wouldn't meet her eyes. "I'm really sorry about your friend, Laura. I'd like to help."

She put the paper in her pocket without looking at it.

"Thanks, Dan. Find out who did it, will you? That'll help more than anything else."

He nodded and then he was gone.

"Seems like a very nice young man."

Laura was still standing at the door, turned to see her mother watching from the other room. "Yes, he is. Can you drive me over to the cabin this evening?"

"If necessary. But if there's anything you need, we could pick it up in town just as easily."

"What I need is to go home, Mother. I can just imagine the mess that's waiting for me."

Mary's eyes widened. "You can't seriously be planning to go back there, Laura. Not after everything that's happened. I can send Del over tomorrow to pack up all your things and bring them back here. We'll lock the place up and try to forget everything that's happened."

Laura shook her head and her voice was firm and even again. "No, that's not what we're going to do. I meant what I said. I'm not running anymore. I'm tired and angry and it doesn't do any good anyway. Whoever is coming, whatever is coming, I'm going to turn and face it. And I'm going to fight on ground of my choosing."

Mary opened her mouth again, then closed it without speaking. There was a long silence before she finally nodded her head resignedly. "All right. I'll take you over after supper. I suppose I should have realized you'd inherited my stubborn streak. Your father always used to say I was the last of my line. That's one more thing he was wrong about."

"No, he wasn't," Laura contradicted. "You are the last of your line, Mother. But I'm the first of mine."

Ashley Sothern's murder replaced Christmas as the main topic of conversation in Dorrance that year. Laura went to see Ashley's parents who both seemed to be walking around in a daze, and she left with the impression that Mr. Sothern felt that she was responsible for the death of his daughter. Kathy called and they met at Foster's, and it was Kathy who cried. Laura had only wept for her friend one time; while cleaning up, she had found the sweater that was supposed to have been Ashley's Christmas present.

Kathy's trip to Boston was still on schedule. "Please come along, Laura. At least for a few days. You need to get away from this place."

"No, that's exactly what I don't need. I'm real good at getting away; it's time to learn to stay put."

She spent Christmas day at the farm. Her mother's tree was small and there were only token presents under it, but Laura hadn't been feeling much holiday spirit and her mother had never been particularly sentimental. It was one of the few times in their lives when their moods seemed to coincide.

On the first Saturday after Christmas, Dan Sievert called Laura and asked her out to dinner. It was low key and barely qualified as a date, but it felt good. They talked about trivial subjects, never mentioning Ashley's death or the ongoing investigation. Dan regaled her with tales of his childhood; he'd actually been a bit of a hellion. "After my adopted father died, the police and I had an adversarial relationship for a long time, but I was lucky. The local beat cop was patient and convincing. He got me to straighten myself out and I guess he's the reason I ended up becoming a cop myself."

"Any luck identifying your parents?"

"Not really. I eliminated a couple more names last week but that's about the extent of it. People around here don't open up much to outsiders, or hadn't you noticed?"

"You should let me see your list of possibilities some time. I don't know if I can tell you anything useful, but this is one local who's perfectly willing to spill the Dorrance beans."

"Maybe I'll do that."

It wasn't a particularly romantic evening, but it was companionable and reassuringly normal. Laura managed to pass three hours without thinking about Ashley or Sean, and when he dropped her off at the cabin, she felt revived and optimistic even though he'd declined her invitation to come in.

"I have to go on duty in less than an hour. Just barely enough time for a shower and a change of clothes and the ride down to the station. I'll take a raincheck, though."

"Stop by later tonight. I'll be up late."

"Maybe. Good night." But he didn't come by, and she fell asleep sitting in the chair beside the woodstove.

She drove by the farm early the following morning. The Jeep was gone and she was turning around to leave when she saw it coming up McAlester.

"Well, this is a surprise. To what do I owe this honor?"

"Boredom, mostly. And I wanted to test your memory."

"About what?"

"Do you remember anything about someone local putting their baby up for adoption? It would have been about two years before you had me."

They were in the kitchen again, her mother already putting on the inevitable pot of hot water for tea, and for a few seconds Laura thought she hadn't heard the question. "I assume we're talking out of wedlock?"

"Not necessarily."

"Is there a reason why you're so interested?"

"I just heard a rumor is all and I got curious. Come on, Mother. You've always had a good ear for the local gossip."

"Well, there were stories about Gloria Chadwick and her parents did send her away for one summer, but I always thought it had more to do with her fondness for shoplifting than anything else. She didn't even have a boyfriend that I know of at the time." She hesitated. "And it's more likely you're talking about Janet Post."

"Janet Post? Any relation to Pete and Edie?"

"Their daughter."

"The one who died?"

"Yes, about a month before you were born. Janet was a strange child, and we all knew there was something wrong with her long before the trouble started. Sometimes she'd fly into a rage for no apparent reason, screaming at people, sometimes throwing things. She was suspended from school almost as much as she attended. Nowadays they'd have put her on tranquilizers, of course, but in those days we all pretended that nothing was wrong. By high school she had a reputation, if you know what I mean, and her luck ran out during our junior year."

"Pregnant?"

Her mother nodded. "She dropped out of school and had the baby and people wondered if that would settle her down. Instead, it made her worse. She was arrested one night breaking windows on Main Street, and a few days later she assaulted one of the neighbors with a rake. Pete and Edie got worried that she'd do something to the child, and they talked to Doctor Werner—he died back when you were an infant—and Werner convinced them that Janet needed professional care. Edie's own mother died in an institution, you know. Bad blood might hide for a generation but it always shows up eventually."

"So they put the baby up for adoption?"

"That's how I remember it. Janet was sent to someplace near Shawcut, but she only lasted about a year. She picked a fight with another patient, inmate, whatever you call them, and he broke her neck before the attendants could intervene."

"Do you suppose Pete and Edie know what happened to the baby?"

"I'd be surprised if they didn't, but Edie died of cancer last year and Pete has Alzheimer's. The state must have records, but I think they keep those things closed to the public."

"Yeah, they do. Thanks."

"Is this important for some reason?"

"No, not to me anyway. I have to go."

Laura drove back to the cabin, wondering if Janet Post was on Dan's list, and whether or not he would welcome the possibility that he was the bastard son of a woman with a history of violent outbursts who had died in a mental institution. Sometimes it was better not to know the truth.

The next time she saw Dan, he was in uniform. He pulled over to the side of the road as she was emptying her mailbox and rolled down the window.

"Good morning!"

"Hi!" She walked over to the patrol car and leaned down. "There's coffee on."

"Not this morning, thanks. I have to go in. We had a little excitement last night. One of the local boys got caught putting something in his date's drink."

"A date rape drug? In Dorrance? Maybe the town has finally left the nineteenth century after all."

"Looks that way. The worst part is that this apparently isn't the first time. Chief Clay has suspected for a while that there's been something shady going on at O'Brien's but he hasn't been able to get the county authorities to sit up and take notice until recently. They had an undercover man in the bar who got suspicious when the little lady took ill and had to be helped out back by two friends so that she could lie down for a while. Ended up with three arrests, a padlocked door, and a very sick young woman."

"Who got arrested?"

"The bartender, Olsen. He's from Nickleby. A local kid named Langston. I don't think I heard the third name."

"Langston? Tommy Langston?"

"Might be. Hope he's not a friend of yours."

"Not even close, but I know him. He killed his girlfriend on Sharp's Curve a while back."

Dan's face changed. "Oh, then I know him, too. Didn't remember the name, but I do remember the face. Comes from money, doesn't he?"

She nodded. "His uncle's a judge. His parents aren't that well off, but Tommy got spoiled by the uncle, who doesn't have any kids of his own. I can't say I'm surprised to hear he's in trouble, although I have to admit, with his looks, I'm surprised he had to resort to drugs."

"Not everyone is a pushover for a pretty face."

"Good point. Hey, when am I going to get to see your list of names?"

"How about over dinner later this week?"

"Great."

Ordinarily, she'd have called Kathy to find out what was going on, but that option was closed to her. So instead she went into town and stopped at Slade's. Edna had heard about the arrests, but didn't know much more than Laura, except that she knew the name of the girl involved. It was Gail Shaw, whom Laura had most recently seen in the company of Mason Cortway.

Her curiosity thoroughly aroused, Laura decided to bite the bullet and drive up to the farm. By now Mary Collier would probably know as much as the police, if not more. Not for the first time Laura wondered how her mother could simultaneously have her finger so firmly pressed on Dorrance's pulse and be so unpopular with her neighbors. Apparently, the drive to gossip was stronger than simple animosity.

Del Huggins came out the front door as she was driving up. He glanced in her direction, his eyes as unfriendly as ever, then turned and walked to his Land Rover without a word. She watched him drive down toward McAlester Road before walking up onto the porch.

Her mother must have been standing at the window because she opened the door the moment Laura reached it. "Come inside, Laura. I assume you know what's happened."

"I'm not sure. What are we talking about?" She followed her mother into the living room where Mary Collier dropped down into a chair, looking older and wearier than Laura could remember.

"The police have arrested Tommy Langston and Mason Cortway."

"Mason? I heard about Tommy and Gail Shaw, but Mason?"

"I know. It doesn't seem possible. He's not a strong person, though, and I suspect the Langston boy talked him into doing something foolish."

"I'd use a rather stronger word to describe rape, Mother."

Mary gestured dismissively with one hand. "Gail's a little tramp. I wouldn't be surprised if she wasn't helping Tommy trick Mason into doing something he shouldn't so that he'd be forced to marry her."

"You've always had a soft spot for Mason, Mother, but I have to tell you, it's one of the few cases I know where you're completely wrong in your judgment of a person. Mason is a worm, and a bad-natured one at that. He never had friends in school and he doesn't have any now. I saw him with Gail just the other night and he treated her like she wasn't even there."

"All the more reason why she'd want to get him into trouble."

Laura rolled her eyes. "All right, forget Mason's sterling character for the moment. Just what happened anyway?"

Laura had to interpolate a bit from her mother's version of the incident, but even she couldn't build a convincing case in defense of Mason. He'd brought Gail to O'Brien's early in the evening. They'd had a few drinks together before Tommy showed up, supposedly by chance, alone, and joined them. No one had actually seen Tommy spike the drink, but the glass was recovered with the residue and more of the drug had been found in a plastic bottle in Tommy's pocket.

Gail had complained of dizziness and nausea and had asked to be taken home. Mason told her to wait a few minutes to see if her stomach settled. Gail had passed out instead. Tommy retrieved a key from the bartender and had helped Mason carry the unconscious girl to the back room, supposedly to rest until she recovered. The undercover police officer had called for backup and confronted the bartender, who had reluctantly produced a duplicate key. Tommy Langston was in the process of removing Gail's clothing when the police opened the door, while Mason stood in the far corner of the room, watching.

"He hadn't actually done anything except watch. He never was a strong boy, you know. Takes after his father."

"His father doesn't have a criminal record that I know of."

"Unfortunately, that's not the worst part of all this."

Laura waited, but her mother remained silent. "All right, you don't have to play up the drama any more. What else happened?"

"Apparently the Langston boy insisted that he was only trying to do a favor for his friend, Mason. You don't have to be a detective to know that was a lie, but Mason wasn't thinking clearly and he must have been led to believe that he was going to end up taking all the blame. So he told the police that Tommy made a regular business out of drugging young women, and that he, Mason that is, only found out about it when he talked to another customer."

Laura waited. "So why is this important?"

"Well, the other customer he named was Del Huggins."

Laura's jaw dropped, and her first instinct was to laugh. But then she thought about it some more, and then even more, and then she gasped. "Oh my god! Joyce Catterall!"

"That would be jumping to conclusions," her mother cautioned. "And Del has just told me that he categorically denied everything when the police questioned him."

But it all seemed to fall into place for Laura. Del was a classic misogynist. His contempt for Laura and her friends had been obvious when she'd lived at the farm, and, if anything, his animosity had grown stronger in recent years. A normal relationship with a woman would not have been possible for Del, but an unconscious, drugged, helpless victim would appeal to him on many levels.

"You'll have to fire him."

"Don't be in such a hurry, young lady. The police haven't charged him and he insists that he's innocent. I won't condemn him because of something Tommy Langston claims but can't prove."

"I thought it was Mason who named Del."

"Yes, it was, but supposedly he was just repeating what Tommy had told him. The police have talked to Del and they haven't arrested him, so there's apparently considerable doubt about his involvement. I just hope he can clear things up quickly. I'd hate to lose him."

"Why, Mother? I know Del works hard and he's good with machinery, but there are half a dozen men in Dorrance who are just as good. The day after he left here, you'd have candidates calling for a chance to come talk to you about the job."

"You're probably right, Laura, but I'm used to Del. He's

been with us for a long time and he understands this farm almost as well as I do. And unlike some, he knows his place. He doesn't always agree with what I tell him to do, but he keeps his mouth shut and does his job. There aren't many who do that nowadays. And frankly, I'm not likely to get anyone near as good for what I pay Del. He never asks for more than I offer to pay, and he never threatens to look for a better position. Del has his faults, Lord knows, but he's very useful to me and to the farm, and I'd really hate to see him go."

Laura thought she might stay for supper, but her mother started to hint that if, in fact, Del left the farm, it would be a good time for Laura to become more involved. "I can't keep up with things anymore. I don't suppose you'd consider helping a little if it came to that?"

Laura sidestepped the questions, avoided admitting that, if anything, her antipathy toward the farm had increased rather than decreased in recent days, and then made an awkward and unconvincing excuse for leaving.

Most Christmas decorations came down more quickly than usual, as though Dorrance was anxious to get the year over with. Laura accepted Dan's invitation to attend a New Year's Eve party at the Trading Post, where she had a very good time and near the end of which she and Dan finally kissed, tentatively the first time, with more confidence later. Kathy sent a postcard from Boston indicating that she was having a great time and urging Laura to come, at least to visit. Tommy Langston jumped bail and left town, and since Gail Shaw was refusing to press charges the police weren't inclined to expend too much effort on a lost cause. Detective Hopper returned in early January and interviewed Laura again, but the tenor of his questions convinced her that he was grasping at straws.

Ashley had been killed by a blow to the back of the head.

Death had probably been instantaneous. Her body had been kept somewhere cold enough that she'd frozen solid, and she'd been dead for at least three days when she was placed in Laura's cabin. She might have died the night she was supposed to meet Laura at Moon Pond, or she might have already been dead when Laura received her note. There were no signs of a struggle, and nothing to indicate where she'd been during the interval between her disappearance and the recovery of her body.

Mason Cortway's partnership with Bud Wiegand became public knowledge during the second week of January because Wiegand had to declare personal bankruptcy. Apparently, in his quest to accumulate even more money he had made some crucial mistakes, including the acquisition of some comparatively worthless property near Moon Pond. Property values on Moon Pond Road actually rose for a few days when rumors of a development project leaked out, then plummeted when it became obvious that the plans were unrealistic, underfunded, and unlikely to attract outside investors. The same realtor who had called to make an offer for Laura's cabin called back a week later to ask if she was interested in buying the property adjacent to hers at a bargain price.

John Dill shocked the town council by announcing that he would not be seeking a renewal of his contract for another two years. "I've done all I can here in Dorrance," read the quote in the local paper. "You need a fresh set of eyes and hands, and I need a new challenge." Mary Collier didn't gloat when she heard the news, but Laura couldn't help noticing how much her mood improved.

Laura's part-time job turned to full time when, as predicted, one of her co-workers gave notice. Most of her work was off the sales floor, but occasionally she filled in at the cash registers. She wasn't tempted to announce that she wanted a career in retail sales or even office work, but it gave shape to her life and made the days pass more quickly. There were times she briefly forgot about Ashley and other times, usually when she was with Dan, when she even managed to forget about Sean.

The weather surprised everyone by being unusually mild; there hadn't been any serious snowfall since before Christmas. It stayed cold, sometimes dropping below zero, but the air was dry and relatively calm. Unfortunately, there was a fresh storm brewing in the Midwest, and an even more violent one developing right in Dorrance.

CHAPTER SIXTEEN

Although Laura wasn't unhappy with her job, she couldn't see herself checking the day's receipts, posting inventory, and placing re-orders for very long. Realistically, if she was going to do something with her life, she either had to give in to her mother's importunities and work at Rustin Farm or leave Dorrance. She had actually spent a good deal of serious thought about the farm before deciding against it. Even if she managed to summon up some minimal interest in the work—a major task in itself—she knew that the future of agriculture in Dorrance was bleak. Several local farms had already closed down, and those that remained were marginal at best. Her mother's savings would probably allow her to continue to work the land, but each year there would be another small drop in their reserves, and sooner or later she'd have to stop the hemorrhaging by ceasing operations and trying to sell the property while it still had some value.

Even worse, in the short term, was that she would be under her mother's thumb again. Mary Collier would not relinquish any serious control over the farm while she was alive. Oh, she'd consult with her daughter over matters and even listen to her when their opinions differed. But in the end, the only changes she'd be allowed to make would be insignificant, concessions designed to fool her into believing she was a partner in the enterprise.

Laura felt uncomfortable whenever she tried to understand

her feelings about her mother and the relationship between them. There was affection, and she supposed there was love, but Mary Collier had always been impatient with sentiment and wary of emotional displays. Laura was certain that this was the root, or one of the roots, of the problem between her parents, but her father's sharpest criticism of his wife had been to sigh and say "you know how your mother feels about that sort of thing." She wondered if he might have stayed with them if her mother had been willing to talk things through, or if he'd been determined enough to force her to listen.

Laura could barely remember her mother during her early childhood. Whenever she had bruised herself or had a question that needed to be answered right away, she always went to her father, or to Betty, the cleaning woman before Alice. She had vague recollections of her mother being in the house, but she had almost seemed like a visitor rather than a resident. That had changed somewhat as she got older. Her mother had taken a more active interest in her, and she had a handful of very pleasant memories—her mother taking her around the farm on a tractor, a shopping trip to Buffalo, a picnic lunch up on the Bluffs.

Then had come her teenaged years. Laura didn't think she'd been any more rebellious than most girls her age, and certainly less so than Ashley, but most of her interactions with her mother—and some with her father as well—had been confrontational and belligerent. Some were the usual things—chafing under curfew rules, a couple of cases of truancy, Mary's objection to some of her boyfriends—but others were more unique to the Collier family. Her mother insisted that she had a duty to the Rustin heritage and to the community at large that required she measure up to higher standards than those of her friends. That meant associating with the right people, getting involved with the student government, and studying subjects that would help in the management of the farm.

She could almost recite her mother's lectures by heart. "The Rustins have been the first family of Dorrance since the town was founded two centuries ago. It's not that we're better than the other people, but we're a symbol of their best hopes, their highest aspirations. They look to us to set an example. I know it seems unfair, but if you want people to respect you, then you have to be respectable."

Mary's interest in her daughter's life might have been considered flattering from some abstract viewpoint. From close up, it was intrusive, obstructive, and maddening. She had personally confronted some of Laura's acquaintances and told them they were inappropriate companions for her daughter, she had vetoed her desire to go to the Junior Prom with Leo Kerner because of his arrest for underaged drinking, and she had torn up a dress Laura had bought with her own money because it was "scandalously revealing."

Mary's attitude was an open, somewhat bitter joke at school, and inevitably some of the resentment had stuck to Laura as well. Only Kathy and Ashley remained close friends among the girls, and most of the boys stopped asking her out, except for Mason Cortway and a couple of other respectable, but deadly dull specimens of whom her mother approved.

Laura had lots of time to think and reflect, and the more she thought about it, the more she was convinced that sooner or later she was going to have to pull up stakes and move on. After all, what was here for her now? Ashley was dead, Kathy was in Boston, her father was hiding somewhere. Only her mother remained, and she and Laura got along better when they were together infrequently. She hadn't made a firm decision yet, but she made an appointment with Ted Catterall to find out what legal problems she'd have if she tried to sell the cabin and move away. Laura also made a mental note to stress discretion about the visit; if her mother caught wind of it, she'd redouble her efforts to lure Laura back to the farm.

The day of her appointment, she drove into town early to cash her paycheck and run a few errands. A crisp wind had picked up and she was walking along the sidewalk with her head down when she almost collided with a figure coming the other way. She backed away, apologizing, and then realized that she was looking at Mason Cortway.

"Mason? Are you all right?"

He looked terrible. His face was pale and his eyes seemed to have receded into his skull. It was obvious that he hadn't shaved that morning, or not completely, anyway. His hair was uncharacteristically long and protruded incoherently from beneath his knit cap. The scarf around his neck was skewed to one side and he was standing with his shoulders hunched defensively.

He blinked at her for a second or two, as though he didn't recognize her. "Laura? Sorry, I didn't see you. I have to go." Mason started past. She almost reached out to grab his arm, but at the last second she snatched her hand back. Their last meeting was still sharp in her memory. If Mason had gotten himself into trouble, then it was his problem. And if he had, in fact, been intending to drug and rape Gail Shaw, then he deserved whatever was coming to him.

Catterall's part-time secretary greeted her when she arrived at the office. "He's going to be a few minutes late, but he should be here any time."

"I hope there's no trouble."

Ann Tabler wasn't quite professional enough to conceal her concern. "He just hasn't been himself since, you know, the accident."

Laura nodded. "Joyce was a wonderful girl. I used to babysit for her."

"If only she hadn't been his only child. And with his wife

gone, too, well, I don't know. He just frets and gets lost in memories and sometimes he loses track of the time. When I called and told him how late it was, he seemed quite surprised." She suddenly seemed to realize that she might have been indiscreet. "Not that his work suffers. Oh no, he's very precise about that. It's the only thing that seems to interest him anymore."

"I'm sure he'll be fine, Mrs. Tabler. He just needs some time to adjust."

The older woman hesitated, then decided she wasn't being disloyal. "I've suggested that he see Doctor Conway, but he insists that he's all right. They say depression can be a disease, you know."

Laura had spent several months taking antidepressants, a fact which she didn't feel tempted to share. "It's perfectly natural for him to be depressed and preoccupied right now."

"I realize that, dear, but I'm worried about him. Sometimes he disappears for hours without telling me where he's going. I've had to reschedule any number of appointments for him. And then he'll drop in on his clients unannounced at the oddest times, or call them in the middle of the night. He woke Mrs. Galway out of a sound sleep last weekend, and he was knocking on Tubby Ryan's door at four in the morning a few days before that. I don't think he's sleeping right, either."

Mrs. Tabler might have been even more indiscreet about her employer if the door hadn't opened at that moment.

"Ah, Miss Collier. I apologize for keeping you waiting. I'm afraid I lost track of the time."

"That's all right. Mrs. Tabler has been keeping me company and actually I only just got here."

"Well, come into my office and have a seat while I get out of this unbearably heavy coat."

Laura watched for any sign that the attorney was losing his

grip, but he was attentive and pleasant while she explained the uncertain nature of her plans and her desire to understand her options.

"Perfectly reasonable. In fact, I probably should have explained all of this earlier. There just doesn't seem to be enough time to get everything done lately. As I told you, I reviewed your aunt's instructions following your first visit. She left quite a bit of leeway and I don't think you'll have any difficulty pursuing whichever course seems best to you. The monies were left in a trust, as you know, for the maintenance of the cottage. I was named as primary administrator. The funds were to be transferred to you once you took up residence on the property, and are theoretically reserved for maintenance and associated expenses for the first year following. There is no requirement, however, that you live in the cabin to preserve your interest, or even retain ownership. Your aunt probably intended for you to remain there, at least for a time, but the phrasing is elastic enough that I think we can safely allow you to do as you wish."

"You said you were the primary administrator. Was there another?"

Catterall looked briefly uncomfortable and his eyes moved away from hers. "Originally, it was your father. After his departure, I appointed Mrs. Tabler in his place."

"Not mother?"

The attorney's face stiffened slightly. "No. In my judgment, she was not likely to honor the wishes of the decedent. If you don't mind my saying so, your mother is rather indifferent to the wishes of those which do not coincide with her own."

Although it was the truth, Laura found herself being somewhat defensive. "Mother has strong opinions, Mr. Catterall, but she always acts honorably as she sees it."

"That might well be true, but she does have a certain

insensitivity to the feelings of others, and her determination to have her way sometimes leads her to run roughshod over their desires."

Catterall's voice had risen slightly and Laura fought to control her own temper. "She's a proud woman, and sometimes she can be overbearing, but I don't think she's ever deliberately hurt anyone or treated them unfairly."

There was an awkward pause, and then the lawyer seemed to relax, or perhaps collapse back into himself. "I don't mean to be offensive, Miss Collier. I wasn't implying that your mother was malicious, just insensitive. She doesn't know what it feels like to have lost an only child. I do. I envy her that ignorance, particularly since it's one I might have shared if she'd agreed to let the town fix that deathtrap two years ago."

"Sharp's Curve."

"Yes," he nodded again, but now all the life seemed to have gone out of him.

Laura made her escape a few minutes later, vowing to complete any further business with Ted Catterall by telephone or mail.

Laura was eating lunch in her cabin two days later when the cell phone rang. The woman on the other end of the line introduced herself as Nurse Cameron. "I work at the clinic here in town. Doctor Conway asked me to give you a call and ask you to come down right away. Your mother's been in an accident."

"An accident? Is she all right?"

"Oh yes, she'll be fine. Some bumps and bruises and a couple of stitches, but nothing serious. But she can't go home for a while yet and she's been asking for you."

"I'll be right there."

The clinic was on the north side of town, almost completely

hidden by a row of spruce trees. Laura navigated the winding driveway and parked in the small lot, then half ran to the entrance. The receptionist in the lobby gave her directions and she found her mother with little difficulty, sitting propped up in a bed in a private room.

"Oh, there you are, Laura. Be a good girl and go find Dr. Conway and tell him to have my clothes returned immediately. I'm quite all right."

"You don't look all right." Mary Collier had a bandage over one ear, an ugly scrape on one cheek, a swollen lip, and the fingers of her left hand were wrapped in gauze. "What happened?"

"Nothing to be alarmed about. The brakes slipped on the Jeep while I was coming down to town and I went into a ditch. I banged my head and apparently broke a finger, but that was the worst damage."

"You might have been killed!"

"Oh, don't be so melodramatic. On McAlester Road? The biggest drop off is only six feet and I managed to avoid that one."

"I don't understand. How could the brakes fail? I thought Del went over the Jeep regularly."

"Of course he does. It was just an accident. We'll have him look at it as soon as I get home." She glanced meaningfully toward the door. "Which will be much sooner if you could rescue my clothing from wherever they've hidden it."

Laura was spared commenting by the sudden appearance of Nathan Clay in that very doorway. He was holding his hat in his hand, but he stepped in without invitation.

"I'm afraid one of my officers already took the liberty of asking Ed Burgess to tow your vehicle out of the ditch, Mrs. Collier."

Laura saw her mother's face tighten slightly and heard a very subtle change in her voice. Mary Collier did not approve of Nathan Clay as Chief of Police. She considered him an amateur and a busybody and, even worse, he wasn't the candidate she had supported. "Well, I suppose that's just as well. I'm sure it needs some body work. I hit the embankment pretty hard."

"Yes, Ma'am, you did. And that's what I need to talk to you about."

"What? Are you going to give me a ticket on top of everything else? It was some kind of mechanical failure, young man. I wasn't drinking or speeding or doing anything I wasn't supposed to be doing."

"No, of course not." Clay was rapidly losing his professional aplomb. "I just got off the phone with Ed Burgess, Mrs. Collier. He tells me that this is the first time he's looked at your Jeep."

"That's right. Del Huggins takes care of all of my vehicles for me. He's very good with machinery."

"Would anyone else have had access to your vehicle during the past day or two?"

Mary's eyes narrowed and Laura caught her breath, realizing what he was implying. "What are you trying to tell me, Nathan Clay? Stop beating around the bush."

He sighed in exasperation. "Your brake lines were cut, Mrs. Collier. Ed Burgess spotted it right after he brought your Jeep in and put it on the lift. It looks to me like someone tried to kill you."

There was a brief, uncomfortable silence. "Piffle." Mary's face expressed disbelief rather than fear. "I'm not sure if I could have killed myself on McAlester Road if I tried. Are you sure it wasn't just a mechanical failure of some kind? Ed Burgess doesn't lead a secret life as a detective, does he?"

"No, but he's a first-rate mechanic and if he says your brakes were tampered with, then I believe him."

"Well, then someone played a prank, a dangerous prank

admittedly, but nothing worse than that. There are far easier and more certain ways to kill me if that's what they wanted."

"That's as may be, but given our recent history," he glanced involuntarily toward Laura, "we have to take matters of this type very seriously. Do you know if there's anyone in town who might have a grudge against you?"

Mary laughed, and Laura almost joined her. "Certainly there are. And your name would be pretty close to the top of the list, wouldn't it?"

Clay frowned and colored and his face wasn't quite as steady when he answered. "I've never held it against you that you were opposed to my getting this job, Mrs. Collier."

"Oh, of course you have. You wouldn't be human if you hadn't. There's nothing wrong with feeling that way. I resent you a bit for getting the job, so we're even. But you've lived here most of your life; you know how this town works. There are enough smoldering resentments and old feuds to provide motives for a shelf full of murder mysteries. Yes, there are people in Dorrance who wouldn't shed a tear at my funeral. You can probably name the best candidates as well as I can. John Dill, Bryant Wiegand, Ted Catterall, Lucy Dumars, Edna Slade." Laura blinked when she heard that last name but didn't say anything. "But I can't see any of them climbing under my Jeep to cut the brake lines."

"Well, someone did just that. I'm going to ask you to take some extra precautions until we get this cleared up. Whoever is responsible might just want to take another stab at it." He put his hat on. "I'll send someone up to the farm later today to take a statement if you think you'll be up to it."

"I'll be fine once they give me back my clothes."

"Then I'll be saying good day to you. Both," he added belatedly and left.

"Don't worry, Mother. They'll catch whoever's responsible."

Mary made an impatient sound. "Double piffle! Nathan Clay wouldn't be able to catch the culprit if he had a videotape of the crime. Now would you please go find my clothes for me?"

"All right." She was halfway to the door when she paused and looked back. "Mother, why would Edna Slade want you dead? She hardly knows you."

Mary drew a deep breath and rolled her eyes. "I guess we never got around to telling you that. When I first met your father, he was engaged to my best friend, Edna Willoughby." Laura looked blank, then her eyes widened. "Right. Edna Willoughby is now Edna Slade. We haven't spoken since the day your father broke off their engagement."

Laura didn't find either Doctor Conway or her mother's truant clothing right away, but she did run into Chief Clay and Officer Enfield talking quietly in the lobby. She couldn't resist the temptation to eavesdrop when she realized that they were unaware of her presence.

"So you want me to bring Huggins in for questioning?"

"Yes, I think so. In view of the other things we suspect about him, he seems the most likely candidate at the moment. He's good with his hands and obviously had the opportunity, and he's not bright enough to realize how obviously it would point to him."

"All right. I'll drive out there right now. I have to tell you, though, Chief, that it doesn't feel right to me. Del may not be too educated but he's as careful a man as I've ever known. He would've covered his tracks better and he would have made sure that whatever he did worked."

"Might have been better if he had. Then the town would have been rid of two troublemakers."

Laura gasped and the two policemen whirled toward her, Enfield startled, Clay shocked. "Miss Collier! I didn't know you were there."

"That's pretty obvious. My mother isn't always the most temperate person in the world, Chief Clay, but I've never once heard her wish someone dead." She turned pointedly to Enfield. "Would you happen to know where Doctor Conway is?"

Clay opened his mouth but didn't say anything. Enfield nodded toward the emergency admitting room. "I think he went in there."

"Thank you, Officer." She walked past them without giving Clay another look.

Doctor Conway assured her that there was nothing seriously wrong with her mother. "She's probably more shook up than she's letting on, but there's no reason why she can't go home. I held her here for a while because of that bump on the head, but I don't think she's concussed. Tell one of the nurses I said it was all right and they'll get her clothes for you. But make sure she takes it easy for the next day or two, and if she gets unusually bad headaches or seems sleepier than usual, call me right away. I offered to give her a prescription for a painkiller but she wouldn't take it."

"Mother doesn't like drugs, particularly painkillers. She says pain is a natural thing, that it keeps you in touch with your body and warns you when something's wrong."

"Well, she's right enough about that, but once the alarm has gone off, there's no reason to let it keep on ringing. But I know your mother. If she changes her mind, call me and I'll fix her up."

"I'll do that. Thanks, Doctor Conway."

Back in the room, she decided not to repeat Clay's comments, but she did mention that the police suspected Del Huggins.

"Why in the world would they think that? If he killed me,

he'd be out of a job."

"Probably because he had the opportunity and he'd certainly know how to do it."

"The Jeep sits outside all night unless it snows hard enough that we put it in the barn. Anybody in town could have sneaked up there in the dark. And half the town knows enough about automobiles to cut a brake line. Damnation, Laura, even I could manage it."

"Right now, let's just manage to get you home."

Although her mother was alert and talkative during the drive home, shortly after arriving she complained of dizziness and took to her bed, asking for tea and light toast. Laura was almost certain it was an act, and got confirmation when she brought a tray up to the bedroom.

"Maybe it would be best if you stayed here tonight, Laura. I'm feeling light-headed and it probably wouldn't be a good idea for me to be alone right now."

Although Laura was absolutely certain this was an act designed to lure her back to the farm, at least on an interim basis, she decided not to argue the point. One night wouldn't make any difference. "All right. I'll just run home for a few minutes to pick up a couple of things."

"Thank you, dear."

Her mother was asleep, or pretending sleep, when Laura returned, but she came downstairs early in the evening, looking as determined and alert as ever. She supervised while Laura made supper, stir fried chicken and potatoes, and they were halfway through the meal when the cell phone rang again.

Laura gave her mother an apologetic look before answering. "Hello?"

"Hi! Where are you?"

"Oh, my God, I completely forgot!" It was Dan's day off and they were supposed to be going out for dinner. "I'm at my mother's place."

"Yeah, I kind of figured that. I stopped by the station and they told me about the accident. How is she?"

Laura glanced across the table at her mother, who wasn't exactly glowering but who clearly still disliked having meals interrupted. "She's fine and she thanks you for asking. Listen, I'm really sorry about missing our date. Why don't you stop by and have supper with us?"

"I don't know if I should . . ."

"It's perfectly all right. Mother doesn't bite. Not hard, anyway. And thanks to the accident, she's even had her shots."

"Well, if you're sure I'm not intruding."

"No, not at all. We have plenty of food and we're tired of talking to each other."

Laura put two more pieces of chicken in the pan and cut up some potatoes, ignoring her mother's sudden and meaningful silence. For a change, she won the test of wills and it was Mary who spoke first.

"You're not getting serious about this boy, are you?"

"He's not a boy; he's a man. A policeman. And no, we're not particularly serious. At least not yet." She couldn't resist the final tease.

"Policemen's wives have a notoriously difficult time, you know."

"Yes, Mother. I do watch television, you know, or at least I did when I had a television to watch."

"You're welcome to come over here whenever you want. My television hardly ever gets used."

"That's because you don't have cable." Laura decided to change the subject. "Just between you and me, Mother, who do you really think sabotaged your car?"

The answer was a while in coming. "I really have no idea, Laura. After all, there really are an awful lot of candidates, aren't there?"

Dan arrived after about fifteen minutes. He was clearly uneasy but relaxed slightly after he'd asked after Mary's injuries and she'd replied politely. Laura had reheated her own half-eaten chicken and ate along with Dan, although her mother was clearly finished. There was an awkward silence at first, then Laura made an offhand reference to the accident.

"Dick Enfield says you already know it wasn't really an accident."

"Chief Clay has a flair for the dramatic," said Mary drily, but it was a halfhearted effort.

"Apparently, Del Huggins, Mother's foreman, is the top suspect," added Laura.

Dan shook his head and looked uncomfortable. "Not anymore. Ordinarily, I wouldn't tell you this, but half the town probably knows already. Your mailman practically made a public announcement down at Slade's that he saw someone standing in your yard early this morning, Mrs. Collier. He said this person was standing out front, and that he walked over to your Jeep just as the mail truck drove away."

"That would be Scott Chadwick," said Mary. "He always did like looking in on other people's business."

"Who was it?" asked Laura, considering this a much more urgent issue than Scott Chadwick's nosiness. "Who was here?"

Dan hesitated again before answering. "We don't have any confirmation yet, but he says it was John Dill."

CHAPTER SEVENTEEN

Dan couldn't tell them anything further and it was late the next afternoon before Laura finally heard the details about John Dill's visit to the farm. She spent the night in her old room, and woke to find her mother up and about with breakfast already cooking and Del Huggins, morose as ever, just leaving by way of the back door. Mary's bruises had darkened and she actually looked a bit worse physically, but her demeanor proclaimed that she wasn't about to let a little discomfort disrupt her routine.

Laura played satellite for a while, sitting near at hand while her mother posted a handful of invoices to her ledger. It was all handwritten, of course. She still thought computers were "toys for boys." Eventually Laura escaped, insisting she had some errands to run, and she did, in fact, stop at the bank and the drugstore, then returned to her cabin, put things away, and confirmed that nothing was amiss. She had already decided not to spend a second night at the farm, but she would return for supper as agreed, in an effort to maintain their fragile truce.

Her mother was quiet but unusually animated when she returned, which meant she had learned something juicy and was waiting for the right moment to reveal it. Laura knew better than to try to provoke her into speaking before she was ready, so she made small talk while helping set the table, in the dining room this time. They were dishing out when her mother finally overflowed.

"Would you believe it? John Dill admitted right away that he was prowling around the house yesterday morning."

"If he was seen, there would hardly be any point to his lying."

"Perhaps not, but his story certainly sounds unlikely. He apparently told the police that he drove up to make peace with me."

Laura's eyebrows lifted. "That doesn't sound like John Dill."

"No, it doesn't, but he has been acting very differently since his wife left him. I wonder sometimes how much of his posturing was a show for her benefit, and now that his audience has left the theater, he doesn't have any reason to go on. I always thought there was a weak and rather shallow man hiding behind all that bluster. Anyway, he claims to have been here for about half an hour, most of that time walking back and forth outside trying to make up his mind whether or not to ring the bell."

"Wouldn't you have seen him coming up McAlester? You've always had a kind of sixth sense about visitors."

"Actually, I spent about an hour in the cellar yesterday morning. It was overdue for a reorganization and cleaning and I decided to stop putting it off. Dill said he eventually did ring, but when no one answered, he assumed I was out. I'm not sure I would have heard the doorbell, so he might be telling the truth."

"Did he say anything about the Jeep?"

"He told the police he didn't remember going anywhere near it, but Chadwick insists he was right beside it."

"Do you think he did it, Mother? God knows he dislikes you, but would it be enough for him to try to hurt you?"

Mary thought for a second or two, then shook her head. "No, Laura, I don't think he sabotaged the Jeep. At his worst, he can be insulting, vindictive, and sneaky. But John Dill is at heart a coward. The chance that his precious reputation might be damaged would discourage him from taking that kind of risk. No, for a change I think he's telling the truth. Now that he's announced his intention to resign at the end of his term, I imagine he's just trying to clear up loose ends. I wouldn't be surprised if he asked me for a letter of recommendation."

"Then someone else must have been at the farm that morning."

"Or the night before. I think that more likely."

They finished the meal in relative silence. Mary made a token effort to convince Laura to stay for another night, but it was obvious that she considered the battle one of form rather than substance.

It was already full dark when Laura drove away from the farm, wondering if this latest incident was connected to Ashley's death. She was determined now to sell the cabin in the spring. When she had first decided to return to Dorrance, it had seemed like an island fortress, a refuge where she could hide away and heal, a place filled with pleasant memories of her childhood, her father, and a time much more innocent than the present. All of that was lost to her now. Every time she opened the door, her breath caught, wondering if she'd find evidence of a fresh intrusion. She had dreamed a couple of times that Ashley was sitting by her bed, and had wakened in a cold sweat. The soothing sounds of the wind in the branches outside now sounded ominous and spooky. She had, in fact, considered moving back to the farm, but she was too stubborn to let her mother claim that victory. It would only encourage her to press the attack on another front.

Her plans after that were still nebulous. She could stay in Dorrance for a while; she'd talked to a realtor and he identified two small houses which she could afford to rent on her budget. She could go to Boston for an extended visit with Kathy and possibly relocate there permanently if things worked out. Or she could pull up stakes altogether and head for the west coast. A complete change of scenery might be good for her. Whatever impulse had drawn her back to Dorrance had long since misfired. It was once again that tightly constricted, narrow-minded prison of her childhood.

On the other hand, Dan was here, and likely to stay. She thought about him with increasing frequency, trying to analyze her own feelings toward him. He was good company, quiet, attentive, thoughtful, perhaps a trifle too reserved at times. Laura liked him a great deal, but she wasn't sure she was ready to trust her emotions to the care of another person just yet. Thinking of him reminded her that she still hadn't told him about Janet Pack, but she wasn't sure if she should. Even assuming the worst case, that he was, in fact, her son, it might be better for him to remain ignorant of his parentage.

The rest of the week passed at a leaden pace. John Dill was questioned and released, and Mary was forced to do without her Jeep until a forensics team could be spared to examine it. Tommy Langston was arrested in Montana on Friday morning and was being held pending extradition. The county officials did finally close down the bar, citing the numerous fire and building code violations which they had previously been content to overlook. No one except his family knew where Mason Cortway had gone, although rumor had it that he was at home and rarely left his room. His father had resumed active management of the family business and wouldn't talk about his son.

Laura spent most of one Saturday morning helping Dan and his brother clean out the basement of the bar, or more correctly, cleaning out part of the basement of the bar. "Uncle was a packrat," explained Paul Sievert. "He bought the Buffalo paper every day and never threw one out. They're all down here, labeled and tied neatly in bundles. He also kept every receipt and invoice for the bar, all of his personal correspondence, and a really remarkable collection of magazines and old books."

"Are any of them valuable?" she'd asked.

Paul had shrugged. "Dan thinks we might be able to sell some of them on Ebay, but I don't know if it's worth the effort. The basement is musty and there's a lot of mildew. A lot of it is ruined."

"And don't forget the bugs," added Dan enthusiastically. "Are you one of those girls who can't stand bugs?"

"I grew up on a farm. There are good bugs and there are bad ones. I don't mind the good ones and I squash the others."

The first two hours were spent clearing space at the foot of the stairs so that they'd have an area in which to sort the rest. The basement was much bigger than Laura had expected, and so full that they couldn't even see most of its contents, let alone physically penetrate some of its recesses. It was also very cold, although they didn't notice that very much once they actually started working.

Paul and Dan ferried the bundled newspapers to the upstairs storage room. They'd go to the recycling center on Monday morning in the back of Paul's pickup. Laura sorted other bundles into categories—ledgers and other records of possible value, old invoices and other trivia for trash, books and potentially saleable items to a third area. There was a layer of dust over everything and all three of them were dirty by mid-morning and positively filthy by noon. Paul made sandwiches for lunch and they washed them down with beer.

Paul glanced at his wristwatch. "We open in two hours. I'd say we call it a day. We'll have to get rid of the junk before we can sort any more."

"Same time next weekend?" asked Laura.

Dan and Paul exchanged looks. "We didn't think you'd be interested in a return match," said Dan.

"Don't be silly. It's like a treasure hunt, except without the treasure." She laughed, perhaps a bit too hard. She was out of practice, after all. "Unless you guys aren't up to it two weeks in a row."

Paul frowned dramatically. "I think she's casting aspersions on our manliness, Dan."

"Can't have that. All right, Miss Collier. We'll see your macho and raise you one. I'll rent a Dumpster and we work Saturday and Sunday both."

"You're on."

On Monday, Detective Hopper called and asked if he could stop by and talk to her briefly. "I'm just in town for a few hours, checking on a few details. I only need a few minutes of your time."

"Sure. I'll be home all day."

Hopper was subdued and unusually polite. He summarized her previous statement quietly and systematically and asked if she'd remembered anything else that might help them.

"No, I've gone over everything in my mind a hundred times, of course, but there's nothing. I still think there was someone out there that night, watching me, but I have no proof. I don't go down there after dark anymore. All I can think of is that Ashley must have been somewhere close, either dead or dying, while I stood waiting to meet her."

"That's possible."

He sounded so obviously skeptical that she turned to face him directly. "But you don't think so. Why not?"

"Well, on the face of it, that seems the most likely case. You received the note setting up the rendezvous, she failed to appear, someone else may have been at the scene, someone who presumably killed Miss Sothern to prevent her from talking to you, and the victim's body was probably kept nearby before it was placed . . . where it was found. And Miss Sothern told you in her note that she had been threatened in some way by a person she identified as your dead husband."

"That's right."

"The dead don't walk, Miss Collier."

"I know that, Detective. I don't know who Ashley saw, but it wasn't Sean Brennan. It might have been someone who looked like him, though. A close relative maybe."

He shook his head. "We've checked into all that quite thoroughly. The only living relative is a very distant cousin. She's blonde, female, lives in Alaska, and is fourteen years old. There was a second cousin but he died of cancer."

"Then a friend perhaps, someone I didn't know. There might have been a chance resemblance, or some kind of disguise."

"That's all possible, of course." Hopper's skepticism was even more obvious.

"What aren't you telling me?"

He didn't answer her right away. Instead, he took out a cigarette, then gave her a questioning look. She nodded and he lit up, inhaled deeply, let the smoke out slowly. "I'm not convinced that Miss Sothern ever sent you a note."

"But you saw it!" She frowned. "You don't think I typed that myself, do you?"

He shook his head. "No, certainly not. If I did, I wouldn't be talking to you about it. But what makes you think your friend wrote the note you received?"

Laura hesitated, then realized that he had a valid point. She had wondered from the outset why Ashley had used a typewriter, or how she had managed it if she was supposedly in hiding. Even the signature had been typed. "I see. Then she might already have been dead by then."

He nodded. "We're pretty sure she was, Miss Collier. The body was frozen and thawed and then refrozen at least once over an uncertain length of time, so the coroner's office isn't willing to be too precise about the time of death. Unofficially, the presiding examiner believes that she'd been dead at least five days when you found her."

"But how?"

He shrugged. "This time of year? There are a hundred places nearby. She could have been kept in someone's barn, in the trunk of a car, or just hidden in the woods someplace. We suspect she was outside because of the thawing and refreezing. The weather warmed and cooled dramatically during the five days after her disappearance. The examiner also found evidence of some post mortem damage; the body was dragged quite a distance across the ground at some point."

"God, that's horrible. Are you trying to tell me that this has nothing at all to do with Sean?"

"I didn't say that. Someone stole your husband's body, Miss Collier, and that note was supposed to convince you that he was still alive or that someone was pretending that he was. I find it hard to believe that those two events are completely unrelated. I think this does have something to do with your late husband, and that's why I'm here. Is there anyone you can think of who might hold you responsible for what happened to him? An old friend, maybe a rival lover?"

Laura coughed to cover a nervous laugh. "Actually there was another woman, Detective, but I don't think that's going to help you very much. When I first met Sean he was having an affair with my best friend, Ashley Sothern. We weren't on speaking terms again until just recently."

Hopper's face betrayed the fact that he'd been taken completely by surprise this time. "I see," he said at last. "No one else? You're certain?"

"No one else, locally at least. I couldn't tell you what happened before he came to Dorrance. He mentioned old girlfriends to me occasionally, but never in any detail, and it wasn't something I really wanted to know about."

Hopper stayed only a few minutes longer, declining the offer of coffee. He left her with another of his cards, just in case she thought of something later. "I know it must seem to you as though we're not doing much, if anything, to catch the killer, but we have so little to go on, and there are so many other cases out there. But I don't like losing, Miss Collier. I promise you that I will follow any lead that comes our way."

She found herself liking him better this time than in the past, and she made an effort to put some warmth in her voice as he left. The moment the door closed, the cabin felt appreciably colder.

Laura had only once been a customer in the Trading Post since Kathy's departure, and that was with Dan. But on the Friday following Hopper's visit, he was on duty and she didn't want to be by herself. Her first thought was to visit her mother, but when she called the house there was no answer. Mary might not be the most popular citizen of Dorrance, but she was always invited to local functions and actually pursued a fairly active social life. As far as Laura knew, there were no men in it, at least in any meaningful sense, but she wouldn't have put even that past her mother.

Thwarted from her first plan, Laura changed clothes and drove into town, telling herself that she was going to stop in at Slade's for coffee, even as she parked at the opposite end of Main Street. It was almost as if her feet had minds of their own, because she was inside the Trading Post before she consciously realized where she was going. The usual crowd was already there, and several regulars waved, nodded, or even called to her. She smiled and waved back and made her way straight to the bar.

Paul came over, already carrying a glass of the Merlot she'd been drinking most recently. "Dan's on duty tonight."

"I know. I just stopped by for a few minutes. Looks like a good crowd."

"Business is indeed picking up, I am glad to say. For a while there it was touch and go. Dan and I put all of our savings, such as they were, into the renovations, and we're in hock up to the bridges of our noses."

"Well, with O'Brien's shut down, things can only get better."

He frowned. "Actually, we haven't seen much of their clientele and I'm just as happy that way. They tended to be a rougher crowd. You know, drugs, things like that. Most of them probably went over to Wallaby's in Shawcut." He excused himself to serve another customer, but then returned to where she was sitting.

"I'm glad you stopped by. Do you know a young guy, sandy haired, wispy mustache, named Kevin Slade?"

"Sure, I've known Kevin since I was a toddler."

"He was in here the other night. And he was talking about you. I heard your name mentioned and my ears perked up. I missed part of it, but I didn't like the part I heard."

"From Kevin? He's just a puppy. He's always been a little slow, but he has a heart of gold."

"Maybe. But maybe he changes when he's had a beer or three."

She hesitated. "I don't think I've ever seen him drinking."

"And I'd have to say I've never noticed him in here before or since. But he was talking to a couple of the regulars and your name came up, like I mentioned. And when I walked by he said, and I quote: 'Laura Collier should never have come back to Dorrance.' And then he might have noticed me standing there because he clammed up and never said anything else that I heard."

She laughed, but it was slightly forced. "Well, he's probably right. There are days when I wish I'd never come back. I'm sure it was meant innocently, Paul. Kevin has had a crush on me since we were kids, and he wouldn't hurt a fly."

"If you say so, Laura, but if I were you I'd be a little cautious around him, just in case. Someone hereabouts is willing to hurt a lot more than just a fly and I'd hate to see anything bad happen to you." He laughed uncomfortably. "Where else would I find someone willing to help us clean out the rest of the basement?"

Laura was sure that Kevin hadn't meant his words as a threat, but there was just a sliver of doubt. Whoever was responsible for Ashley's death and everything else that had happened lately must be someone she knew, and she certainly couldn't rule Kevin out. Feeling more depressed than ever, she finished her wine quickly and then went home.

They didn't finish clearing the basement of the Trading Post that weekend, but they at least managed to bring some order to the chaos. When they stopped working in the middle of Sunday afternoon, the debris had all been sorted into categories and the obvious trash had all been removed. Among other discoveries were a rusting filing cabinet filled with old family records and photographs, a neatly boxed and labeled collection of World War II memorabilia, newspapers dating back forty years, a coin collection that might possibly be valuable, old furniture which definitely was not, a variety of dead animals, mostly mice plus one squirrel and, oddly enough, a couple of birds, and a case of now very-well-aged whiskey.

Although the final disposition of some items had yet to be determined, Paul declared the project effectively finished and suggested that they all have supper at Foster's to celebrate. "My treat." He glanced at himself and his companions, all of whom were covered with a substantial layer of dirt and sweat. "After showers all around, of course."

Laura and Dan decided this was an admirable idea. It seemed unusually bright outside, but they'd spent most of the day in what was essentially a windowless cavern. It was also bitterly cold again and a major storm was supposed to hit them some time after midnight.

Back at the cabin, Laura tossed her dirty clothing in the wicker hamper, added wood to the stove, and showered. She ached all over from the lugging and carrying and would have preferred a luxurious and relaxing bath, but a shower was all that was available, and it was, in any case, so chilly that she didn't want to spend a long time undressed. Shivering, but clean and relatively dry, she slipped into her best pair of slacks and second-best blouse, quickly adding her warmest sweater. She was beginning to understand why her aunt had so rarely left the cabin; if the stove wasn't constantly tended, the interior cooled off very quickly.

They met at Foster's. Dan and Paul were already sitting in the bar when she arrived. There was no problem getting a table. Trade at Foster's had declined along with commerce in Dorrance in general. Laura wondered how much longer they could stay open. Although they had a fair amount of traffic at lunchtime, she'd never seen the parking lot crowded during the evening, and tonight less than a quarter of the tables were filled.

Paul was in good spirits, more animated than usual, in fact, or perhaps that was an illusion created by Dan's unusually quiet and thoughtful demeanor. Laura wasn't feeling very talkative, either, but they had two drinks before the food arrived and a third to accompany it, and by then she'd begun to feel more relaxed. "You're awfully quiet tonight," she ventured at last.

"Just tired I guess."

"I can't imagine why. Paul and I did all the heavy work." She blinked her eyes rapidly to show that she was kidding.

"You were doing such a great job, I just didn't want to interfere."

Paul reached over and tapped her arm. "Don't let him fool you. He's thinking about that filing cabinet full of family records."

She didn't understand at first and glanced back and forth between the two. Then it came to her. "Do you think there's anything there about the adoption?"

Dan shrugged. "I won't know until I've looked. I glanced through a few of the papers and they're from the right period, but Uncle's filing system seems to have been sequentially by date and the hell with the subject matter. If there's anything there, it might take weeks to find it."

"I could help."

"Thanks for the offer, but I'll spare you the boredom of going through old tax returns, letters from Aunt Blanche, shopping lists, and appliance warranties. If there's anything there, it can wait until I have time to find it."

Laura suddenly remembered that she had half promised to stop at the farm this evening. "Oh my god, I'm in big trouble." She fumbled in her purse and found the cell phone. "Mother's been pretending to be clingy and dependent ever since her accident. I have to at least call."

Mary Collier's voice was calm and emotionless when she answered. Laura asked how she was doing, knowing she wouldn't be told even if her mother was in excruciating pain. "I thought I'd come by in the morning instead of this evening, if you're going to be home."

"That's all right. The police have released the Jeep, so I'm not marooned anymore. Burgess dropped it off a couple of hours ago."

"I don't suppose they've found out who was responsible?"

"Nathan Clay couldn't find his own ass with both hands. He

still thinks John Dill did it."

"Well, he might have."

Her mother's sigh was audible through the phone. "You've always liked easy answers, Laura. I suspect that this problem is a lot more complicated than that."

"You're probably right. Hey, I have to go. About nine tomorrow?" She broke the connection and set the phone down beside her plate.

"Is everything all right?" Dan must have seen the fleeting expression of discontent on Laura's face.

"Sure. I'm going to have to do some penance tomorrow for breaking our date tonight, but I'm an old hand at that. Mother is never happy when her plans are disrupted, unless she's the one doing the disrupting."

"She does have quite the reputation," said Paul. "When you tend bar, it doesn't take long to find out who's feuding or sleeping together or just got out of jail or doesn't put out on the first date. Sometimes I feel like a priest in a confessional. The first night I opened, this big guy with a scar on one cheek came into the bar and started drinking boilermakers almost as fast as I could make them. I thought I'd just met the town drunk, but he hasn't been in since. Anyway, after the fourth or fifth drink, he started in on this woman he claimed ruined his life. I'd never heard the name before so I didn't know who he was talking about until a couple of months later when I found out Mary Rustin and Mary Collier were the same person."

Laura sat there with her mouth half open. Dan leaned across the table. "Are you all right?"

"What?" She recovered herself. "Sorry. You caught me by surprise, that's all. I know in my head that a lot of people don't care for my mother, but it's still a bit of a shock to hear it said out loud like that." She spoke quickly, covering the real reason for her stunned reaction. The man with the scar on his cheek was almost certainly Del Huggins.

The meal arrived just then and Laura had an excuse not to talk for a while, and by the time their plates were nearly empty, she had recovered her composure. But she was suddenly very tired, declined the offer of coffee and dessert. "Sorry, guys, but I'm just about wiped out. I'll take a raincheck. But stay if you want. We came in separate cars, anyway, so you don't have to see me out."

They both stood up, exchanging uncertain looks, but it was obvious that Paul was really looking forward to the lemon meringue pie displayed in the dessert stand. "Really, I'm fine. And I'll be home in ten minutes. Thanks for the supper, Paul."

"My pleasure. And the next time I have to clean out an old basement, I'll give you a call."

"Yeah, well don't hurry on that one. I'll be coughing out dust until spring. Good night, guys."

She had taken half a dozen steps when Dan called her name. He was reaching across the table as she turned, and she saw his hand touch the cell phone she'd forgotten to return to her purse. The angle was awkward and it wasn't quite within his reach. His fingers brushed it and it started to spin, and he overcorrected trying to grab it and instead knocked it off the edge of the table.

It shattered when it hit the floor.

CHAPTER EIGHTEEN

Laura was surprised at how isolated she felt without the phone. It was beyond repair, of course, and she and Dan had done a little dance about who was going to pay for a replacement. The prospect of waiting several days while a new one was ordered did not cheer her. She didn't want to mention it to her mother when she visited, because she had already provided enough ammunition for a lecture without adding the telephone, but if she didn't, her mother would try to call and possibly panic when she couldn't raise her daughter.

Not that the farm had proven itself to be much of a refuge lately. A prowler, a sabotaged Jeep, and a resentful employee who seemed interested in her private records. Laura had never mentioned her suspicions about Del before, but after hearing about his outburst at the Trading Post, the mysterious encounter at the house had assumed a sinister cast in her mind. Del certainly wasn't a friend, and she owed him no particular loyalty. On the other hand, if her mother did fire him, it would give her more leverage, provide another reason why Laura should return and help run the farm.

The storm had stalled during the night, dropping only four or five inches on Dorrance, and Laura was deprived of an excuse to cancel the morning's visit. Occasional flurries of light snow hung suspended in the breeze, but the sky was almost clear when she went outside. She arrived feeling irritable and almost spoiling for a fight, a mood her mother correctly diagnosed and disarmed by being unusually pleasant. For a change, she even made coffee instead of the inevitable tea, and Laura finally started to relax.

"Are you nervous about it? The Jeep, I mean." It had been parked in its usual spot when she arrived. "I think my heart would stop the first time I had to use the brakes."

"Nonsense. I took it out this morning to make sure Ed Burgess fixed it properly. And I've asked Del to take a look at it when he has time, just in case. I assume you've heard about Mason Cortway?"

Laura shook her head. "Nothing recently."

"The family is trying to keep it quiet, of course, but it's hard to keep a secret in a town as small as this one."

"What secret? What are you talking about?"

"Money, my dear. When Mason had his little breakdown after the incident with that girl, his father had to unretire himself to run the store. It seems he found some money missing."

"And you think Mason took it?"

"Oh, there's no question about that. He'd invested it in some foolish land development scheme with Bud Wiegand, apparently."

Laura nodded. "I'd heard about that."

"Did you know they tried to buy the cabin a while back?"

"Yes, I think you mentioned it. Someone did, anyway."

"I don't suppose they approached you. I told them that it was your property at the time, but I wouldn't give them your address. It was right after Christmas last year."

"No. In fact, I haven't been on good terms with either of them if you remember correctly. And it sounds like their big development scheme has been unraveling for a while now."

"Apparently they ran into a number of problems, financial and otherwise. Now they own a lot of undeveloped land that no one wants, along with loans they can't pay."

"It's a shame really. I've been thinking about selling the cabin later this year." She hadn't meant to say that, but it slipped out before she realized what she was saying.

Her mother's reaction surprised her.

"I wouldn't do that, dear."

"Why not, Mother? You've never liked the place."

"No, I haven't. It's too rustic for me. I may be a farm girl, but I do like modern conveniences. And I don't think it's a fit place for you to live on a regular basis. But your aunt wanted you to have it, and it meant a lot to her when she was alive."

"I believe you told me she was a foolish, sentimental old woman."

"Yes, I'm sure I did." Mary turned and stared out the window. "I guess as I've gotten older I've contracted the same failing."

"You don't have a sentimental bone in your body, Mother."

"Don't be so quick to judge. You'd be surprised at how complex this old lady can be. In any case, even leaving aside the personal connections, this would be a particularly bad time to sell. Now that people are hearing about this ridiculous failed attempt to build a resort, any property near Moon Pond will be of even less value than before. Wiegand and the Cortways will be trying to dump what they own to cover their losses."

"We'll see. My land has the best access to the water, and that should make it more valuable. I'll decide what to do when winter is over."

"If you'd like, we could open up the wall between your bedroom and the guest room to give you some more space."

"No, Mother, I'm not moving back to the farm. I'll either find some other place in town or somewhere else. I'm still not sure what I'm going to do next, but my options in Dorrance are pretty limited."

"You could help run the farm while you're trying to decide.

You wouldn't have to make a long-term commitment."

"No I couldn't. Don't try to lure me into your trap. It won't work. Aren't you ever going to accept that?"

Mary was silent for a long time. "Eventually, perhaps. It's just hard for me to believe that the Rustin blood doesn't run true in your veins, Laura. You've always been more Rustin than Collier."

It was meant as a compliment, but Laura felt mildly offended and remained sullen for the rest of the morning. It clouded over and began to snow in earnest around noon, so she used the weather as an excuse to leave right after lunch. "I need to pick up some groceries on the way home and I want to get back before the drive is all drifted in."

"You could always stay here for the night. We have plenty. I worry about you out there by yourself."

"Don't start, Mother. Nothing is going to happen."

The snow came down thick and fast, huge flakes that accumulated quickly. There was almost no wind but her wipers were barely able to keep the windshield clear. She was concentrating so hard on her driving that she completely forgot that she had meant to go into town on the way back. By the time she reached the cabin, there was already a further two-inch accumulation on the ground and it was falling heavier with each passing minute. She could hear it whispering through the branches. It had grown warm enough that the snow was wet and heavy. Laura was in the cabin and had just started to take off her coat when she remembered the market. She was out of milk, and bread, almost out of toilet paper and coffee.

"Damn!" It was quite possible that she'd be snowed in for a couple of days. She had enough to eat if she wasn't too picky, and she could live without toilet paper if she had to, but life without coffee was insupportable. The Chevy was already covered with snow, but she brushed it off and backed it out onto Moon Pond Road. The market was normally less than a ten-minute drive, but tonight it would probably take longer.

In fact, it took half an hour to get there, and almost double that time to get back. The wind had picked up, and the snow was so thick that it was literally impossible to see the hood of her car. Laura inched along with her window open so that she could be sure she was still on the pavement. There were no streetlights on Moon Pond Road, and the short trip felt interminable. She was reminded of a story she'd read in high school, about a traveling salesman who finds himself all alone on a highway one night. He's running low on gas and he passes a sign that says the next exit is five miles. Five miles later he sees the same sign again, and then again, and the needle on his tank doesn't move and he's stuck on that dark lonely road forever.

She almost went right past her turnoff. At the last minute she recognized a twisted tree and took her foot off the gas. The turn was quite an adventure in itself and she had to abandon the Chevy almost immediately once she was off the pavement. The snow around the cabin was now thick and heavy.

Laura managed to get all three bags into her arms. The snow had begun to drift and some of it got inside her right boot. She cursed but resisted the urge to move faster. If she fell in this stuff, she'd never be able to find her scattered purchases. By the time she reached the door, she was shivering and her headache had achieved epic proportions. She set the bags down in the snow, plastic not paper, and took the keys out of her pocket.

That's when she realized that she'd forgotten to lock up when she left.

Laura wouldn't have thought it possible, but suddenly she felt even colder than before. She turned the knob and pushed the door open, peering in carefully. She'd thrown a couple of pieces of wood into the stove before leaving, and it seemed to be chugging along happily. The flickering flames threw bizarre distorted shadows onto the walls and ceiling, shadows that now seemed fraught with menace.

She had oiled the hinges and the door swung open almost silently. Laura waited until she could be sure no one was concealed behind it, then stepped over the threshold, leaving her groceries behind. Other than the crackling of the fire and a faint susurration of snow behind her and on the roof above, there was nothing to be heard. Impulsively, she walked directly to the center of the room and turned her head to peer into every corner. Other than the bathroom, she could see everywhere in the cabin; she had even taken the blanket down from in front of the bunk beds.

There was no sign of an intruder. Everything looked just as she had left it. Laura relaxed slightly, but she didn't feel comfortable until she'd checked the bathroom, with the same results. Laughing nervously at herself, she retrieved her half frozen purchases and put them away, but only after making sure that all the doors and windows were secured.

The wind howled all night and the snow was still falling when the sun came up in the morning, although not as intensely as it had the night before. Laura turned on the radio and learned that twelve to eighteen inches had already fallen and that at least another foot was expected during the day, with the skies finally clearing in the early evening. She resigned herself to spending at least a couple of days snowbound; Moon Pond Road would be the last one plowed in Dorrance.

Laura had enjoyed being alone during the months following Sean's death, or at least had fooled herself into thinking she was happier by herself. The cabin had seemed an ideal fit with her new lifestyle and she had expected to live in it for the foreseeable future. But now she felt isolated and trapped, with no telephone, her car buried under a remarkably large drift of snow, not even a television to keep her company. So much snow had drifted up against her front door that she couldn't push it open, so she spent the morning clearing off the back porch. An hour after she was done, the wind had blown a good portion of the snow back, as though taunting her.

Perhaps simply because she couldn't leave, Laura felt the confinement more acutely as the day wore on. The snow eventually did stop falling, but the wind kept up and the later snow had been drier, more prone to blowing and drifting. Visibility was still very limited, and the sky lightened but did not clear. Eventually, she heard the plow go by on Moon Pond Road, but the prospect of shoveling out the Chevy, and then the twenty or thirty feet between its rear bumper and the pavement, was sufficiently daunting that she resigned herself to involuntary exile for at least another day. Maybe Mother would send Del over with the truck to plow her clear, or maybe not. Their parting the previous day had been quiet, but as frosty as the glaze on her windows.

She tried to read, but couldn't get interested in either of the two newly purchased books on her shelf, and the local radio stations seemed to have largely gone over to sports talk shows and country and western music, neither of which interested her in the slightest. Bored and restless, she cleaned the already nearly spotless bathroom, rearranged the stock in her makeshift pantry—twice, finally managed to force the front door open far enough that she could go outside, but only by wading through hip-deep snow. Although she made a start at shoveling a path to the road, wide enough for her but not for the Chevy, it was cold and blustery and she had only made it halfway when she finally gave up and went back inside.

By early evening, she had resolved to leave the cabin the next day, one way or another. If necessary, she'd finish digging the pathway to the road and walk into town. The pavement would be clear and it wouldn't be that long a hike. She promised herself lunch at Slade's, a new pair of gloves, and she still had to order a replacement for her cell phone. One way or another she'd entertain herself for the day, although she would have to remember to leave enough time to walk back while it was still daylight. Unless she could find someone willing to give her a lift.

The sky began to clear just a little too late to do any good. Laura spotted the moon from the back porch. From this vantage point, she could also see its milky reflection on the surface of Moon Pond, which probably explained the name. Although this wasn't the original cabin, it had been built on the same site as that of Owen Wainwright, whose holdings had rivaled that of the Rustin family until his death. None of his children had wanted to remain in Dorrance, and the property had been sold piecemeal. All of the shoreline of Moon Pond had once belonged to the Wainwrights, but the family was extinct, locally anyway.

It was a pretty place. She'd always loved coming here as a child, and she was still fond of it even now. But it didn't feel the same. Perhaps it was a function of being older, but more likely it was because everything seemed to have taken a turn for the worse since she'd come back, reversing the progress she'd made since Sean's death. It had all started with the dead cat, she realized. Then the trouble with her still unidentified intruder, the nerve-wracking wait for Ashley near the ruined dock, and finally the discovery of her friend's frozen body. The cabin had stopped being a safe haven; now it was just another place she couldn't think of as home.

Laura tried reading again after eating a light supper, and this time finally managed to get involved with the story, more through desperation than because of the author's skill. The private detective hero had just been slugged from behind, somewhat predictably as far as Laura was concerned, when she was startled by a loud thump. Something had struck the wall of the cabin, around the side under the window she'd had repaired. She set the book aside and stood up, more curious than alarmed. At first, she tried to look out through the front window, but the angle was too acute for her to see anything, and the porch windows were no help at all. The side window was set high under the cathedral roof and she didn't have a ladder, but she thought she might just possibly be able to look down through it if she moved the table and climbed up onto it.

The table was heavier than she thought and she was about to abandon the attempt when something slammed into the back wall, right between the two small porch windows. Laura jumped, startled, and ran to the closest window without thinking. It was windy, though not nearly as violent as it had been the night before, and blowing snow rushed by almost horizontally. For a brief second she thought she saw a shape moving outside, right near a line of low brush, but it was gone almost immediately, if it had been there at all. It was more likely that the wind had picked up some debris, a dead branch perhaps, although the impact had seemed much louder than she would have thought possible from such a chance collision.

She put on her coat, but didn't zip it up, and stepped out onto the porch. Enough snow had blown back that it took her a few seconds to solve the mystery. A foot-long piece of firewood was half buried in a tiny drift. It was certainly heavy enough to have made the thump, but far too heavy to have become airborne in anything less than gale force winds. A more likely explanation was that an owl or another nightbird had gotten disoriented in the snow. If so, it had apparently recovered and departed. She put the piece of wood under her arm and retreated into the cabin, carefully securing the door behind her. It crackled and steamed when she put it into the woodstove.

Perhaps ten minutes later, the cabin was struck again. There was a sharp snap this time, and a rattle of glass; Laura's head jerked around immediately and her breath caught in her throat. She stood cautiously and crossed to the window, discovering, to her relief, that it was intact. A gust of snow swirled suddenly toward her and she flinched before realizing that it was just a playful twisting of the wind.

"Where's that damned flashlight?" It took a minute to find it because she'd rearranged so many times that she'd lost track of where she'd left it. Holding her face and the light close to the glass, she used it to check the porch, then carefully examined the window from top to bottom. Part of the upper frame was splintered and she was pretty sure the damage was new.

She didn't want to go out there again, but it would be worse not to know what had happened, an uncertainty that would gnaw away at her until she investigated. This time she zipped her coat, put on boots and stuck her heavy gloves in her pocket. Snow had drifted up against the door, but she was able to push it away with minimal effort. Something cracked out in the night and she whirled just in time to see a good-sized limb fall from a nearby tree, laden down with heavy, wet snow. Considerably reassured, she clicked on the flashlight and examined the damaged window.

A small section of the upper frame had shattered. Laura leaned very close and was disquieted by what she saw. She couldn't be certain, but it looked to her like the impact of a small-caliber bullet. Some form of missile had certainly struck the wood, and she couldn't think of any other explanation. No windblown object could have done this kind of damage.

Laura turned and stared out into the darkness and suddenly felt that she wasn't alone.

She slowly backed toward the door, slipped inside, and locked it behind her. Her hands were shaking and her heart was racing.

Her first thought was to call the police, but then she remembered the broken cell phone. Her second was to arm herself, and she went looking for the rifle.

But she didn't find it.

She searched the entire cabin, even the bathroom, and then searched again, even though she knew she hadn't moved it during her reorganization. Although she hadn't missed it at the time, she realized now that she hadn't seen it at all that day, and couldn't remember seeing it the day before, either. Someone had removed it from the cabin. But how and when? The locks were all secure, the windows unbroken. She hadn't had a visitor for almost a week, and she knew the rifle had been standing in its usual corner more recently than that.

Then she remembered her hasty departure for supplies before the storm, and the fact that she'd forgotten to lock up when she went out. It was the only possible explanation. Someone had entered the cabin that evening in her absence, and had made off with the rifle.

It might even have been her own weapon that had been fired at the window.

"This is not good," she whispered aloud. "Not good at all."

She had the small hatchet that she used to chop wood for the stove, but it wouldn't be much defense against an armed opponent. It felt slightly better having it near at hand, though, so she put it on the kitchen table where it would be handy if needed. Cautiously, keeping as low a profile as possible, she made her way from window to window, peering out into the night, her imagination fooling her eyes into finding shapes among the shifting currents of airborne snow. Once she saw actual movement, but it was just the lower limb of a nearby spruce, waving in the wind.

Something struck the roof, almost directly over her head, then slid down the sloping side with a series of clatters and thumps. Laura whirled toward the window, saw something dark fall past, and rushed across the room. It was another piece of wood from her woodpile, freshly split, and like the first it could not possibly have been propelled by the wind.

Someone had thrown it up onto her roof.

Laura could probably block both doors with some of the furniture, enough to make it difficult for anyone to break in. They could break one of the windows, though; she couldn't possibly block all four of them as well as the doors. To make herself less of a target, she turned off all the lights. The glow from the woodstove was enough for her to see by and hopefully wouldn't provide too distinct a silhouette if she passed in front of a window.

Briefly she considered making a run for it. Her incomplete pathway would get her halfway to the road, but even if she waded through the snow and got clear, it was at least a half hour's walk to town and she'd be without cover for all of that time. The chance that a car would come by at just the right time was too small to be worth considering. The possibility that she might end up shot dead on the roadway, or even worse, left there wounded to freeze to death, dissuaded her.

The better part of a half hour passed without further incident. Laura had almost started to relax when she heard a distant crack, then a closer one. A spray of glass flew across the room as one pane of the rightmost porch window shattered. There was an immediate freezing draft and a flutter of loose papers. Laura ducked under the table, biting her lip, and waited, her teeth chattering and not just because of the sudden drop in temperature.

It was anger that finally got her to move. She felt humiliated squatting under a table, scared out of her wits, and unable to fight back. Keeping her head low, she moved on hands and knees to the cabinet, found her roll of duct tape. The window pane was small, less than twelve inches square, and there was a picture mounted on the wall that was pretty close to the same size. She stood up just long enough to pull it down, ripped off the back and slid the glass facing out. Then another crawl and a cautious look outside, even though it was still impossible to see more than eight or ten feet with any reliability.

It was getting cold quickly. Laura stood up between the two windows, pressing her shoulder against the wall. She gently set the glass over the broken pane, relieved to discover that it covered the opening quite nicely. It only took another couple of minutes to tape it firmly in place. Sitting on the floor once again, she waited while the stove managed to overcome the worst of the chill. Another half hour passed uneventfully. Laura hoped that was a good sign, but she wasn't ready to bet her life on it. With the hatchet in her lap, she curled up in a corner of the room where she could watch both doors, wrapped herself in a blanket, and waited for the morning.

Eventually, she fell asleep.

She woke at first light, stiff and sore and half convinced that she'd dreamed the previous evening's incidents. The patched window dispelled the illusion. It didn't seem as menacing in the daylight, but it was still enough to convince her that she had to get out of the cabin and get help as quickly as possible. She'd walk to town and notify the police, even though she was beginning to share her mother's doubts about Nathan Clay's administrative abilities. On the other hand, she still had Detective Hopper's card in her wallet. If she could convince him that this was connected to Ashley's murder, and she was sure that it was, he'd investigate it himself, she was certain, even if Chief Clay didn't call him in officially.

Breakfast could wait but she wasn't about to venture outside without coffee. She drank two cups, finishing the second as she was donning her winter gear. The front door was blocked again;

apparently the snow had drifted back during the night, and this time she couldn't budge it at all. She finally went out by way of the porch, feeling incredibly exposed. The wind had settled to a gentle breeze and the snow had stopped falling, so she was able to examine her surroundings quite readily. There was no sign of an intruder, and if they'd left tracks the night before, they would have been obliterated long since.

Laura managed to avoid most of the drifts, resulting in a somewhat circuitous route around to the front. When she turned the corner, she stopped in her tracks, staring in shock at her front door. It wasn't the snow that had blocked it this time. Someone had pushed her trash barrel flush against it and filled it to overflowing with cut wood. It wasn't that that made her breath catch in her throat, though. It was the words scrawled on the door, apparently with a felt marker.

"Did you miss me?" And it was signed "Sean."

There were a couple of surviving boot prints, or half prints at least, but they were featureless depressions now, with no visible detail by which they might have been identified. She left the barrel untouched, however, just in case there was some clue to be found by more educated eyes than hers.

Much of her path had been filled in, but she made it to the road, sweating inside her heavy clothing. With a last look back at the cabin, she turned toward town and started walking as quickly as the treacherous footing would allow.

CHAPTER NINETEEN

The desk sergeant listened patiently to Laura's story, then asked her to take a seat. Chief Clay himself appeared a few minutes later and she repeated the entire account while he nodded and attempted to look professional. It was more likely that he resented her for disturbing his day with yet another mysterious and probably unsolvable crime.

"I'm afraid I'll have to ask you to stay away from the cabin for the time being. Is there someplace else you can go?" He obviously already knew the answer to that question.

"I'll be up at the farm."

"That's probably best. I'll have someone drive up and look around right away."

Laura almost spoke up because she was afraid that whoever the chief sent would be as likely to destroy evidence as discover it, but she closed her mouth and settled back into the chair. It probably didn't matter. The storm would have taken care of any possible footprints and the surviving physical evidence was pretty obvious.

"Is there a phone I could use?"

He nodded toward one on the corner of the desk.

She called the farm and her mother answered on the fourth ring. "Hi, it's Laura."

"Good morning. Isn't it a little early for you to be up and about?"

271

"I've had some trouble. Would it be possible for you to come pick me up?"

"I suppose so." Mary's voice was thick and raspy. "I assume they've plowed up your way by now."

"Yes, but I'm not at the cabin. I'm at the police station."

There was a short pause. "All right, I'll be right down."

Laura was standing in the vestibule when the Jeep pulled into the crescent-shaped driveway. She was outside and opening the passenger side door before her mother had time to kill the engine. "What's happened this time?" Mary's nose was red and her voice hoarse.

"Are you all right? You sound terrible."

"Oh, it's just a cold. Now tell me what's going on."

"Someone was out at the cabin last night. Whoever it was shot at the windows and left a message on the door. And they signed Sean's name to it."

Mary sighed. "Sometimes I wonder if he really is dead. Oh, I know his body died, but maybe something of his spirit stayed behind."

"You're the last person I'd expect to hear that from, Mother. I thought you told me that superstitions are all nonsense."

The older woman chuckled softly. "So I did. But as you get older and closer to death, sometimes you start wondering how it can all just end. Ten years after your grandfather died, we were still talking about him as though he might be just in the next room, and we certainly wouldn't have done anything that he might not have approved of. And I've felt my father's presence at the farm from time to time. I'll be faced with some difficult decision and wondering what to do and it's as though a voice whispers in my ear and I know it's him come back to help me."

Laura shook her head in disbelief. "I can't believe this. My mother has turned into a mystic."

"Well, I did tell you that I could sense your father around from time to time, even though he isn't really there."

"But we don't know that Daddy's dead."

"No, we don't. But I think he must be. Ben had his faults, but he was rarely inconsiderate and he truly loved you, Laura. He might not have come back, but he would have made sure we knew he was all right. I think he went someplace to think and that we would have heard from him eventually, but something happened, an accident perhaps, or a stroke. They ran in his family, you know."

Laura should have been shocked, but in some deeper level of her mind, she had come to the same conclusion long ago. Instead of shock, she felt sadness and loss, as though by saying it aloud, her mother had made it real. "Chief Clay is sending some people up to the cabin, so I won't be able to use it for a while, probably a couple of days."

"I think it would be unwise of you to go back there at all, except to pick up your things and even then in broad daylight and with an escort."

"Mother, we've been through all of that. I'm not going to be driven out of my home any more than you'd let someone drive you out of yours."

"But you'll be much safer at the farm."

Laura shook her head, exasperated. "Will I? I seem to remember something about a prowler trying to break down your back door, and it was the Jeep that was sabotaged, not my car. Del Huggins isn't lurking in dark corners and searching through my files." Too late she remembered that she had never mentioned the suspicious encounter with Huggins.

"Would you like to explain that last comment, dear?" Her mother's voice was smooth as velvet over a framework of cold steel.

"I'm sorry. I forgot all about it until now. It wasn't a big deal.

That first night when you were away visiting the Hallworths I stopped to check the house and I surprised Del inside. He was probably just making sure nothing was wrong, but I had the impression that he'd been looking through some of the files in your office."

"I see." There was an extended silence that lasted until the Jeep was parked beside the house and they were getting out. "I think it's time that you and I had a little talk about Del Huggins."

"If you want. But I don't want to get him in trouble over nothing." They climbed onto the porch and Mary unlocked the door.

"Oh, it was something all right. I have no doubt that Del was searching quite thoroughly and I know exactly what he was looking for. But he wouldn't find it in my office. Let's have some tea."

Laura made a pot of tea while her mother disappeared upstairs on some mysterious errand. When she returned, she was holding a plain, legal-sized envelope. Laura poured and then sat across from her mother at the table, waiting patiently for an explanation.

"Del has always been a good worker, but in his heart he's basically a very weak man. Some years back, he gave in to a particular failing of his and made the mistake of leaving some of the evidence where it just happened to fall into my hands. I confronted him with what I'd found and we eventually came to an understanding about the terms and duration of his employment. I told you that I couldn't possibly replace him without paying significantly more money, if you recall."

Laura felt as though time had suddenly come to a stop. "Mother, are you telling me that you've been blackmailing Del into staying here?"

"More or less, yes, that's what I've been doing."

"Isn't blackmail still a crime in New York State?"

"Technically speaking, I suppose it is. But there are unusual circumstances in this case."

"What kind of unusual circumstances?"

Her mother picked up the envelope and drew out a fairly thick stack of photographs. "I think you're old enough now to see these." She pushed them across the table, her expression calm but her eyes intense.

They were facedown. Laura reached out and took the top one, flipped it over. She recognized the scene immediately. It was a secluded cove on Moon Pond not far from her cabin. The day was bright and sunny, the trees in full leaf; the picture had obviously been taken during the summer. Three young women were swimming in the cove, or rather one was swimming and two were standing on the beach, gesturing at the third. All three appeared to be about sixteen and all three were completely naked.

She recognized them. Kathy Peebles. Ashley Sothern. Laura Collier.

There were forty-eight photographs, all shot that same day, all from the same position. Some were funny, some very revealing. A disproportionate number of them concentrated on Laura herself.

"I don't understand. How is this possible?"

"A telephoto lens and a good camera. Del has a tiny darkroom hidden in his basement. You weren't the only young girls he photographed up there and elsewhere, but I let him keep the rest."

"I'm no lawyer, Mother, but doesn't this make you an accessory to his crime?"

"No, I don't think so. I was certainly within my rights to confiscate everything involving you. The negatives are in here as well." She tapped the envelope with a forefinger.

"But you should have gone to the police. This is a crime. It's, I don't know, kiddie porn, invasion of privacy. Something."

"I'm not so sure of that. It certainly isn't pornographic, and he took the photographs in a public place. It's probably no more than a misdemeanor, although I grant you it would certainly make things very uncomfortable for Del if this got out. He would have to leave town, of course, and that would have left us without a foreman for the farm. So, instead, I made him sign a confession, promise to stop spying on young girls, and agree to continue with his present duties at an adjusted rate of compensation. Frankly, I think my punishment was far greater than anything the authorities would have done to him."

Laura opened her mouth, but words failed to come.

"You see, dear, that's why I was quite certain that Del had nothing to do with my accident. The last thing he would want is for something to happen to me before he managed to find this envelope."

"Maybe he didn't mean to kill you. You told me yourself that it was unlikely you could have been seriously hurt running off McAlester Road. Maybe he's just trying to frighten you, frighten us. He lives by himself, and most of the time he's alone during the day. He could be the person responsible for everything that's been happening. He could be Ashley's killer!"

"Oh, I rather think not. It's all a bit too subtle for poor Del. I grant you that he's mean enough, and he's certainly strong enough to have moved that barrel in front of your door, but I can't see him writing notes on your bathroom mirror and there's no reason at all for him to break into this house. He has a key, after all."

"Didn't you tell me you loaned him one of Daddy's guns?"

She nodded. "Yes, to shoot rats. Laura, this is farm country. Del was probably one of the few people in town who didn't already have some sort of firearm. You're reading too much into this."

"Am I? I don't know about that." She looked away from her mother, thinking furiously. She ought to tell the police, but if she did, her mother would be in serious trouble. But if it was, in fact, Del who was responsible for Ashley's death and she didn't say anything, he might kill someone else, perhaps Laura or her mother or both of them.

Mary gathered up the photographs and returned them to the envelope. "Maybe I shouldn't have told you this if it troubles you so much. But take my word for it, Del Huggins is a weak man and a shallow thinker. He couldn't come up with anything this subtle, and even if he did, he wouldn't have the nerve to follow through."

"Then who do you think is behind it all?"

"The way I see it there are two possibilities. The first is that Sean had a friend somewhere that none of us knew about, probably someone here in Dorrance, although I suppose it could be an outsider. Strangers tend to be obvious around here, though. We don't even have a motel."

"The cabins on the other side of Moon Pond are occupied," suggested Laura.

"That's a possibility, I suppose. But maybe there's another motive entirely, and this business about Sean is just a cover. You're a little young to have mortal enemies, dear, but it's not unheard of."

"Unless it's one of your enemies, Mother, and let's face it, that would be a pretty long list. Maybe I'm just a way for them to get back at you."

"I considered that, but I don't think so. It's the other way around. You're the one they're after."

"What makes you think that?"

"Ashley. She meant nothing to me. I didn't even like the girl particularly. But the two of you were very close."

It was a valid point. Laura felt more confused than ever. "I can't talk about this right now. Get those things out of my sight. I have to think."

Her mother disappeared for a while, taking the photographs with her, presumably to return them to their hiding place. Laura thought furiously, trying to find a pattern, a clue, something that she had overlooked. The only result was a blinding headache and a sense of helplessness like that she had felt after realizing that Sean's temper tantrums and irrational behavior were more than just passing moods or quirks. But she also had an uneasy feeling that the solution was right there in front of her, waiting for her to move the puzzle pieces into just the right combination.

But if a pattern was there, it was too obscure or too subtle or perhaps too cluttered with other information. She finished her tea, using the last of it to wash down some aspirin. Mary was still upstairs and Laura wandered up, found her changing the sheets in her old bedroom.

"I just thought I'd freshen the room up a bit."

"I could have done that. You don't have to fuss over me."

"I meant what I said about knocking down that wall, you know. I haven't used that guest room since you've been gone and I certainly won't miss it. You could turn it into a little office."

Laura felt her gut tighten. "I've already told you, I'm not going to move back here. Not permanently. I just need to stay a couple of nights while the police do whatever it is that they plan to do out at the cabin."

"You're not thinking of going back there! Not after everything that's already happened."

"Yes, that's exactly what I'm planning. I don't want to quarrel, Mother, and I don't want to hurt your feelings, but you're wasting your time. I'm not going to come back to the farm, not now or after you're gone. In fact, why don't we both leave? I know you're not making much of a profit anymore. Let's sell the property while it still has some value and move someplace where half the town doesn't flinch when we walk into a room."

"You can't be serious."

"Oh, I'm completely serious. I've been completely serious ever since high school." Her head hurt, she was tired and frustrated, and the revelations about her mother's little extortion hobby had set her nerves on edge. Her voice was rising and she knew it and suddenly she no longer cared. Just this once she was going to say what she felt and if her mother didn't like it, well, she'd just have to get used to it.

"There's nothing you can say or do that will ever convince me to stay on this farm, Mother. It bored me when I was a child. I disliked it when I was a teenager. And right now I hate it. I hate it because of what it did to you and Daddy and what it's doing now to you and me. You've let this place, and the holy Rustin tradition, become an obsession. All my life I've seen you make decisions based on what was best for the farm, not what was best for us."

"But . . ."

"Don't interrupt me. I have to get this out. The farm has always felt like a silent, invisible member of the family, someone you loved the best. I think that's why Daddy left. He knew he couldn't compete. When you were first married, he got caught up in the farm, too, but as he grew older, he realized that wasn't enough."

"I loved your father, Laura."

"Yes, I think you did. But not enough. Not as much as you love this farm. When I was dating, I could always tell which boys you were going to like and which ones you wouldn't. It had nothing to do with their manners or their appearance. You liked Mason because he always talked about the family business and how important it was to keep up tradition. Billy Walker was okay because he was planning to take over his dad's farm, and when you found out he'd been caught stealing you told me it was just a phase he was going through."

"I was only trying to help. You have to admit some of the boys you dated were trouble."

"Well, it's hard to get dates when your mother is feuding with half the adults in town. I couldn't be as choosy as I liked, and, frankly, your favorites didn't work out so well in the long term. Billy Walker ended up in prison for car theft, and Mason isn't exactly a model citizen."

"All right. It's not always easy to judge people at that age. I'm not even sure I understand you and you're my daughter." Mary was beginning to sound angry rather than apologetic, but Laura wasn't going to back off this time.

"That's just it. You don't have any right to judge people. You can't predict how they're going to turn out, and you have no right to try."

"I was certainly right about Sean Brennan, though, wasn't I? I told you the marriage wouldn't last, that he was a trouble-maker."

Laura froze, aghast. It wasn't so much the words, which were bad enough in themselves, but the tone. Her mother was angry, understandably, but her words also held a note of triumph, of vindication.

"That's low, Mother. Really low. I don't think I want to talk to you just now."

She spun on her heel and headed for the stairs. Cold or not, she was going to take a walk, a good long one. Mary came out onto the landing and watched her descend. "I was wrong about one thing more," she shouted. "I thought there was more Rustin blood in you than Collier. Apparently, that's not true, either.

Rustins don't quit when times get rough. They just work harder and do whatever is necessary to get the job done. You have too much of your father in you. You want to cut and run rather than face up to your responsibilities."

There was more, but Laura was out the door by then and she didn't hear the rest of it.

It wasn't as cold as she had expected. A warmer air mass had chased the storm through the area and the snow was already melting into mounds of mush. It was sloppy going but the footing was considerably less treacherous than it had been first thing in the morning. Laura still had to pick her way carefully, and she was only halfway down McAlester, her eyes focused on the ground in front of her feet, when she realized that someone was calling her name.

It was Dan Sievert, sitting in his personal car, though still in uniform.

"Are you all right? Can I give you a ride someplace?"

"No, and yes." She crossed the road and walked around the back of his car. He leaned across the seat and pushed the door open.

"I got called in for a couple of hours and I heard what happened this morning." His voice was raspy and Laura realized that like her mother, he was coming down with a cold. "Hopper and the mobile crime lab showed up pretty damned fast this time, and they had a bunch of troopers with them, so my services are no longer required. I was just going to stop by and see how you were."

"I'm fine." Her voice was still brittle and she told herself to calm down. "Mother and I had a little disagreement and I came out to cool off, that's all."

"It's certainly cool enough. Do you want me to take you back?"

"To the farm? Definitely not."

Dan leaned forward on the steering wheel and gave her a long, slow look. "Where to then? Breakfast at Slade's?"

She shook her head. "I'm not hungry. Unless you are, I mean. I could have coffee."

"No, I'm fine. I was eating when the call came in. So where do you want to go?"

"I don't care. Someplace quiet. I need to think."

"All right." He sat back and the car moved forward. They turned around at the farm entrance and drove back down McAlester and then into town. Laura felt only mild curiosity about their destination; at the moment she really didn't care so long as her mother wasn't there.

"Hopper's going to want to take a statement."

"Fine."

"Want to tell me what happened? Off the record?"

She did, explaining in minute detail, not so much to satisfy his curiosity as to reorganize everything in her own mind. Laura was convinced that the solution was within her grasp, but she couldn't quite move the pieces into the right combination. Dan listened without interrupting and she became so caught up in her narration that she didn't notice where he had taken her.

"Where are we?" The car had stopped in front of a small house on a street heavily overgrown with pine trees.

"Grosvenor Street. My place. Want to come inside? I can probably manage some drinkable coffee."

"Sure."

Dan's house was surprisingly tidy and clean. The front room was rather plain, with generic landscapes hanging on the walls and a large pot of artificial flowers by the door. He put their coats in a tiny closet under the stairs and led the way to a small, but efficient and spotless, kitchen. There was a table in one corner, surrounded by four chairs. She noticed that his cookware, though limited in range, was of very high quality, and his spice rack was large, and showed clear evidence of frequent use.

"Are you into cooking?"

"A little. Mom was head chef for a restaurant back in Rochester. She taught all us kids the basics, and I was curious enough to ask for the advanced course. It's not as much fun cooking for just myself, but sometimes Paul comes over and I show off."

She peered around the corner and saw a small bathroom, beyond which was a closed door. "That's my office," explained Dan, following her eyes. "Come see."

He led the way into a room too small to have been intended for dining. The house seemed even smaller on the inside than it had from without. There was a computer sitting on a small wooden desk, two black filing cabinets, and a locked, glass-fronted gun case behind which she could see half a dozen handguns and four hunting rifles.

"Do you hunt?"

"Not recently. I still do some target shooting, but now that I carry a gun on the job all the time, I try to relax without one."

They had coffee, and Dan called the station to tell them where Laura was. Half an hour later the phone rang and Dan ran her out to the cabin where Hopper made her go over the events of the previous night three times before he was satisfied. She was amazed at how much things had changed in just a few hours; the snow on the windshield of the Chevy had already melted, and part of the cabin roof was clear. The police had completed the path she had started, but it was obvious that it wouldn't be necessary much longer. Someone had even shoveled out her car, although they hadn't cleaned it off.

Hopper looked angry and discouraged. "I won't lie to you, Miss Collier. There's not much here for us to go on. The marker looks like the same one that was used in your bathroom, and we've already determined that's a dead end. Any footprints or tire tracks would have been obliterated during the night. Someone did shoot at the windows; we haven't found the round yet, but the splintered area on the frame is unmistakable. When this all melts," he gestured with his arms, "we'll go over the whole area again. Probably tomorrow morning if it stays warm like this."

"But you don't expect to find anything, do you? Anything useful, I mean."

He shrugged. "It's always possible. Everyone makes mistakes. But I wouldn't count on it, and frankly, Miss Collier, I'd strongly recommend that you find someplace else to stay, someplace where you're not alone. This individual, whoever he is, has been playing with you up till now. I wouldn't take any comfort from the fact that he could have killed you more than once and hasn't."

"I know that. It galls me to be driven out of my home, Detective, but you're right. It's time to go."

Hopper appeared rather surprised, as though he'd expected more resistance. "I think that's the right decision."

"How soon can I move my things?"

"You can take some clothes and other personal items now if you'd like, but we'd prefer you leave as much as possible until we're done. Late tomorrow afternoon would be fine."

"All right. And thank you for trying, Detective. I know how frustrating this must all be."

She packed an overnight bag and went outside. The trees were shedding melted snow so quickly that it felt as though it was raining. Laura started back toward Dan's car and noticed that while she'd been inside, he had cleared off the Chevy and shoveled around its wheels.

"Want to give it a try?"

A couple of the state troopers were embarrassed into helping push, so it took less than ten minutes to back the Chevy out onto Moon Pond Road. Dan, red-faced and breathing hard, leaned down to peer in the window. "Going back to the farm?"

"God no!" But where was she going to stay? There wasn't even a motel in town.

"I have a spare room."

She shook her head. "No, I couldn't."

"Why not? Afraid you'll get a bad reputation with the locals?"

Laura laughed. "Point taken. But I really don't want to put you to any trouble. You've already been a big help."

"We protect and serve, remember? Come on, it'll give me an excuse to do some fancy cooking."

She thought about it, knew she shouldn't, then nodded her head.

"Great. Hold on, I'll follow you back."

Gritting her teeth, Laura called her mother and told her not to worry. "I'm staying with a friend. I'll talk to you tomorrow."

Mary's response was cool and noncommittal.

They had missed lunch so Dan made an early supper, insisting it was a simple stir fry although it tasted better than the occasional expensive meal she'd had at Foster's. Dan opened a bottle of wine and they had a glass, and then he showed her the upstairs. His bedroom was closest to the bathroom. One of the remaining three rooms was empty, one was obviously set aside for storage, and the third held a bed, a very small chest of drawers, and a squarish table, all unfinished.

"I've been meaning to stain these, but I never got around to it."

Laura put her bag on the bed and they went downstairs and had another glass of wine while they were cleaning up, and somewhere during that process they came quite close, and then they were standing with their arms clenched tightly around one another, and all Laura could think of was how wonderful it would be to be lost in this embrace forever.

She eventually slept comfortably and peacefully that night, but not in the guest room.

CHAPTER TWENTY

Dan got out of bed early the following morning, but Laura rolled over and went back to sleep. When she woke the second time, she found herself alone in bed, wrapped herself in one of Dan's robes, and went downstairs to find out where he'd gone. He was sitting in his office, paging through a spiral notebook filled with neat rows of handwriting.

"What's up?"

He glanced back at her. "Oh, nothing really. Just checking to make sure I've transferred everything into my database."

"Your private research project?"

"That's the one." He closed the book and swiveled around to face her. "It really is more of a hobby than anything else, honest. I'm not obsessed with discovering my roots."

"I didn't think you were." She suddenly remembered Janet Post and her expression grew more solemn. "I completely forgot. There's something I heard that might help." She bit her lip. "But it's not all good news."

"Tell me."

So she repeated everything her mother had said, about Janet's violent history, the unwanted child, her death in a state home. "I wasn't sure if I should mention it at all."

"Trust me, if there is a history of mental illness in my ancestry, I want to know. But you can set your mind at ease. Janet Post is definitely not my mother."

"Oh. You knew about her, then?"

"She was one of my prime candidates early on. But I was able to eliminate her almost immediately. I'm not sure what happened to her baby; the records are sealed. But I do know that I'm not her child."

"How can you be sure?"

His mouth twisted into an exaggerated smile. "Because Janet Post's baby was a little girl. And there's something else." His expression was completely unreadable but some sixth sense told Laura that he was hiding something. "I know who my parents were, Laura. I was going through some of my uncle's papers this morning while you were asleep and I found what I was looking for."

She felt a flush of excitement, not entirely pleasant. Was this good news or not? "So tell me already!"

He shook his head. "Not yet. But I promise I won't keep you in suspense for long."

Laura was unpacking her bag in the spare bedroom when the phone rang. Dan answered it, but she couldn't hear what he was saying, and when she came downstairs he had already hung up.

"Breakfast is just about ready, or I guess this is actually lunch." A very large omelet was sizzling on the stove.

"I'm hungry enough to eat both." She poured herself a cup of coffee from the nearly full pot. "And that smells delicious."

"I told you I was a fair cook." His face became serious. "Will you be all right here on your own? I have to go in. They're juggling schedules again, thanks to the storm, the flu, and Detective Hopper's requests for additional manpower."

"I'll be fine. Hopper said I could take my stuff out of the cabin this afternoon so I'll probably go over and get that over with."

"I'm not sure you should go out there alone."

"I doubt I'll be alone. The state police will be scouring the landscape for evidence again."

"Do you need any help?"

She shook her head. "No, not really. Everything I owned at the time fit in the back of the Chevy when I got here and I haven't added that much since. When my mother calms down I'll ask her to send Del over to take everything else back to the farm. I just want some more clothing and my makeup and the book I was reading and some personal things."

"Well, be careful anyway. I don't think the person we're dealing with is entirely rational."

Dan ate quickly and then started cleaning up, but Laura told him she'd take care of it. "It's the least I can do."

"All right, I've really got to get going. I'll try to call you later on."

She felt odd being alone in his house. Although he'd already given her a grand tour, including his bedroom, she felt like an intruder. After cleaning the kitchen, she went back upstairs and finished putting her clothes away. She wasn't sure how long she would be staying here, but for the moment it was a refuge, a place where she was free of mysterious visitors in the darkness and free of her mother's interminable campaign to recruit her into the Rustin cause. There was even a television and a satellite dish, and she spent two hours channel surfing, reassuring herself that there was indeed an outside world.

It was almost three o'clock when she realized how late it had become. The Chevy was low on gas, so she drove in to Ed's garage and filled the tank, then cut over to Moon Pond Road and drove up to the cabin. As she had expected, the police van was still there, along with a single patrol car, but Hopper was gone. A young man who looked like he only needed to shave on alternate days met her and reluctantly admitted that it was all right for her to take anything she wanted.

"We're done with the interior, but we're still working on the porch and out that way, so if you wouldn't mind staying clear, we'd appreciate it."

"Have you found anything useful?"

He looked distinctly uncomfortable. "You'd have to talk to Detective Hopper about that, Ma'am."

It took her longer than she had expected to sort through her stuff. A lot of things she'd brought with her no longer seemed worth keeping. She'd bought some new clothing recently, and several of her older slacks and tops looked almost as though they belonged to someone else. Perhaps she was finally putting her past behind her. She packed what she wanted to keep in her two mismatched suitcases and put them in the trunk of the Chevy. Books, makeup, and other personal items went into two cardboard boxes that fit nicely in the backseat. She carried those out as well, then went through the cabin again, this time composing a mental list of what should be salvaged. The remaining food could go to the farm, but the cookware might as well stay with the cabin.

The police officer she'd spoken to rapped on the door and told her it was all right for her to go out onto the porch if she wanted. "We're packing up now. We'll be out of your way in just a few minutes."

She thanked him and, in fact, did venture out onto the porch to examine the damage. An inch-long piece of the window frame had been neatly cut and removed, presumably finding a new home in a police evidence bag. Someone had filled in the spot with some kind of putty that was already hardening.

Laura felt a sudden sense of loss. She might come back to the cabin at some point, but it would never be home again. The pleasant memories of her childhood adventures here were overladen with darker ones, and she doubted that it would be possible for her to sleep here again. She felt a wave of loss, an emotion so strong that she put one hand on the wall to support herself until it had passed. "There went my childhood," she said aloud.

There was no reason for her to stay any longer, but she hesitated, caught up once more by the feeling that the answer to the mystery was within her reach. Something about this place, or what had happened here, or something that she had heard elsewhere was percolating in her subconscious. She glanced at the sky. Dusk was coming up fast, but there was still time for a quick walk down to Moon Pond. She knew it was foolish to do so, that she should get in the Chevy right now and go, but if she did, she might miss the chance to figure this all out.

She bundled up in her warmest clothes and started down toward the water.

The surface of Moon Pond rippled only very slightly. There was no ice and the water level was quite high. She could hear the rushing of melted snow pouring down from either side, swelling the waters below her. Laura turned to her right, walked directly to the ruined pier, the spot where she had found Ashley's scarf. There was a large flat stone not far away and she sat down on it, staring at the rotting posts, trying to travel back in time to that night.

She systematically recalled all of the relevant events since her arrival in Dorrance. There was the dead cat she'd found on her first visit to the cabin, the broken window, the theft of Sean's body, Ashley's disappearance, the subsequent incidents here, and her mother's experiences at the farm. No great truth revealed itself. The jigsaw puzzle remained scattered and without form. She concentrated on each potential suspect in turn—Bud Wiegand, Ted Catterall, Mason Cortway, Del Huggins—and then the less likely ones—John Dill, Edna and Kevin Slade, even Tommy Langston. Was one of these people responsible or was it someone else entirely, possibly even some friend of Sean's that she'd never met?

Laura lost track of time and didn't move for so long that her hips and thighs were stiff, and not just from the cold. Even worse, darkness had somehow managed to arrive without her noticing and she hadn't even brought her flashlight. Much of the snow had melted, but there was enough left to make footing treacherous and, as the temperature dropped, it was beginning to freeze again.

It took her much longer than usual to get back to the cabin, and she half fell once, banging her knee and bruising her shoulder. Cursing herself for her stupidity, she continued even more carefully, stumbled around the side of the cabin to the front door. She hadn't locked up when she'd gone out, but it didn't matter any longer. She was only going to pick up the last small bag of items she had collected and leave, and the next time she came to the cabin, if ever, it would be to get it ready for sale.

It was still warm inside, although the fire in the woodstove was foundering and sputtering and cast just enough light for her to see her way around the room. She closed the door behind her as she entered, but only took three steps before coming to a stop.

Across the room, two figures sat at the table, facing in her direction. One was shrouded in a heavy coat and hood, its face hidden; the other wore only a plain blue suit. The suit he'd been buried in. It was Sean Brennan, propped in a chair, slowly defrosting in the heat.

Laura could see his face clearly, or what was left of it. Apparently this wasn't the first time he'd been thawed. She was a bit surprised at herself, at her lack of emotion. There was no fear, no sense of loss, not even a feeling of horror or revulsion. He was dead, gone, would never threaten her again, had not threatened her since his tumble down the stairs back in

Vermont. Sean Brennan was not the cause of her present problems. He wasn't even the excuse. She knew the answers now, at least to the big questions. It had come to her in the moment that she had swung open the door, the door which was no longer blocked by her oversized trash barrel.

Laura turned to the hooded figure and spoke evenly. "Hello, Mother. Would you like some tea?"

The two women sat across the table from each other, quietly drinking tea. Mary Collier used her left hand somewhat awkwardly because her right hand was clenched tightly around the handgun she'd brought with her. Laura had put fresh wood in the stove and it had quickly warmed up inside, but she kept her heavy coat on anyway.

"How long have you known it was me?"

"I realized it just now, as I was coming in."

"I had the feeling that I'd slipped some way, but I couldn't for the life of me think what I'd done wrong. I've been very careful, you know."

"You made the classic bad-guy mistake. You mentioned something you couldn't possibly have known. You told me that Del was strong enough to have moved the trash barrel in front of my door. I hadn't said anything about that."

"Ah, of course. When you know what's actually happening, it's hard to remember what's been told to you and what hasn't."

"Are you going to tell me why?" Laura finally asked.

"Come now, you're a bright girl. I'm sure you know the answer. I tried everything I could think of to convince you that your future lay at the farm, right from the first. I drove out here that first day and left one of the farm cats on your porch, hoping to dissuade you right at the start. You're a Rustin, Laura, deep down inside. But you've been corrupted by the Collier blood. I should have known when I married him that Ben was weak, that there was a danger that his weakness might breed true."

"You killed Ashley just to get me to move back to the farm?" The idea still seemed so absurd that Laura had trouble feeling any emotion about it. Or perhaps she was just in shock.

"I never did like that girl, and she was hardly a great loss. She'd already messed up her own life, caused so much trouble for her parents, and she was a bad influence on you even when you were children. Little Ashley didn't care for me, either. I'd offered her a ride before that afternoon, you know. I had intended to kill her much sooner. But she turned up her nose and refused and I couldn't very well force her into the Jeep. That storm was a godsend, though. She was looking pretty bedraggled when I happened upon her, and I knew instantly that it was the right time. And it was. She wasn't happy about accepting a ride, but it was starting to sleet and she still had at least another mile to walk. But don't worry, dear. She didn't suffer. Just one quick blow on the back of the head."

"I see. And you typed that note. The one setting up the meeting."

"Of course. I used your old typewriter, as a matter of fact. It's still up in the attic. I knew you wouldn't believe that Sean had come back from the dead, but I thought it might convince the police that there was someone from the outside involved."

Laura's voice shook. "I can't believe you dug up his body! How did you manage that?"

"Remember my mercy visit to Lydia Hallworth? Did you really think I'd spend that much time on the old biddy? She was always criticizing me behind my back when she was in Dorrance and I haven't heard from her since she moved."

"And the drink in the bar?"

"Tina, the barmaid. She's not at all a nice girl, but she knows to keep her mouth shut if she's paid enough. Particularly when

I showed her some of the pictures Del Huggins took the day he spotted her screwing Nathan Clay up at Pierce Grove. Tina's husband isn't the forgiving type."

Laura digested that quietly. "My compliments, Mother. You seem to be as skilled at blackmail as you are at farming."

Mary tilted her head to one side. "If that was meant as a cut, it didn't work. I make use of whatever tools come to hand, Laura."

"But what about the Jeep? And the prowler?"

"The prowler never existed, dear. I bent the lock myself. And when I saw John Dill pacing outside the house that morning, I knew it was too good a chance to miss. I waited until he gave up and went away, then cut the brake lines myself." She laughed softly. "I'm afraid that didn't go quite as planned. I had meant to run off the road into the field, not a ditch."

"So where has he been all this time?" Laura nodded toward the corpse, which had settled somewhat since they'd been talking.

"Most of the time he's been in one of the utility sheds out at the farm. These warm spells have been troublesome, you know. At one point I'm afraid he was quite ripe." She reached over and patted Sean's knee. "He's not quite so handsome now, I'm afraid. It's a pity. I thought that was his only good point. For the last three days he's been even closer, right under your nose, in fact."

Laura looked puzzled and her mother laughed unpleasantly. "The crawlspace underneath the cabin. I was quite concerned that those troublesome policemen would stumble upon him, but apparently it never occurred to them to pull off one of the boards and look down below. When you were kind enough to tell me that you were going to retrieve your things after the police had gone, I decided that it was time for the family to be reunited, for one last time. All four of us."

Laura frowned, confused. "Four?"

"Why, yes. Your father's here, of course. I buried him under the cabin right after I killed him. There was no point in keeping him around."

The cabin seemed to spin around Laura's head and she gripped the arms of her chair to keep from falling. "You killed Daddy?"

"Well, I had to." Her mother's voice seemed almost matter of fact. "He was going to take a lot of money. Money that we needed to keep the farm running."

It took a couple of tries before Laura could speak. There could be no doubt now that her mother was insane. "He had a right to a share. You could have just let him go."

"I suppose you're right, but we quarreled rather harshly that day, and he came out here to spend the night. I thought I'd make one more effort to convince him that he was being foolish, that we could work out some compromise, but then we argued again and he said something about writing when he was settled someplace and that he was going to urge you to leave as well. There was this hatchet standing in the corner of the room and I just grabbed it and hit him before I could think what I was doing. I didn't actually mean to kill him, you know. I turned the blade away. But I'm afraid he wasn't as hardheaded as he thought he was." Mary laughed, and the laugh sounded strained and uncertain.

"I always thought you were cold, Mother, but I had no idea you were as bad as this. You lived with him for almost twenty years. You loved him once. Are you telling me that you didn't feel anything?"

"Love wears out sometimes, Laura. Are you still in love with him?" She nodded toward Sean.

Laura considered the question seriously. "I think I'm still a little bit in love with what he was, before he changed. But Daddy didn't turn into a homicidal maniac." But Mommy did, said a little voice inside her head. "I can't believe you left him there, dead and alone, for all these years."

"Oh, but he's not alone. Not anymore."

Stunned, Laura couldn't speak. She opened her mouth to say something, but the words wouldn't come out.

"Colleen Dill is there to keep him company. But don't worry. Say what you will about your father, he was always faithful. I'm sure that if their ghosts are down there, they're just friends."

Laura tried to speak again, her voice a thin croak. "Colleen Dill?"

"It was a simple matter to lure her out here. I simply called and told her that her husband had a deep, dark secret and that I was acting as an unwilling agent for a blackmailer. She was very good about drawing out the money to pay for Dill's imaginary sins and meeting me out here where we wouldn't be disturbed. They were real love birds, those two. I meant to be merciful. I had nothing against the woman, just her husband. But she moved just at the wrong moment and I hit her shoulder instead of her head. If she hadn't been so tiny, it might all have gone wrong. But, eventually, she was still and I dragged her down under the house and buried her right next to your father. I took her keys and went to their house and left a message on that computer thing of theirs, then drove out West, used her credit card to buy some gas, doubled back and dumped her car in the river. The hardest part was walking back to the cabin after-wards."

"But why? Just because you didn't like her husband?"

"It was a tactical maneuver, dear. Dill was talking to someone in Albany about a connector between the interstate and the old truck route. That would have meant building an exit right where our northeast field sits. I couldn't let him do that. We're barely breaking even as it is and that's our most profitable land. With his wife missing, he had other things to think about, although not even I expected him to fall apart as completely as he has. In the end he was just another weak man propped up quietly by a stronger woman." She glanced at Sean's body, which she had propped up in the chair, and smiled to herself.

"So now what? Am I next?"

"I'm afraid so, dear. I'm sorry about that, but I couldn't very well let you sell the cabin, now could I? Someone would be bound to look underneath it someday. I knew it would be all right until the spring, but I was determined to get you out of here before then. You have to admit, I did my very best to convince you to come back to the farm."

"Yes, Mother. You always do your best to get your way. So how are you going to explain it all?"

"I don't intend to. I'll leave you here with your husband," she nodded to the corpse again, "and scribble a message for the police. Something to the effect that you ruined his life and left him behind in Vermont and now you'll be together forever. Detective Hopper already seems half convinced that the killer is someone from Sean's past. I have to confess that I made up a few choice tidbits while he was questioning me. Just enough to whet his curiosity without being specific enough for him to actually find anything, you see."

"Can you really do it? Can you really shoot your own daughter?"

Mary leaned slightly forward, and there was no emotion in her face or her voice. "Yes, I can and I will. I'm sorry, Laura, but a Rustin does what is necessary, regardless of the cost or the consequences. If you really had the Rustin blood in you, you wouldn't have to ask that question. You'd already know."

"I do know, Mother." Laura's hands had been clenched inside her coat pocket and now they emerged. In her right hand was the revolver that Dan had insisted she borrow, just in case.

Mary's eyebrows twitched, but her face didn't change expression otherwise. "Well, well. Maybe there's more to you than I realized, after all. But I'll ask you the same question. Can you really do it? Can you really shoot your own mother?"

Laura answered by squeezing the trigger. The recoil was stronger than she expected, but her father had taught her to fire handguns as a child and she knew enough not to jerk the trigger. The sound was surprisingly loud in the confined space, and she jumped back, startled, afraid that she'd missed. But Mary Collier had jerked backward with a shrill cry and her own weapon had gone skittering across the floor into a corner.

Laura stood up and walked around the table, the revolver held ready. Her mother lay on her back, gasping softly, her left hand clutched around her right elbow. Even in the darkened cabin, Laura could see the glint of fresh blood. Mary looked up at her daughter and grimaced. "Good shot."

"Daddy taught me. Remember? How are you doing?"

"I'll live, unless you decide to shoot me again. That might be best."

"I don't think so." Laura felt surprisingly calm. Her mother looked helpless now, but she retrieved the fallen weapon and put it in her pocket before coming any closer. "I don't have a phone and I can't very well leave you here so we're going to have to wait for a while. I'm sure Dan will be here when he doesn't find me back at his place. We need to stop the bleeding before you go into shock."

"Why bother? This is the end of everything anyway, isn't it?"

"The end of one thing is always the beginning of another."

Mary coughed and her body jerked as she jostled her mangled elbow. Her voice was weaker when she spoke again. "I don't suppose there's anything I can say at this point to convince you to keep the farm? After I'm gone, I mean."

"No, there's not. It's just a piece of land, Mother."

"But the Rustin name . . ."

"Deserves to vanish," she interrupted. "Most of the people in Dorrance hate the Rustins and the rest just don't like us. You and grandpa and his father always treated the town like villagers outside the castle walls, useful for the services they could provide but never to be treated as equals. You interpreted their resentment as envy and kept everyone at a distance. Well, the walls are down, the treasury is nearly empty, and the villagers are rebelling. We're not aristocrats anymore, Mother, just farmers. And I don't like farming."

She would have said more, but Mary Collier had fainted. Laura bandaged her arm as best she could and wrapped her in a blanket with her head on a pillow. She was still sitting at the table, watching over her mother, when Dan Sievert drove up an hour later.

The excitement and confusion that followed the arrest of Mary Collier largely passed Laura by. There were reporters in the yard for several days, but they eventually got discouraged when she wouldn't speak to them. The only visitors she allowed inside were the police, and no one seemed to notice that Officer Sievert was there every day, some days until very late in the evening. Her mother was expected to make a full recovery from the gunshot wound, although she would probably never regain full use of her right arm.

Only one mystery remained, and that didn't occur to Laura until almost two weeks had passed. Dan had brought fresh groceries and was cooking them supper when she suddenly remembered. "Dan! I completely forgot! You said you'd found out who your parents were."

He nodded. "That's right. I'd meant to tell you over a fancy meal somewhere." He gestured toward the food simmering on the stove. "This isn't quite as fancy as I'd planned."

"Tell me anyway."

"Only if you promise never to tell anyone else. You and Paul are the only ones in Dorrance who I can tell."

She frowned, puzzled. "All right, if that's what you want."

He nodded and stirred their supper. "Well, it seems that Paul and I can't call ourselves brothers anymore."

She frowned. "Why not?"

"Because it turns out we're cousins. Uncle Jake was my father. My mother was named Doris Goodall."

Laura shook her head. "I never heard of her."

"No, but you've met her."

"I have? But who is she?"

He sighed. "She's an unhappy woman who just once in her life did something risky and unorthodox and paid for it by getting pregnant by someone other than the man she had agreed to marry. Uncle Jake took care of everything, arranged for me to be adopted by his sister and her husband, and never told them the truth. My real mother got married a few months later and now has a family of her own."

"That's great. That you found out, I mean. Isn't it?"

He turned toward her, his expression a blend of conflicting emotions. "I suppose so. But you might want to reconsider our relationship."

Laura frowned. "Why would I want to do that?"

"Oh, maybe because Doris Goodall married Joshua Cortway. That means Mason is my half brother."

"Well, as long as we don't have to invite him to the wedding."

"Oh? Is there going to be a wedding?"

She stood up and walked over to where he was standing, and their supper slowly began to burn as she convinced him that there was, indeed, going to be a wedding.

ABOUT THE AUTHOR

Don D'Ammassa is the author of one previous murder mystery, *Murder in Silverplate,* as well as novels in the science fiction and horror genres, and two reference books dealing with fantastic literature. He has written over one hundred short stories for a variety of magazines and anthologies. He lives in Rhode Island with his wife Sheila, two cats, and 50,000 books.